The Killing of Mindi Quintana

The Killing of Mindi Quintana

Jeffrey A. Cohen

Welcome Rain Publishers
New York

For my sweet Janine

Acknowledgments

I am deeply grateful to novelist David Bradley for our long friendship, and for his wise critique of several drafts of this novel; and to my editor Alan Rinzler for his friendship and wonderful work. I am also indebted to veteran Philadelphia attorney, Thomas Quinn, for his assistance and legal insight. All deviations from current Pennsylvania and federal law, and from actual Philadelphia practice and procedure, whether intentional or otherwise, are my work alone.

1
—

The China Manager

Freddy Builder, Chanet Department Store's manager of china and glass, arrived in the morning to find Jill, one of his salesgirls, beaming at him in his display area. She glowed as though she'd been skating. Her lower lip trembled and her body twitched like she was close to some kind of orgasm.

She yelled at him, "Manager of the Month! That's twice in a row!" and leaped into the air like a cheerleader.

All of this was a sword through him, and he held up his hand to forestall the cartwheel she seemed to be measuring.

"Thank you, Jill, it *truly* is an honor," hoping to shut her up.

"Oh, congratulations!" she squealed. "Congratulations!"

She threw two balls of streamers onto the floor, keeping the ends in her hands. The balls rolled past him on either side.

"I was going to hang them! Surprise!" and did her cartwheel anyway.

She giggled.

He hated her.

She began stringing the streamers, pulling furniture over to stand on, babbling all the while, faster than he could think. She skipped. She *hummed*. She stopped, a new realization growing steadily over her face.

"Mr. Builder," she began.

Go away, he thought.

"Oh, Mr. Builder," she said.

"Don't," he said.

"Do you know, do you realize, you—*you* could be *Manager of the Year!*"

He stared at her—"They'll bronze your face!"—and stared through her, seeing his face, bronzed with all the others on Chanet's concrete storefront.

"You'll be Store Symbol!"

A year of his personnel picture staring at him and everyone else from newspaper and television ads. Buses. The greatest manager. Store mascot. Ronald *fucking* McDonald!

"No," he whispered.

"*Yes!*" she screamed. "The first floor manager ever to be Manager of the Year!"

He knew they wouldn't, he was only a lower—but then again, some upper-middles had scheduled lunch with him for noon and he wondered if this could be why. He was shaken and had to reassure himself that they would never do it, make him that ridiculous creature. He was only the china manager. A lower. They wouldn't do it. His heart slowed down. But when he looked at Jill again, he experienced a violent pulse and forced his look away.

"You're not supposed to be here," he told her. "You know the rule about being early."

Jill sucked a lip into her mouth. She'd come early to hang streamers for her boss. She was holding the ends again.

"You're fired," Freddy told her, walking past her to the men's room.

"No . . . please," she said softly, turning with him as he passed.

"You're fired, get out of here," he called back. "We'll mail you your check."

"*Please*," she called after him, her voice echoing.

Freddy sat in his stall, pants up, staring through the vertical slit at a bright white slice of porcelain sink. He'd put Jill from his mind and was now holding fast to another white flash.

The white parka of a college girl. He'd been in college, too, and was walking home from class. Parked cars tightly wound the street next to him.

It was winter. He wore a long coat. The air was frigid, the evening, purple. Clear ice and frozen snow made the walking hazardous, but he went staring straight ahead. Past the West Philly houses which forty years before had been the fine homes of the well-to-do. Even from the sides of his eyes, he'd thought he'd seen them as they'd been, that he had their sense. Again the homes were exuberant.

He walked without gloves, not at all willing away the cold but simply oblivious to it. He had been twenty-two and, though gazing only ahead and within, his surroundings had pressed upon him. They seemed both super real and surreal. Sky so purple, it was virtually black. The homes complete again and warmly lit, their missing bricks and porch planks given back by the night. He saw his breath, watching through it evergreens in the street light and bushes so deeply green, so saturated with green they might have dripped green droplets.

Now, in the tile-porcelain-metal bathroom, Freddy's balls shrank in his pants. His eyes riveted still to the bright white segment of sink, he felt again the cold that had pierced him next so completely.

A flash of brilliant white had taken his eye to the right that night, and he'd stopped. Standing there on a porch several feet above the street was a girl in her parka, looking at him. He felt she had been watching him for some time. He took a deep breath through his nose. And looked at her.

She was strikingly beautiful. Dark complected—Latina, he thought—and delicately featured. She had the longest black hair he had ever seen; it stopped short inches above her knees. Some of it moved easily over her white parka.

"No gloves," she said.

He fumbled in his pockets for his gloves, but his hands were so cold he could not tell if they were there.

3

"Hey, I've seen you in the CW office, haven't I?" she said.

He pulled his pockets inside out. He had one glove.

She laughed as though borne out. "A writer. It was you in Gibson's office, wasn't it?"

"Yes."

"But you're not in the program. I've never seen you in a class."

"Marketing. I've taken some though."

She put her hands in her pockets and pressed her arms to her sides. "I'm Mindi," she said. "Come on up, I'll give you some hot chocolate. You'll be needing those hands if you're going to write."

He'd climbed the bowing porch steps. He'd gone inside with her and stood next to her while she heated the milk for the hot chocolate. It seemed the night came in with them, everything vivid and textural. She'd lit a low flame in the next burner for him to warm his hands, and when the hot chocolate was made, she asked if he wanted to drink it outside, which he very much did.

They'd stepped back out, and he found the night had kept its strange quality. The sky had lost its hint of indigo and was absolute black. He thought it must be him, that he'd just never been out in a night so strong that it in fact buzzed. It seemed animated, that was it.

So he'd thought it was him, but she gave a short laugh that sounded a little afraid.

"It's like something's stretching the sky and whatever it is, is going to tear through any minute and get us," she said. Some of her hair touched his face.

Nobody was on the street. No cars passed.

"What's your name?"

"Frederick."

"What were you thinking about tonight, Frederick, that daze you were in?" She smiled at him.

"A story." But that wasn't true. He didn't think he'd been thinking at all.

"I'd love to read your work."

And he'd thought the night must be filling in his defects, too.

He sat on the toilet with his teeth clenched. A spigot was running, and there were voices in the bathroom now, but they did not cut through meaningfully. He'd dated her, and sometimes she'd tell him he was moody or interesting. That she wanted to understand him, that she understood people best through their writing. She'd say, "Let me read the one you were thinking about when we met."

But her father had been arrested just a couple of months later. He'd owned a construction company or something and he'd bribed somebody. The case was in the papers and her parents had wanted her to transfer away. Between semesters, she moved to Colorado.

A year later he was an assistant buyer at Chanet's. And then it was three years, and soon it was five, and then it was six, and this moment, and he was Manager of the Month again and still here in this store. And, like at other such times when he still thought of her, he told himself, *Maybe if I'd shown her something,* meaning, perhaps, since he kept such thoughts murky, that if he'd conquered his fears then, he would never have joined Chanet's. Maybe he'd be off now doing what he should be doing, though he didn't reach into the haze for exactly what that was. He stood up and flushed for those who would see him leave.

The store was open now, Jill was gone, and Freddy was in his display area again. He felt the holes in the arrangement of his merchandise. Felt them, the way he felt the formation of the displays themselves, which were his job to design and maintain. The old display was carcass. The customers had picked at it, buying and moving, until they'd killed it. Not even they would be interested in what was left.

The holes bore into his back like doubts. He saw one and thought, *If I don't leave this place soon, I'm gonna die here, in retail,* and another, *Maybe this is all I'm good at,* and another, *Why the lunch today with the upper-middles?* He felt the new tension grow in him, and the tension always there.

He looked at the mahogany étagère against the wall, with its wood shelves set inside it at staggered heights, from the top, first right then left. The customers had just about stripped it of merchandise. He turned, remembering a piece that had just come in. A beautiful long-necked Lalique crystal vase, cut in a hundred flat oval faces, facets, windows, mirrors. It would be the new center and he knew where he wanted it.

He strode into the stockroom to fetch it, turned with it, strode back out, and placed it exactly on the second left shelf, just below the middle. Now the display would build itself. He would use pieces of the carcass and bring it alive again. That brown glazed bowl, a Paul Chaleff, round and earthy with a round hole at the top. It should be on the lower right shelf.

He swung to bring it over, and put it into place. It attacked the vase for attention, but the vase won. More was falling into place. Flutes, the long-stemmed glasses. He needed two groups, one with shorter stems. He rushed across the floor to a series of step ledges and brought some back with him. Put them by group on each of two shelves, the taller to the right on the top right shelf and the slightly shorter ones far right on the low left shelf. He stood back. The glasses stretched and tried to pull the vase toward themselves at angles, but it was the vase that anchored them.

Suddenly, the beginnings of something else came to him. But could he leave the étagère yet, would he lose it if he did? He beheld it again. It was far enough along. He knew that whenever he looked at the étagère, what needed to be done would come to him. So he dismissed it and desperately grasped at the retreating new images. The square rosewood table. He went to it near the sidewall and placed its contents hurriedly on the floor. The inkwell.

"Ahem."

Freddy looked up. A short round brown man with bulging eyes

looked at him. Two tall white skinny men, one slightly shorter than the other, stood to either side of him. Standing in front of the étagère, they blocked all but the vase. They wore name tags from Sporting Goods.

Freddy brushed by them and grabbed the inkwell he wanted from a far shelf, brushed back past them again and placed it—no!—just *past* midway on the table. But the ink, he needed to add—

"Ahem."

This time Freddy saw it was the round man who spoke.

"I'm busy," Freddy growled as he went around them again, but they were forcing him to attend to them . . . he felt conscious thought coming to the forefront . . . and it was all stupid again. He walked the blue-black ink jar he'd retrieved back to the table and left it anywhere. He turned to the men.

Emissaries from Sporting Goods coming for advice, obviously. The other department managers were constantly hounding him with questions but they seldom came themselves. They sent underlings instead to save face. Politics.

"What do you want?"

The short man spoke again. "Fishing rods aren't selling."

"Fishing rods aren't selling?" He stood blinking at them. "Maybe it's the ice on all the water."

One of the tall men gave him a penetrating look. "But they're supposed to sell better."

"I'm in the middle of something."

The men looked at each other huffily. "Should we come back?" said one of them.

Freddy gave them his back. "Yeah. When it's warm."

The men went away.

"He's building one of his *famous* displays," floated back to him.

Freddy stood looking at his display. It pulled at him to continue building it. But for what? For the customers? They put their gum in his spoons. They bought what he told them to and never knew he had spoken.

For the buyers, the middles, the uppers? Buyers begged him to put their pieces in positions of prominence, which to them meant at eye level, and management oohed and aahed at his sales figures, not at what had achieved them.

For himself? He despised the displays. They brought him the Manager of the Month awards, they threatened him with much worse. But the holes attacked him: *Fishing rods aren't selling . . . write? Write what? . . . the motherfuckers, the motherfuckers, the motherfuckers are going to make me Manager of the Year, aren't they?*

Only by building his displays could he find release in this place, and then only by plugging their holes could he have peace. It was only later that they became ridiculous, caricatures of creativity.

He was still being drawn to the table, he needed to finish—but before he could move, a fat face wearing heavy black-rimmed glasses peeked out from behind a mirrored pillar.

"Uh, sir? I'm sorry to bother you. Could I have a moment?" it asked. A hand fixed its glasses.

It was the new chocolate manager, Freddy recognized him. The chocolate stand was the least prestigious managerial position in the store. Poorly performing managers were moved there as a last stopping place on the way out. This chocolate manager had come himself, a sign of weakness. He had no emissaries.

The man came out from behind the pillar and approached.

"Congratulations, sir, by the way. You must be very happy."

Freddy put a finger in his mouth and pulled it out with a popping sound. Made a circle with it in the air.

The waist ties of the chocolate manager's apron dragged behind on the floor. Freddy guessed they were not long enough to get around him. The chocolate manager leaned over and whispered to Freddy, who felt his hot breath in his ear.

"I'm having trouble with chocolate pretzels." He stood back and turned his palms up. "Can you help me? Please? They're not selling."

Freddy looked him over. Chocolate pretzels were the least of the man's troubles. He was dying the store death. There was nothing Freddy could—or wanted to do—for or regarding this walking corpse, except have it walk away.

In the lingo of retail he admonished, "You must use your fixtures productively."

"I'm *trying* to use them productively," the chocolate manager protested. He pled with his arms. "I taped some of them on the glass, but the lights melted them into the other candies. I gave out free samples. Now I have three pounds of stale broken chocolate pretzels that the middle-middles are taking out of my check. I say 'yummm, yummm' to the kiddies and point at them, but"—he shrugged—"they just laugh at me. They call me 'fatty.'"

Freddy closed his eyes. "Try moving them next to the pistachios, fatty," he said.

The chocolate manager's eyes widened. He sputtered his thank-you and stumbled away, mumbling it would make a difference, he would soon be back in Home Appliances, really he would, certainly he would. *The flicker*, Freddy thought, watching him go.

At noon, Freddy looked up from tea sets and saw that the upper-middles had appeared to take him to lunch. They were a group of five altogether, four of them standing in a semicircle blocking his view of the étagère. The fifth—the leader, Freddy surmised—stood in front of the others.

Of the four, two were women, both prim, one with blond hair and black rims, and the other the other way around. They wore dark business suits, as did the two men between them. The two men were youngish, had high hairlines and fresh-scrubbed faces. They were bright-eyed and had slapped on some Chanet's aftershave, the store brand, Freddy could smell it. Only kind they used, he was positive they'd say if he mentioned it. Standing there, the four looked like they would sing or try to convert him to their religion.

Freddy recognized the leader, Robert Jamison. He occasionally ran the buyers' meetings, which floor managers also attended. He was a thin, tall man with feathery brown hair and an angular face, wearing what looked to be a custom-made Italian suit. He had an unlit cigarette in a mother-of-pearl filter. No pinholes in that lapel, no, no. In fact none of them had name tags on their suits; they were of middle-management stock after all.

"You were supposed to be ready at noon," Jamison said. "Where's your coat?"

Freddy looked at the five. None of them had coats. Nevertheless, he apologized and went into the stockroom to retrieve his own.

"Well, then," Jamison said when Freddy returned, "let's be off." And he started immediately away with the others. Freddy had to hurry to catch up with them.

On the escalator, Jamison turned to him and said, "You don't need a coat, actually, we're eating in the store. But you couldn't have known that and should have been ready to go outside. We've got to be careful that we maintain the proper respect. But don't worry, we like you, we like you." Freddy's grip tightened on the escalator arm as the others picked invisible lint from his suit.

The five left the escalator on the second floor and Freddy followed. He guessed they were going to Tweed, a fancy restaurant on that floor where the food was rumored to taste like . . . tweed.

Ze maître d', who was dressed in tweed, took *zem* to *zere tableh.* As they followed through the high-ceilinged room, the place already crowded with ladies who lunch and men discussing documents over eyeglasses low on the nose, Freddy noticed the rash on the maître d's neck where his tweed shirt had infected him.

The upper-middles forced Freddy to sit in the center of the semi-circular booth, with two of them on either side. Jamison sat in a chair directly across from him. Little fibers from the tweed cushion poked through Freddy's pants and irritated the backs of his legs. His tweed napkin stuck to the tweed-covered table like Velcro and he had to peel it off. Nobody else seemed bothered.

"My name is Mr. Jamison," Jamison said. "But," and he leaned forward to touch Freddy's arm, "for the purposes of this meal, mind you," he raised his brow in qualification, "you can call me Bobby," and he smiled, for it was still pretty damn wonderful of him. There were sharp intakes of breath around the table and Jamison settled back for Freddy's reaction to his shocking good fortune.

Their eyes tore into him. "Thank you . . . Bobby," Freddy said. The others clapped him on the back and introduced themselves. Carried away by the moment, Freddy was to call them by their first names, too.

The waiter approached and asked for their drink orders. Jamison said they were ready to order their food, too, since "their esteemed guest from the lowliest level of management" had only an hour. Jamison gestured charmingly for Freddy to order first. Freddy opened his menu and hurriedly scanned it while they drummed their fingers. He ordered the Steak Tweed and some Plaid Potatoes. Jamison ordered the Salmon Ella. So did the others.

"How about a drink first?" Jamison encouraged Freddy.

"Okay." He ordered scotch.

"Iced tea, for us," Jamison said disapprovingly.

When the waiter left they congratulated Freddy for his Manager of the Month award, Jamison handing over his framed certificate. It wasn't often someone from lower management won, let alone twice in a year, but, they told him, he deserved it.

"But I hope you're not thinking about Manager of the Year," said Jamison, to Freddy's great relief. "It would be quite out of the question for a lower to be Store Symbol." The rest agreed vigorously.

The waiter returned with the drinks and set them down on little tweed coasters. Inside them were soggy tweed-lined swizzle sticks. Jamison raised his drink and the others followed suit. "To this month's Manager of the Month. Middle-management material!"

"Middle-management material!" they all repeated, drank, and leaned over to clap him repeatedly on the back.

"Drink, drink!" Jamison said because Freddy hadn't yet. Freddy tried to sip at it but kept getting fuzz from the swizzle in his mouth.

"There's no telling how far a talented fellow like you might go, how high a floor you might someday have an office on," Jamison said.

"Think of that!" said the others.

"And there's no telling the number of wildlife prints they'll put in that office for you," Jamison said.

"First there's the *Tiger in the Grass* print," confided a fresh-scrubbed face.

"Then the *Zebra in the Grass* print," let on the other.

"Then," said Jamison, "the *Cow but Without Any Grass* print, because," and they snorted at his joke, "the cow's eaten all the grass!" They urged Freddy to laugh with them. He sat sweating, surrounded, without recourse, and still they continued.

"In a few years, if your potential bears fruit, you might even have an office with two windows," said the brunette with blond rims. Freddy looked into his drink.

"But," said the blond with brunette rims, "you would not be moved to a new office for this."

There was a pause for him to ponder the paradox. They squirmed in their chairs, unable to stand his suspense. He squeezed his glass.

"Five years ago our efficiency-minded company concluded it was far too costly to actually move people about," said a fresh-scrubbed face, drawing it out. They were biting their lips and looked like they needed to pee.

"Today," the other blurted, "*every* office has two windows—but one is boarded up!"

"Imagine," said Jamison, making crowbar motions, "prying those boards away and seeing the city in both windows now. Aahh."

"And scraping those *City in the Grass* posters from the glass, when you warrant a real view," said the black-haired woman from behind yellow frames.

Freddy mentioned that he really wasn't feeling well and perhaps should be going, but they just clapped his back some more to make him feel better. And they continued.

"Soon," Jamison said, "you do get a bigger office. They just move your adjustable wall out four feet to the right and everyone else down the row has to compensate."

Yellow-hair-black rims laughed. "After two such moves on a floor, the person in the last office has to turn his desk sideways."

"With the third move, they either promote and move him upstairs a floor, or fire him, based on our promotion equation," said a fresh-scrubbed face.

"A merit calculus, really," Jamison explained. "It measures performance over time as a function of available office space."

Yes, siree, Bobby said, there was a great big beautiful world for Freddy inside the store, but, his new friends warned him, he should not set his sights too high, too fast. Not if he wanted to keep them as his friends. And they stopped smiling and kept silent for five minutes to let him know they weren't joking. When they started in again, it was to assure him that middle management, though hard work, was great fun.

In that vein, Jamison looked now like he had just a dumpling of a thing to tell him.

"Each new lower-middle," he said, "gets a turn at firing the choco-late manager."

There were titters. Jamison said that if there were no new promo-tees, an upper-middle got to do it. "The chocolate terminations are wonderful fun," Jamison explained, "because they are videotaped and shown at the upper-middle-management Christmas party. The idea is to come up with the most outlandish—hence amusing—pretense for termination!"

"I told my chocolate manager we suspected him of spying for Iraq," said the well-dressed young man on his left.

"Oh, you kidder." Jamison flipped a hand at him.

"I fired mine for making anti-chocolate statements at an anti-chocolate rally," said the man on his right.

"Moved out your wall twice for that one, as I recall," Jamison said. The man nodded humbly. The women looked at each other and begged Jamison, "Tell him how you fired yours, tell him how you fired yours!"

"Oh, all right," Jamison said. From the inside pocket of his jacket, Jamison withdrew three folded eight-by-ten glossies and dropped them in front of Freddy, who glanced at the one on top. It looked like a group of atoms.

"Don't look at them yet," Jamison said.

The others were chortling now and covering their mouths with their hands. Freddy wanted only to leave. He picked at his meal; the restaurant had done something to his steak so that it resembled a swatch of tweed. The fries were plaid.

Jamison's face was a blossom of mirth. "I called my chocolate manager in and had him sit down. I dropped the pictures in front of him, just as I've done with you. I'd already explained my game to the video camera. And I said, 'Mr. Chocolate Manager—' The man was shaking from the outset, by the way, we start rumors before we send for them so they're primed. 'Mr. Chocolate Manager,' says I. 'Every so often we should check that our dispenser of chocolate and candiful treats is a competent purveyor of our goods, should we not?' I don't think he knew what I was saying, but he agreed since I had indicated with my question that I wanted him to.

"'Well, sir,' I told him, 'I am pleased that you concur, for I have arranged to administer you our chocolate test. Your continued employment, by the way, depends on your passing.' Well, now the man was in a thorough tizzy! I told him to pick up the photos and look at them, and when he did, he had to hold his one hand steady with the other just to see them. I said, 'These are pictures of three different molecules. One is a chocolate molecule, one a beer molecule, and one a washing machine molecule.' Look at the pictures,

Frederick, what do they look like to you?" Freddy forced himself through them.

"The same molecule," he said.

"Precisely! A water molecule!" The others were beside themselves now and they kept clapping Freddy's back until he made laughing sounds and showed them some teeth.

"And I said, 'Your job is to pick out the chocolate molecule.' He started jabbering about his wife, which I let him for a while—the height for the audience, you know—and I told him I sympathized and fully expected he would pass.

"Well," Jamison said, "that man spent an hour—more film than we had—trying to distinguish between the pictures, holding them up to the light, searching with a magnifying glass, begging for clues, but never reaching the issue—and this is the *really* funny part—never reaching the issue of which distinguishing feature, once found, would indicate chocolate!"

Freddy's new friends were doubled over the table. Freddy doubled over, too; the plaid fries weren't agreeing with him. Black-hair-yellow-frames to his left whispered in his ear that the chocolate manager had developed an interesting white froth at the corners of his mouth before the film had run out. Freddy moved his head to the other side of his plate and yellow-hair-black-frames elaborated. "Like the dogs in that psychology experiment."

"Well, Frederick, we're going to promote you after the first of the year," Jamison said suddenly.

Freddy pulled his head up a few inches from the table. They were staring at him.

"Thank you," he said.

"Think you can top my chocolate termination?" Jamison asked good-naturedly.

It was a rhetorical question. But Freddy thought he could. He brought himself straight. If they promoted him, he'd top this man who was signing the check now with such flourish. Then he'd tell them all to fuck off. Not now, not yet. He needed this job, he needed the money, yes, even the release of the displays and his small authority over others. But soon. Soon.

He said nothing.

"And we have *another* surprise for you," Jamison said. "We're firing the new chocolate manager 'by committee,' since middle-management promotions won't go through till next year. A group effort—and we want you on the team!"

By committee. Freddy stared at his plate.

"Don't worry," Jamison said, misunderstanding. "You'll get to do one on your own." He grinned again. "But this guy gets his pension if we don't hurry, so we can't wait for you!" The others agreed with guffaws.

"Right then. There'll be a principals' meeting soon, and we'll let you know your part. We hire outside actors for these things—fake FBI agents, spies, contract killers, whatever we need—and they'll be there, too."

Jamison stood and the others stood with him. Freddy stood, too. A fresh-scrubbed face pointed out he had some plaid on his mouth. He wiped sharply at his lips with his napkin and drew blood. He spit out tweed fuzz. On the escalator, Jamison put his arm around him and said to keep on calling him 'Bobby.' The others put the invisible lint back on his jacket. They left him in his department.

There was the display to finish. He built savagely, ending up where he'd begun at the étagère. He stood in front of it, watching, it all coming through him so strongly, what had to be done. He made the trips to the stockroom and back, with piece after piece, building, arranging around the vase. Five rocks glasses in a group, on the middle left shelf, four around one, made the display complete. He turned and went to the back, then turned again to look. The display swirled furiously away from the crystal vase. And held.

2

Centerpiece

Dressed in jeans and a white winter sweater under her ski jacket, Mindi waited at the corner of Fortieth and Baltimore for the trolley east into center-city Philadelphia. They weren't the forties-style trolleys anymore that had still ridden the tracks, clanging that bell, when she was in college. These were "sleek and aerodynamic," as the SEPTA commercials boasted, they were part of a "fleet." Well, at least they didn't hover yet. Something still said roasted chestnuts while you waited for them looking at the tracks.

Christmas was in six weeks, and on New Year's Day her parents would be married thirty-four years. It would be the first anniversary in five years that her father would spend in his home with his wife. The first Christmas in five years that she and her mother didn't pack the presents and the goose, *pupusas* (tortillas with cheese inside), and Christmas cookies in the back of the of the car, then drive silently to the prison at Allendale. When your father was in jail, it was silent with your mother on the way to the prison on Christmas. You wrapped the presents when your father was in jail even though the prison flyer informed you it was a waste.

But this year they would have a tree again, it was her father's job to find a great one. This year, her father said, he was cooking the meal, everything, the goose, the cookies, the *pupusas*, and they would let him have a try. But they would have an extra goose on hand just in case.

Her father was still almost manic, it seemed, wanting to do things, see things again. Still, though, sometimes, she would do something

17

characteristic, say something, sometimes her father would just be looking at her, and he'd say, "I forgot you did that," or he wouldn't say anything.

The trolley stopped for her. She stepped on, dropping coins in the box, which thanked her in a whole bunch of languages.

"Transfer, baby?" said the woman behind the controls.

"Nope, thanks," Mindi said. The car was nearly empty. She took a seat near the middle and put her knees up against the back of the seat in front of her. The trolley made gradual turns through the University of Pennsylvania campus and for a while she watched out the window.

It was early to be shopping for her parents' anniversary gift, but there was a particular thing she wanted for them and it was going to be difficult to find. It had to be like the one that had always been in her mother's kitchen, the one that fell and broke soon after he'd gone away. She hadn't really noticed its absence while her father was gone, but now, every time she went to their house, she felt it missing there. Mindi had two hundred forty dollars to spend on one just like it. She put down a leg and pulled the bills from her jeans, counting them again to be sure.

A friend of hers, Stuart, had suggested she look first in Chanet's. She'd been at the Warsaw Café with him, her best friend, Lisa, Des Moines, and the woman directing Des Moines's play at Annenberg, Penn's theater, about a block over from where the trolley was now. Stuart was designing the sets for the play.

Over dinner she'd asked for their ideas on where to look, and Stuart had asked if she'd been to the china department at Chanet's. She knew the building, of course, a downtown Philly landmark housing the city's most venerable department store for almost a century. Close to both the literary magazine she helped edit and to the gallery where Lisa rang up sales and painted, they passed it together when they met up after work. But, no, she'd never seen the china department. Well, the displays there, Stuart said—he had used the word "breathtaking."

They'd raised their eyebrows some, and Lisa had made them laugh with, "You should see the shoe department. Now *that's* breathtaking."

But the director had defended him, saying, "Your friend Stuart here'd be out of a job if he couldn't communicate ideas with his sets and the objects he chooses. So would any museum curator."

Then she'd added, "The interesting question is, why bother in a department store?" And Stuart said he didn't know why, but that if Chanet's didn't have what Mindi was looking for, whoever did the displays would know where to send her.

Mindi got off the trolley at the City Hall station, zipping her jacket. She climbed the dark stairs that the sun painted yellow three-quarters of the way up, and emerged into the City Hall courtyard amid a Saturday crowd of parents and bundled children. As she did every time she crossed the yard, she headed for the brass marker in the center. She liked the thought of touching the very center inch of the city, even if it wasn't really the very center inch anymore.

A prison bus crunched by over the cobblestones at a couple of miles an hour and she saw profiles in the fenced windows. It turned and stopped in the yard at the north archway. A similar bus had stopped once in the same place and her father had come out of it. On the morning of his arraignment, the day after his arrest. That day, as reporters and photographers swarmed the bus, one had asked her how she felt. One asked her, would she pull her hair in front and bow her head a little. One asked, was it true her father had ties to organized crime "elements." Her father, who'd sent his family away twice when bidding against mob concerns. In whose house *"hijo de puta"*— "son of a bitch"—had always been the "mister" for mobster.

She reached the marker and stepped on it. She turned and watched a few guards plunk down from the bus. She wanted to see them better, and the prisoners when they came down, so she moved closer, stopping by a concrete bench near a tree. She'd been standing in about the same spot, her mother next to her, the reporters in front, and cameramen, when her father came down and raised his cuffed hands to cover his face. She felt a tenth of that now, a hundredth of that sinking, but it made her want to fish out her cell phone and wake him up to come shopping with her.

She smiled to herself. She'd let them sleep. She was shopping for their gift anyhow. An icy wind whistled into her face, making her close her eyes. You didn't care. You ran to your father even though there were guards, and you kicked them when they wouldn't let you past, and you fought your mother to get to him, even though you were twenty, even though the cameras were clicking and film rolling and you'd been told the most important thing in the world today was to be strong in its face for your father. When your father was in jail, you could kind of lose your mother, too.

She opened her eyes. The guards were smoking near the front of the bus. Some were handing dollar bills to another who walked off with the money. One of them was looking at her. A few more came out from City Hall and joined the rest. The prisoners still sat in the bus and she watched their faces through the windows. In cells all the time, and still they sat in profile. The wind was blowing her hair in her face so she gathered some with one hand and held it to the side.

The guard who'd been looking at her started over in kind of a half jog. One hand strayed to the gun at his waist to make sure the butt was still outside his jacket. He was thin and dark, sinewy, she could tell it even with him inside a bulky black coat with fur collar. Latino for sure, she would have known that by the way he was moving without more. He got younger as he got closer until he stopped in front of her at about twenty-four. It said Arturo Rodriguez on his name plate.

"*¿Porque tan triste?*" he asked.

"I'm not sad," she said. He smiled at her, showing good white teeth. It made her smile. "Okay?"

"Sure." It was his word for "yes." He said it that way and without the emphasis that normally made it mean "of course." But he made no move to go back to the bus. Instead he shook a Camel Light from a pack and lit it with the first match. He cocked his head toward the bus. "They are very bad men on the bus," he said. She thought about that while he blew out the smoke.

"All of them?"

"Sure." In that matter-of-fact way again that gave the word a sincerity and persuasiveness it seldom had. He pulled more smoke from his cigarette. *"Con ellos,"* he said, "you got to know how to handle yourself."

He held up a jacketed biceps, turning a second to make sure his friends were watching, and another year fell off him. He turned back.

"Here, feel this." The guards were leaning against the bus, looking over, and they cheered him now. Arturo's grin was in his eyes but nowhere else. "It's okay," he said, "go ahead," the cigarette in his mouth. "It's strong."

"Gee, no, I don't think so." She was still keeping her hair from blowing with one hand. She let go now to search her pocketbook for ChapStick.

"Come on," he said, while she searched. He said in Spanish, "For the gringos."

So she stopped looking and gave his arm a squeeze. She put on a suitably impressed expression for his friends. His arm was as hard as she thought it would be. There were whistles, and he was considering his cigarette. He ground it out now and the loose tobacco blew away.

One of the guards called over, "He's got another muscle he wants you to feel."

Next to her, Arturo's look turned angry. She'd found the ChapStick in her jacket pocket and was putting some on.

"But it ain't as big," called another, and the rest of them laughed.

"Shut up," he called over his shoulder. He lifted his shoe and a leaf the wind had pinned to it moved on. She'd bet the shoes near the bus weren't as shiny. He turned slightly and nodded toward it.

"Who you got in there? You got a boyfriend coming down?" He nodded again toward the bus but kept his eyes on her face.

"My father," she said, she wasn't sure why. Maybe because it had been true once.

"*Lo siento,*" he said. I'm sorry.

"He's not a bad man, though."

The guard who'd gone away with the dollar bills was back. There was an orange and white Dunkin' Donuts box on the hood of the bus and he was handing out Styrofoam cups of coffee from a cardboard cup-tray. There was an extra cup for Arturo Rodriguez and the guard put it on the ground behind the front tire.

Arturo brought out his pack of cigarettes.

"Listen up," he said, looking at the pack. "I'm going to marry you."

The pack was empty. He crumpled it and dropped it on the ground. It was still a second, then the wind came and sent it away like a miniature tumbleweed. She had laughed and was grinning now although he probably couldn't see that with the wind blowing her hair again. She liked Arturo Rodriguez.

"You're already married." She indicated his ring. "Or I would think about it," she added.

"I divorce her at lunch and marry you."

She just shook her head and took her hair out of her face again. The guards moaned. He ignored them. He spoke in Spanish now.

"Where are you from?"

"El Salvador. And you?"

"Guatemala." He looked at her another moment, and nodded twice. "Okay, point out your father when he comes down. He'll have steak his first night back at Holmesburg." He turned around and jogged back to the bus.

In a minute they were bringing off the handcuffed prisoners and Mindi looked for the meanest looking of them all. She settled on a huge bald man made of muscle and fat, with eyes so small she wondered if they saw, and feet so big it could have been a joke. He had a guard of his own, rifle ready.

When she pointed at him Arturo's face went slack. Then he called over, "Brian Stamp *es tu padre? Hijo de la gran . . .*" Brian Stamp is your father? Son of a . . . Mindi waved at him, and then at her "*padre,*" who waved back with both hands and emitted something that sounded like a moo.

The last prisoner went into the building followed by the final guard. Arturo Rodriguez's coffee was still behind the front wheel of the bus. Mindi turned and ran back to the marker, again touching it with her toe, and then just walked. There was the smell of popcorn in the shadow of the east archway and of urine as she left the square. She crossed through Broad Street's heavy traffic and entered Chanet's through the revolving doors of the main entrance. She took off her coat and passed the rumpled guard on his stool with his face in someone's red store bag.

As Mindi went by the chocolate stand, the chocolate manager was taping a sign to the register:

TRY OUR CHOCOLATE COVERED PRETZELS!

THEY'RE TASTY!

ON SALE!

(THEY'RE GOOD)

The man looked so blue she bought a pound. The chocolate manager perked up with the sale.

"Was it the sign?"

She nodded, biting into one of the pretzels.

"Ahha!" His round face glowed.

And riding the escalator, she turned around to see the floor below. She found it was organized into perfect square sections. In one stood a husband and wife, each of them holding a hand of the little boy between them, the parents' heads bobbing back and forth between two refrigerators with a salesman's finger. In another, teenagers leafed through racks of CDs, shuffling a step to the right to begin each new row.

As she neared the eighth floor, the directory hanging from the ceiling informed her the china department would be to her left. Stepping off, she walked the aisle, peering into the merchandise areas at briefcases, pocketbooks, expensive jackets, lamps, chairs and couches, her shoes *vvvvippping* on the rug in a way that had her anticipating a shock when she touched something metal.

China.

She stepped into the display and felt cut off from the rest of the store, swallowed by an arrangement she recognized instantly as inspired. A huge mahogany étagère stood in profile to the side of the entrance, the tip of the display wedge formed by three surrounding walls of glass shelving. The shelves were filled with brightly hued tea sets, china, and stemware, but also with dramatically formed red, violet, and yellow glass flowers, blown stained-glass balls with metallic finishes or magenta-colored or firebrick, and delicate, translucent sea forms of glass—shells, waves, jellyfish, water clear or tinctured pink.

There were fascinating, colorful off-kilter bowls and glass baskets, as well as earthy porcelain objects. Larger bowls and other unique glass pieces stood centered on bases in carefully chosen places throughout.

The sets of china and silverware, which were mainstay, were only artful background. Colors complemented here instead of moving incrementally by shade. Size relationships were pleasing; if unpredictable, they were intuitively right. Light splashed through glass to play on the floor with light spilling through still more glass. She felt as if she was in a museum of modern art or some glass blower's palace.

She noticed the absence of store music in here, was grateful for it and relaxed further. She was about to move around to look at the étagère head-on, but noticed a simple dark-stained writing desk with an inkwell on it and moved there instead. The inkwell was crystal with brass corners and mouth. It was elegant, and she held it up to eye level wondering that in a department store someone would think to fill it only—but exactly—halfway with blue-black ink. She was careful, without thinking about it, to put it back in just the same place.

There was more to this display. She felt the lines of it converge behind her and began to turn, but spotted a pair of glass baskets about the size of umbrella stands, on a rough-hewn barn-door table by the sidewall. She went to look. The table still had its ancient metal bracket and the baskets were signed by the artist, Dale Chihuly.

The baskets were beautiful and lopsided, leaning into themselves like they were still molten. The combinations of color were amazing—the one she liked most a glowing gold inside, with windswept yellow giving way in licks to stormy greens, streaks of blue, wisps of red outside. Their shapes reminded her of the dripping objects in Dalí paintings, and the colors made her think of the majestic tumult of fire in a gathering storm. Now she understood the barn door.

Turning, she spied a series of lacquered boxes of various sizes on the opposite wall and went to them.

Freddy was pinning his name tag back to the lapel of his jacket as he emerged from the stock room to see the long black hair and beautiful body moving away from him toward the sidewall. His first thought was of the girl he had dated years before. But he was always so reminded when he saw long black hair, and had stopped seriously considering the possibility long ago.

But when the girl reached up and moved a lacquered box into the exact spot it had been before some customer must have moved it, in the instant before she turned toward the étagère and in surprise pointed at it, he knew.

"Can I help you?" is what came out of his mouth.

She turned to him, but without recognition. "That vase," she said pointing to it again. She gave a startled but delighted laugh and brought her hand to her mouth. "It's the same one," she said, and went over to it.

She took the long-necked crystal vase off the shelf and returned with it to where Freddy stood. It was the piece that had started him building. He looked again and saw the two of them standing together in its facets a thousand times.

"It's for my . . ." Didn't she know him? ". . . parents. You're—"

"Parents," he repeated.

"—Frederick Builder."

"Yes."

Mindi went to the shelves where the vase had been and put it back down for a moment. She backed up and looked at it from there. Then she retrieved it again and came back, framed by the étagère. She became a strobe for him with each step, wrecking his display, perfecting it, as she returned.

"You did this display," she said to him.

"Yes."

"It's wonderful." She looked down at the vase and then back up at him questioningly.

"Do you remember that night?" he asked.

She knew which *night*, though. Why was it there at the tip of her memory? Yes!—but she hadn't thought of it in years. She'd dated this man for maybe two or three months, yet she'd recognized him from that night.

"Hot chocolate," he said.

"Yes, I remember," she said. Then, "How *are* you. Are you still writing?"

"Yes. Short stories, I'm working on a novel. How about you?"

"I'm writing, too. I'm an editor at *Getting Feathers*."

He shook his head.

"It's a literary magazine."

She brought some hair behind her ear with a finger, then shifted the vase from the crook of her arm and held it up to him.

"Since I was a child my parents had a vase like this one in the kitchen. Ours broke. I thought they must have stopped making them. I just wanted something close."

"They make a few," he said.

She asked, remembering it was important, "How much is it?"

"Six hundred dollars."

She closed her eyes. "I don't have it," she whispered, and opened them.

"You could lay it away. No problem."

"Yes, please, could I?"

They moved to the register. Freddy filled out the slips and took the vase and the cash she'd brought. "I'm maxed out on the card," she said sheepishly but still excited. "I'll come back with the rest before Christmas," she said. "Okay? And pick it up?"

"No, take it with you," Freddy said. "I'll trust you for it." He grinned to cover the confusion he felt, the Manager of the Year smiling snidely at him—his picture adorned Chanet's boxes and bags—as he boxed it up for her.

"Mindi," Freddy said, putting the box in a store bag and keeping his eyes on what he was doing. "Could I have your number?"

But she was looking at the display again. It seemed to swirl out from where the vase had been—and now it buzzed with an intensity that reminded her of that strange night she'd met him. She was sure it was only because she was meeting him again now. But she had the same sensation she'd had standing with him on the porch, when she thought something might tear through the sky.

She'd heard Freddy ask for her number. And she wasn't sure how to convey interest in friendship but not more. There was something about him that she still found interesting, it was here in his display and would probably be in his writing. But she remembered there was also something lacking; she remembered concluding in Colorado that what she thought was hidden might not be there. She looked back at him. And went to the counter and wrote down her number.

As he watched Mindi leave his display with his vase, most of what he felt ran through him unnamed. But amazement, there was that. And hope, of making writing real, of having her again, of being seen out with her by every one of the pompous upper-management assholes— but he felt threatened, too, and terrified.

And *shame!* Now it hit him. Shame she'd seen him here. As though he'd been masturbating and the girl in his fantasy had walked through the door. For what were these displays except masturbation? The effort and the sweat of self-expression for himself, by himself. Yet she had admired him for it. She'd understood, if not what she'd walked in on, that she'd walked in on something. She'd gone to the center, hadn't she? Think what she would feel if she saw it in his writing instead of here in this dead medium. If she read the stories he'd written over the years. This time he'd show her. He wanted—

"Nice ass."

Freddy started and turned to see who had spoken.

"Not yours," Jamison said, mistaking Freddy's surprise, "the girl's." Lighting a cigarette despite the prohibition, he nodded toward Mindi as she was just disappearing down the escalator. Blue jeans, parka, simple brown bag strapped over her shoulder. The top of her head, and she was gone.

"I've been watching you work," Jamison said. He indicated the pillar. He took another drag. He said significantly, "A bit of a scouting expedition, you might say," and smiled weightily. He teased. "Not the smoothest of sales techniques, a bit staccato." His lips were pursed in minor criticism. "But"—now brightly—"but"—the sun shone—"you got the job done." A clap on the back. The misplaced pride of a nonexistent, Freddy thought. Jamison was waiting.

"Thank you . . . Bobby."

"Tut-tut," Jamison said, "I'll let you know when it's Bobby, eh?"

"It's just that at lunch you said . . ."

Jamison stared at him and Freddy looked away.

"That was lunch, this is now," Jamison said. "We wanted you to see that we don't take ourselves so seriously in upper-middle management. That little hierarchical distinctions are not so very dear to us there." Then, with swash and buckle, he relented. "You know what? Go ahead, call me 'Bobby.'" Magnanimous, self-effacing, Bobby.

Finished with his cigarette, Bobby twisted it from the filter. "We've got the plan almost finalized for that chocolate manager, by the way," Jamison said. He held the butt by its filter, looking around for a trash can. "Thought it up myself," he said modestly. "Let you in on it soon, but for now just keep in mind that it was my idea to put you on the team. I'll be counting on you."

"Yes, Bobby."

"Yes, Bobby what?"

"Yes, Bobby . . . sir?"

"Good. And, oh, yes," he said. "You fired an untouchable a couple days ago," using management's shorthand for submanagement personnel. "A Jill Caracino?"

"Yes."

"How come?"

"I think she was stealing."

Jamison nodded. "Well, then, good show." He got very serious now. "One more thing," he said, draining his voice of affect. "I noticed you took that customer's telephone number." He made his eyes big. "That's against the rules, as you well know. You're not supposed to do that." He paused to let Freddy be afraid. Then he laughed, "But that's okay," clap on the back, "Fuck her up that beautiful ass of hers and tell me all about it." He laughed again, happy with the camaraderie such comments engendered between the men who exchanged them.

He put an arm around Freddy's shoulder. "For a minute, when that chick was holding the vase, she looked about twelve years old," he said. "Don't get me wrong," he said, putting his hand up and winking. "But you know the problem with sex with twelve-year-olds, don't you?"

"You've got to kill them afterwards."

"Heard that one, huh?"

Freddy nodded. Jamison laughed, shaking Freddy's shoulder. "You'll tell me all about it, right?" he said, and when Freddy didn't respond, "Right?"

"Right," and to Jamison's sudden stare, "Bobby, sir."

"Grand, grand," and Jamison went away, back to his upstairs office.

Freddy looked at the spot where the vase had been. Somehow, the display did not fall without it, there was no need to fill the space or to build a new display.

Perfecting it.

The coffee was still behind the tire as Mindi walked back through the courtyard.

3

Murphy's Twelfth Street

Lisa had come to Mindi's, bringing the dress she planned to wear this weekend to the Lincoln Home charity ball. The plan was to rummage through Mindi's closet and find a dress for her, too, then leave for the party they were going to tonight. They'd just sat down for pre-rummage coffee in the small alcove at the back of Mindi's apartment, Lisa on the couch against the wall between end tables, and Mindi on one of the easy chairs bracketing a small coffee table. Mindi's phone rang and she leaned to answer it, setting down her coffee on the end table at her elbow.

There was a pause after her hello and then, "Hi, Mindi, this is Frederick Builder," the tension in his rhythm if not his words.

"Oh, hello, Frederick," she said, Lisa giving her a puzzled look and Mindi raising her eyebrows in response.

"How's my vase?" he said with a laugh.

His vase. She looked several feet away to where it sat by her bedroom door. "It's beautiful. I'm not going to wrap it till about five minutes before I give it to them. I'm just scared I'll break it." She lifted the cord over her coffee cup, stood up and sat down cross-legged in the armchair.

"I was wondering if you'd like to meet for a drink tomorrow. After work tomorrow. I was thinking we could go to a place you like." He was still a little jittery. She smiled, complimented.

"Okay," she said.

"Where's good?" he asked.

"How about Murphy's?" she said, naming the pub by the magazine where she and Lisa had drinks after work. "It's on Market."

31

"I know it. I pass it in the morning. The one near Twelfth?" He sounded surprised. Murphy's was on the disadvantaged end of Market Street east of City Hall, that was probably why.

"On Twelfth, uh-huh. Would you rather go somewhere else?"

"No, no, that's fine," he said quickly. "I guess I'll see you tomorrow. Oh. How's five-thirty?"

"Fine, five-thirty's great."

Mindi leaned over and put down the phone. She took back her cup.

"Who might this Frederick be?" Lisa asked. Blond hair and green eyes, she had her legs curled under her on the couch and held her cup of coffee on a saucer.

Mindi laughed, pointing at her. "'Who might this Frederick be?'" she imitated, and took a dainty taste of her own coffee. "Is that Swiss mocha, a soothing, mellow roast you're sipping, or a scintillating peppermint blend?"

Lisa wrinkled her nose. "Really, *deah*, you're too tiresome. I merely inquired as to who your gentleman caller might be. But if you'd rather not say . . ." She looked away, taking a "bored" sip.

"He's Sir Frederick of Builder, though it's extremely none of your business," said Mindi. "From the kingdom Chanet's."

"On Broad Street?"

"Quite," Mindi said. "And he's a caller only in the strictest sense of having reached me by telephone."

"I take it then that you shan't be bringing him home after cocktails tomorrow." Lisa placed her cup on the table and sat up primly.

"No, I shan't," Mindi said, throwing a pillow from the chair at her. Lisa batted it back and it landed on the floor.

"The guy who sold you the vase?"

"Uh-huh."

"I still can't place him, Mind. You went out with *so* many men in college."

"Right," Mindi said, resisting the bait.

"Did, too," Lisa tried again gamely.

Mindi rose in reproach. "We have to get ready for the party, Lisa." She picked up the pillow, flipped it onto a chair, and went into her bedroom, leaving Lisa grumpy on the couch. "Besides," she called out from her room, "at least I didn't sleep with the entire football team."

"It was so cute," Lisa called back, happily engaging. "How could I say no?" She got up and walked their dishes to the sink, laughing silently. "And what about you and the soccer team?"

"They swore they would marry me, the bastards. Come in here, dope, help me find a dress."

Lisa came into the bedroom and Mindi held up her hand, saying seriously, "I've got it narrowed down."

They stood in front of Mindi's open closet and Mindi indicated the section she'd made with the dresses she was considering. "Not much to choose from, I know."

"Seriously, Mindi, what are you going out with him for if you're not interested?"

"You can't have too many friends, you know." Then she looked at Lisa, as though reconsidering that.

Lisa was about to respond, but Mindi held her hand up again.

"Don't start, I'm sorry. Find me a dress. But no, Lisa, he's a writer, first of all. Second of all, he's an interesting guy. Really, you should go see his display."

Lisa seemed to think about it. "No, I don't think I will."

Lisa stopped at a dress, and then flipped past it. She stopped again at Mindi's favorite black one.

"Good," Mindi said cheerfully. "Think Tom will like it?"

Lisa looked at her friend appraisingly. She nodded.

"He'll love it."

Tom was one of Lisa's friends, a lawyer, who had invited them both to the Lincoln Home Ball, an annual event organized by the legal community to benefit the old-age home for which it was named. They'd be a threesome on Saturday night, keeping the pressure off.

"What's he like?" Mindi had asked when Lisa first brought him up.

"Oh, let's see. He's divorced. He's tall with black hair and a beard. He's the gallery's lawyer. Fair painter, too. Loves to dance, that's why you'll like him. He drives a great big motorcycle, though—don't get your hair caught in the spokes."

Lisa laid the dress out on Mindi's bed, next to her own dress, which was brand-new and powder blue, and sat down. Tom had a friend he'd wanted to bring along for her, too. But the Lincoln was a legal thing and maybe—

"Think that public defender will be there?" Mindi asked reading her mind, which by now surprised neither of them.

"Could be," Lisa said, as if not important either way. But then, "Turn me down for a drink. Maybe he's brain damaged," she added hopefully.

A week ago, she'd plunked down at their table at Murphy's and told Mindi about meeting him in the gallery.

"This guy came in today," she'd said when the waitress had their drink order. "He'd been in a couple months ago with his wife and bought four paintings for her. His wife, though, Mind. She was—well, she seemed—what's the word? . . . Distant, maybe."

"A bit out the door?" Mindi asked.

Lisa nodded. "Yeah. But not so's you'd notice, you know? He sure didn't," she said. "Dummy," she added. "When he came over to ask me how much for the paintings she liked, it was over five thousand dollars. And he winced." Lisa laughed. "He really winced. It's amazing how shocked people are. But they don't wince."

"Uh-oh," said Mindi.

"Yeah, I really liked him." She held up her finger. "But I'm no home wrecker.

"Anyway, today he comes in again. And he's got the paintings with him. And he wants to know if the gallery would want to buy them back.

"Mrs. Josin took them at a fraction. I tried to talk to him while she did the receipts. Philip's his name. Turns out he's a lawyer, a public defender. But he was dead out, Mind. Nothing in the guy.

"I probably shouldn't have said it, but I said, 'I remember when you bought them. Your wife didn't seem very nice.' Something like that."

"You said that?"

Lisa nodded.

"I think he liked it a little. I mean, for a minute. That I'd say it. But he just sort of kept looking at brushes through the counter glass. I even asked him to come out with us here for a drink. But he said, no, he couldn't. Mrs. Josin came over with the check"—Lisa shrugged—"and he left."

They'd both been quiet a moment.

Mindi had said, "People need time, Lisa."

Yeah, Lisa thought now, looking at her dress on the bed again. People need time. But if that Philip showed up at the ball, she was going to knock him dead with that dress.

Mindi was at the bed now, holding her black dress in front of her. She looked over it at Lisa's. "Hey, you should wear my gold earrings," she said.

"Okay."

"Does Tom like black?" Mindi asked.

Lisa laughed, bringing herself back. "How should I know if he likes black?"

"He's *your* friend."

"We haven't talked about black."

"Well, does he use black in his paintings?" Mindi glared at her.

"Yes, he likes black. He loves black." Lisa stood up with her dress, too. "What do you think of mine?"

"Beautiful." She moved closer for a better look. "Pretty sheer, isn't it?"

Lisa smiled impishly.

"You'll have to wear a bra," Mindi said.

Lisa's look said it wasn't in the cards. "You can practically—no, you *can* see through it, Lisa."

"Yours isn't exactly nipple-obscuring, kiddo."

"You—" Mindi stopped and shook her head. "I'm taking my shower," she said, swinging a towel from the floor over her back and going into the bathroom.

Inside, she undressed and folded her jeans and sweatshirt next to the sink. She took off her bracelet. The catch was getting loose, she had to get it fixed. She put it in the pocket of her jeans. She turned on the water and tested it with her hand.

Why *was* she going for a drink with Frederick Builder? She wasn't attracted. Was she? No. She had told Lisa the truth—she was going to make a friend. But even while she was saying that she realized there was more to it. She was intrigued. Why *was* this guy in a department store? He could be in a museum, like that director said, or design sets like Stuart.

She stepped under the hot water and closed the shower door. And she'd been thinking about that first night she met him. That she remembered it at all had interested her, but that she remembered it so clearly still really surprised her. After Chanet's, she'd come home . . . and that night had rushed back in minute detail.

She had been studying for a midterm and had gone outside for a moment to clear her head. But the night had been extremely uncommon, so clear and tight that she had stayed out watching the street and the neighborhood. She had felt as if she could only have seen them through gauze before. She had thought of calling up to Lisa to say, "Hey, step outside," because it already looked like a painting, one of those done with a thin, sharp brush.

At the edge of the porch she'd had the view up and down the street. Then from one corner a dot moved. It had become human, a shabby overcoat and no hat. And as Frederick came closer, she noticed his hands at his sides had no gloves on them. A few times he slipped but he just kept looking ahead, letting himself slide the few inches until his foot hit pavement again. He hadn't fallen, she thought in the shower, probably for the same reason babies didn't die sometimes falling out of windows. She had thought immediately, maybe he's a writer, too. How wonderful that naive thought seemed to her now, either full off the mark or magically correct. He had stopped and looked at her, and she'd realized she'd seen him before in Lewis Gibson's office. "A writer," had positively flopped out of her mouth. But he had been dumbstruck. Dumbstruck!

It was amazing she could remember all that when so much had happened soon after. Her father being arrested, moving to Colorado. Having to read about the trial online or in the Philly papers she bought at a campus magazine shop, because her mother wouldn't tell her anything, really, and she hadn't wanted to ask her father. And her father calling her after the verdict. In a voice she'd never heard before saying,

"I am sorry."

"For what, *Papi?*"

"For making you the daughter of a criminal. For giving you my name."

"No, don't say that, *Papi*. Don't."

"I paid that man the money." He whispered that.

"Do you think I *care?*" She'd shrieked it and her roommate got up from a bowl of soup and quietly left the room.

There was only silence, him breathing. Then he said, "Mr. McDonald is doing the papers. You are going to have your mother's family name."

"No."

"I am not asking you."

When he said that there was only one answer: *Sí.* But she'd said nothing.

"Do you hear?"

Nothing.

"Do you hear me? You will do it."

"If you don't want me to have your name then change yours."
She'd hung up. She'd left that night for Philadelphia and he'd slapped
her face—he'd never hit her before—and ordered her, shouted at her
to sign the application for name change. Mr. McDonald, her father's
lawyer, was standing there holding out a pen. Her mother yelled at her
and finally begged her just to do what her father wanted.

Her mother pulled her aside. "In a month he'll realize he wasn't
thinking. Change it and change it back!"

"You are crazy, Mom."

"You have not disobeyed him, today is not the day to start."

"Crazy, I'm his daughter."

"He needs you to obey him. Do you understand? Don't you see
what it would do to him?"

No, Mindi said, only what it would do to him to sign. She was over
eighteen, she said, and was not signing. And that was it. "And do not
hit me, Mom. You're about to. Don't."

The shower door was steamed over and she closed her eyes and
faced the shower, letting the water wash away the soap, lifting her
arms, letting it wash it away. Frederick had slipped easily into her
past, more easily than others before and others after. She might have
felt some sadness that she had to leave just at the beginning of their
relationship. But there was too much going on.

And he hadn't really let her inside him, and so she hadn't let him,
though he'd been pretty persistent the few times she'd stayed at his
place. She remembered almost giving in after her father was arrested.
But he'd kept a funny distance, a sullen, even angry one it seemed
later, and she'd resisted. The distance had seemed at first like the one
men often kept when she first met them . . . a nervousness, really, that
always made her feel guilty, and so she'd thought it was that. But it
had lasted longer and, she realized later in Colorado, had had a
different quality.

Still, she had seen something in him, some artistic sense, and that had been borne out in his display. She thought of the intensity, maybe anger—because she thought now that might be what it was—in the display. Maybe that was what he'd been keeping from her back then. It would almost certainly be in his writing, even if he didn't think so.

Freddy had written down "Murphy's Twelfth" and was walking there now.

Jamison had come by before lunch to tell him the date of the principals' meeting for the "by committee" chocolate termination and to see that he marked it down. He'd tried to entice Freddy to ask for hints about the plan by telling him the outside actors had been hired. But Freddy didn't bite.

Jamison was coming to like him tremendously, the thought of which would have sickened him more if he weren't on his way to meet Mindi. He'd thought often during the day of which of his stories to show her, he planned during their drink to ask if she would read some. And he regretted not spending as much time writing them as he should have, but there were the responsibilities of his job, which, as much as he disliked it, was draining and required long hours.

He wished again that he had been collected enough on the phone to suggest a bar where the store people hung out so they could see him with her. He knew Murphy's Twelfth Street, he passed it every morning coming out of Reading Terminal, the regulars lined up with shaky hands to enter. It was in this dirty, teeming three blocks of commercial district between City Hall and the terminal, on the north side of the street where addict entrepreneurs hung in front of record shops selling fake Rolexes and bags of marijuana, for about the same price. You might as well smoke the watch, though, and wear the weed, he thought, because neither would do what they were supposed to. He'd bought his own Rolex from them and had to tell *it* what time it was instead of the other way around. He turned to the clock on City Hall and set it as he walked.

He arrived at the bar before Mindi did. There wasn't much of a crowd yet, though people were coming in behind him as he stood just inside. A man missing two teeth approached him with a tale, asking for money to get back to North Jersey. Moving away from him to the bar, Freddy told him to hitchhike, advising he show some leg.

At the bar, he couldn't see what they had through the dewy refrigerator door, so he had the bartender go through the beers while he watched the entrance for Mindi. He ordered a Molson and took it with him through the bar to the tables, selecting a small one against the back wall, away from the other patrons and with a clear view of the door. He moved his chair to give him the best view and downed the beer quickly. Getting the waiter's attention, he ordered another to take away the edge before she got there.

Just before five-thirty, he saw Mindi enter and looked away quickly, not wanting her to think he'd been awaiting her anxiously. He wasn't worried about her showing, no indeed. He was relaxed and enjoying the interesting photos on the wall, to which he now inclined. Still watching peripherally, though, he saw her spot him and leaned closer to the wall to make out a particularly difficult detail in a particularly engrossing photo. The name of the sponsor on the softball team uniforms, if she asked.

When she didn't arrive at the moment he anticipated, he looked her way again and saw she was talking to the guy he'd suggested should thumb it. He stood quickly, hoping to save her before she saved herself, but then she did just that and started toward him again. He turned back to the wall of photos, sitting down slowly.

When she made it to the table, "Hi, I'm here," she said sunnily, and all the show melted out of him. He began to stand as she sat down and was caught for a moment in an awkward crouch. But the waiter appeared then, greeting Mindi by name, and Freddy sat down while they exchanged pleasantries. The swell of her breasts under her sweater made him remember having them in his hands. He looked at her face, then away. Of course she was achingly beautiful, he'd thought he'd come ready for that.

Come on, he told himself angrily to look her in the eye again. Mindi smiled her "sorry" past the still-chatting waiter and Freddy smiled back, coming back to himself a bit.

She still wore that simple silver bracelet, he noticed, given to her by her grandmother in El Salvador, and had on turquoise and silver earrings, too, but that was the extent of her jewelry; understated but with potent effect, like herself.

Now she was asking for a coffee and Kahlúa and when she finished he ordered another beer.

"Sal says sorry about asking you for money," Mindi said, the waiter taking his leave. She was gesturing to the guy at the bar.

"No problem at all," Freddy said. "He seemed like a nice guy."

"He is," she assured him. "Do you remember my friend Lisa?"

"Your roommate?" He vaguely remembered a blond roommate in sweatpants.

Mindi nodded. "That's right."

"Sure I do."

"She's in Philly, too. We come here all the time. That's how we know Sal."

"It's a great place," he said. "Interesting photos." So Mindi pointed to the one of Bruce Willis on the crowded sidewall and told him how he'd stopped in from a shoot at City Hall.

The waiter was threading his way back through the crowd with their drinks and set them down. While Freddy poured his beer into the mug, the waiter told Mindi "Frank's" latest joke. The head overflowed some and Freddy put his napkin around the glass to absorb it. The waiter got to the punch line and Mindi groaned, which made the waiter laugh.

"I'll tell him you said so," the waiter said, picking up Freddy's empty bottle and going away.

"Frank's the owner," Mindi explained. Her earrings shone in front of her hair. "He thinks bartenders are supposed to tell jokes. That one was typical." Freddy hadn't heard it. He laughed and swallowed more beer. She shook her head and said solemnly, "He must have missed joke day at bartending school."

He lifted his mug. Under her open, friendly gaze, he was feeling everything he'd brought with him to say slip away from him again. He sipped his beer and turned again to the photos, trying to think of anything at all. He suddenly despised himself, and Mindi some, too.

"I know I keep thanking you for the vase," she said, breaking the silence. "My parents are going to love it."

"You're welcome," said Freddy. He was careful to make it seem as if he'd found out what he'd wanted to from the picture before turning to her.

"You have a good eye."

"Really?"

Freddy laughed a little now. He tilted his glass on the table and held it in place with a finger on the rim.

"How long have you been back in Philly?" he asked.

"About four years," she said. "I went to grad school out there and came back after that."

"I remember your father . . . Is he out?"

"Two months ago. That's why I wanted the vase."

"I knew it was something. I mean, six hundred dollars for a vase."

"I know," she said, wilting. She perked up to say, "I'll be bringing the rest to the store very soon."

"That's fine," he said. She began talking about her job at *Getting Feathers*, but he was able to avoid the department store. When she had almost finished her drink, Freddy ordered another round.

Feeling more comfortable now, he took advantage of the lull after the waiter brought it over to remark, "You know, it was pretty strange seeing you like that the other day." He regretted it instantly, because she tilted her head and he knew she was going to ask him why.

She said, "For me, too. Why do you think?" She leaned forward, her earrings moving back and forth on tiny silver chains.

"Well—" he stopped. He couldn't say any of the things he was thinking. "I'm not sure," he said finally.

She lifted her glass and leaned back. "So, you're writing."

"Short stories, a lot of short stories. I'm working on that novel." "Working" was close, he knew how to start it. "A number of my short stories have been published." He had got two into obscure publications while still in college. "Mostly the old ones, though. I haven't been sending them out recently." Hadn't sent any out since starting at Chanet's, though he'd turned out quite a few.

"What's your novel about?"

"Well . . . it's about transformation," he said shifting uncomfortably.

Mindi put down her glass. "Transformation from what? Into what?"

"I don't really like talking about whatever I'm working on at the moment." He swallowed some beer and dried his mouth with the napkin.

She laughed. "You never would talk about your writing."

"I'll show it to you when I'm further along, I promise."

"Well, if whatever comes out of you in your displays comes out in your writing, I'm sure it will be worth reading."

"My displays?"

She was stirring with the straw. "The one I saw was something." She looked up. "There was so much emotion in it."

Now Freddy laughed derisively. He looked at his hands on the beer bottle.

"Well, I thought so anyway," she said, sounding a little offended.

"I'm sorry," he said, looking up. "They're nothing, though. I just do them to keep busy in that place."

"Oh." She did not pursue it further, but she did not sound convinced.

"I really would like it, though, if you'd read some of my stories," he said.

"Of course. I'd like to," she said.

"And tell me what you think of them," he said, growing more animated. "Maybe you'll have some ideas for me . . . where I should send them."

Something seemed to occur to her. "You know which one I want to read?" She reached over and hit his hand. "The one you were thinking about the night you almost froze your hands off."

He grinned. "That's how you know people best, right? By reading their work?"

"Did I tell you that?"

"Only about a million times."

She took another sip of her drink, finishing it. "You don't like people getting to know you?"

"I still have the story. You can see it."

He finished his beer and Mindi excused herself to say something to Frank at the bar. The crowd was mostly male and he watched as eyes rolled up from beer and sandwiches, as even a chair or two scraped as she went by. And then as the eyes turned back to see where she'd come from and respected him.

He made his look indifferent and watched her lean into the bar. She shook her head and more of her hair fell to the sides. He drank from his beer and noticed something glittering on the floor. He leaned closer: It was her bracelet. He glanced over toward the bar and she was coming back. He quickly bent and scooped up the bracelet, put it in his pocket. Then he turned once more to look at the photos. To see if the pitcher wasn't a buddy from high school, if she asked.

He wanted to take her to dinner and dancing, to be seen with her by everyone. He wanted to sleep with her, he believed that in her arms he would somehow be reborn. He begged her in his mind, *Please Mindi, let me be reborn!*

"Hey," he turned too soon and began while she was still several feet from the table, "what happened to your bracelet?"

She stopped in her tracks, looked at her wrist and gasped. "I don't know," she said. "I had it."

She came the rest of the way and started moving things around on the table. "The catch is loose." She was looking on the floor by her chair. "I have to find it." He knew why the bracelet was so important. Her grandmother had died soon after giving it to her, just as civil war in El Salvador was escalating, and Mindi hadn't been allowed to go back for the funeral.

"I'll help you," he said. She left the table to retrace her steps to the bar, and Freddy went to the other end near the entrance. There he took out the bracelet and walked over to Mindi who was on her hands and knees, with the waiter kneeling next to her. Freddy held the chain out in front of her face.

"Oh, thank you," she said getting up and hugging him tightly. "God, my grandmother—"

"Your grandmother gave it to you," he said. He was smiling at her. "I remember." They went back to the table again. She looked at him gratefully and put the chain in her pocketbook. "Listen," he said, "if you're not doing anything Friday night, I was thinking we could have dinner. Afterwards we could go dancing."

She put the pocketbook on the table. "I'm sorry, Frederick, I'm supposed to have drinks with my workshop Friday. But thank you. I hope you'll bring your stories to the magazine, though. Maybe if you have time next week, we could have lunch and talk about them."

"Well, how about Saturday night?"

"I already have plans Saturday, too."

Freddy waited.

"I have a dinner to go to," she said. And when he still said nothing, she added uncomfortably, "It's for this home for the elderly." She stopped. "It's this—" She stopped and sat straighter. Something about him.

Freddy shrugged and rushed in. "No problem," he said. "You don't have to explain."

"Okay. Will you bring by the stories?"

"I will." Then he said, "Didn't mean to push."

She grinned and shook her head. "If I'd lost this . . ." She held up her wrist, then pointed to her pocketbook. "I've really got to get it fixed."

He said, "By the way, where is your office?" and took out a pen. She told him and he wrote it on a napkin. The waiter appeared and Freddy asked for the check. He handed the waiter some money before she had a chance to protest, if she was going to. Then he walked with her to the subway station under City Hall. As the train came to a stop and the doors opened, she said good-bye, and he kissed her quickly on the cheek. As close to her mouth as he dared.

"Good to see you again," he told her.

He let her go and told her to hurry before the doors closed. When the train disappeared, he went back up the stairs and crossed the courtyard, and then the street. He walked the south side of Market again, looking at none of it.

4

The Lincoln Home Ball

Saturday evening, as Philip got ready in his West Philadelphia row house, Mindi and Lisa dressed at Mindi's, and Michael Leopold, first assistant district attorney, masturbated in his town house. Having nothing more titillating than the bar association magazine, he sat bare assed on the edge of his desk chair stroking himself to the woman on the cover. The woman had made partner at a top firm at the mere age of thirty, according to the cover squib.

Thirty. He tried to imagine her breasts through the severely tailored jacket and white shirt she wore buttoned at the throat. He tried to imagine her with no panties on under her neatly creased pinstripe suit skirt.

"Partner at thirty," he murmured, and stroked himself faster.

There was that little quote next to the briefcase that distracted him but resonated: "I did it by delaying gratification."

He stroked, thinking that delay of gratification was a wonderful thing and something at which both he and Sharon, his fiancée, were expert. Sharon's hurtful jest aside (that he might try delaying his a little longer), delay of gratification had taken them far: him to the position of first assistant district attorney and her to the position of SVP of a major pharmaceutical—not to mention daughter to the mayor and patron of the arts. They could delay gratification so well, they often joked, they didn't even need it anymore.

He had to hurry, which was never an issue, unless he needed to hurry. Sharon was waiting for him to pick her up. They were going to the ball at the Four Seasons, hosted this year by Judge Willison. When a man like Judge Gunther W. Willison asked if you'd like to buy tickets, you liked to. Willison might be the closest thing to Oliver Wendell Holmes Pennsylvania would ever see, but nobody in this town was above paying back a slight. And Michael needed all the good will he could garner. What he really needed, he thought, was a *big case.*

With that he came into the Kleenex he had at the ready and was up from the chair before he'd even stopped spurting. He rushed into the bathroom, put himself away, flushed the wad, washed his hands thoroughly, and washed them again. He opened the hamper and brushed in the smelly argyles he had worn at the gym from atop the sink. He splashed on some of that terrific-smelling Chanet's brand of aftershave, the one with last year's Manager of the Year smiling on the label, and straightened his bowtie in the mirror.

He looked at his eyes looking at his eyes and said out loud, "Your big case, Mikey." He retrieved his tuxedo pants from his desk, fastened the cummerbund, slipped on the shoes, grabbed the hanger with his jacket, and hurried out to the car.

Hanging the jacket inside, he got in and turned the key. He'd made a name for himself, he thought, pulling away from the curb. Had the best conviction rate in the office, and a shot and a half at being the next district attorney. And he was only—he shook his head at his good fortune—thirty-three years old. He was young, everything was ahead of him: beautiful Sharon who could throw a party like nobody's business, a kid or two, there was no telling how far he could go. God! Just give me that case! When they arrived at the ballroom of the Four Seasons, Michael had to admit he was even more impressed than he'd expected to be. This was a gala event, always, but this year, Willison presiding, it was especially grand. Men in black tie held brandy or scotch, women in formal gowns carried white wine, and the place was replete with the legal, business, and political elite. He was conscious that Sharon, in her clinging, low-cut beige dress and diamond earrings, the mayor's daughter and easily one of the most beautiful women in attendance, was a tremendous asset here. He squeezed her elbow in a burst of affection then sidled away a moment to say hello to Sam McDonald, a most respected defense attorney. Coming back to Sharon, he found her oohing at an older woman's brooch.

"It's been in my family for generations," the woman said.

"Isn't the *congressman's* wife's brooch gorgeous?" Sharon asked him. Cody's wife, right. He looked at the blackened piece of twisted metal—it looked like it should be smoldering. He oohed it.

"It's survived plague and famine," said the sixtyish redhead. "Wars."

The thing probably wounded somebody in one of those wars.

The crowd was most dense near the hors d'oeuvres tables, and he went over, leaving Sharon still oohing. On the tables were arrayed a multifarious mix of delightful delectables. Delicate slivers of several kinds of quiche, goose liver pâté, sushi, artichoke hearts, brie, jack, and some cheeses not even he, who had been to a million of these, recognized, caviar, all were arranged on gleaming silver platters. Bar kiosks dotted the place and he moved to one nearby. The drinks were all top-shelf, of course, but there was even a bordeaux from a darn good year and a domestic pinot noir he knew to be excellent. No little hot dogs or microwave quiches here, he mused, waiting for a glass of the bordeaux for himself and the pinot for Sharon.

When he saw the two women, though, he realized the food was not the only reason the guests stood so thick here. Both of them, gorgeous, the Latin American one absolutely stunning, standing together near the tables laughing with two men. Lots of eyes flitted to them. Michael couldn't help revising the pecking order with Sharon down a tier. He was glad to be handed his wine and move clear.

Across the floor were the raised dais and the podium from which the judge, before dinner, would thank those whose presence he'd extorted. Michael surveyed the ballroom, observing the couple of hundred of his colleagues in the trial bar, as well as the judges and politicians, and the recognizable business leaders in attendance. Sharon's father, the mayor, was here.

49

Reaching Sharon, he said, *"Clos Pegase,"* handing her the glass. She made an impressed look. "The 2002." She was impressed again.

Seeing her father, Sharon made a move toward him, but Michael caught her eye over the bordeaux: They should wait until the mayor was talking to somebody better.

He went on with his visual survey of the guests, starting a frictionless, fluid pan as if on greased ball bearings, which brought Philip smoothly into view and left him ever so close to behind, but Philip looked up. If he hadn't, Michael's circle would have continued without nearly pause, because Philip was one in whom he had not the slightest interest. Had a chandelier fallen on the man's head, Michael couldn't believe he'd raise an eyebrow, though they had for a time been friends.

Philip had started at the defender's office at about the same time Michael had started with the DA. Both had great rookie years and they had gotten to know each other. When Michael started dating Sharon about four years ago, it turned out she'd gone to school with Philip's then new, now soon-to-be-ex wife, Cindy. Sharon had even been in Cindy's wedding party. Michael and Philip had become doubles partners, but because of Philip, they sometimes beat the wrong people. He was not, Michael found—and apparently Cindy had, too—sufficiently ambitious. After a while, Michael stopped bothering with plausible excuses for breaking the dinner plans Sharon kept making for Cindy's sake. And now he would have to say hi.

Philip, for his part, had not felt Michael's look, the detachment at its source so profound. He'd just happened to look up after his own survey of the room and caught his eye. As was typical with these things, his colleagues were waiting in patient lines with their wallet-sized children and life-sized spouses, to whisper greetings and veiled requests into the ears of as many judges as possible before dinner. He'd been glad to be here stag, with an empty chair next to him to look forward to at dinner.

The judges dotted the room like so many Mafia godfathers. They nodded slightly or didn't, smiled slightly or didn't, clucked little photograph chins or didn't, in approval and disapproval of the attorneys, their requests, their children, and their chuckling, horse-grinning spouses. Consiglieri clerks stood by, straining to see and hear, so as to keep accurate record of the favors given and refused. On Monday a host of pending motions would be granted and denied, while others fell off the earth to be forever "under consideration."

Their eyes having unfortunately locked, though, both Philip and Michael smiled, "happily surprised," and made their way toward each other. Both wished for lightning.

"Long time no see," said Michael. They shook hands.

"Hi, Mike," said Philip. "How goes it?"

"Locking them up, locking them up. You?"

"Keeping them out."

"Not what I heard," said Michael good-naturedly. "Brian Stamp's bye-bye, isn't he? Bzzzzz," pulling the switch.

"Not your notch, though." He sucked the last of the vermouth from his Manhattan.

Michael smiled. "Oh, we don't do notches these days. We've got these little gold electric chair stickers now."

"How about that."

"Hey, too bad about you and Cindy."

"Yeah, thanks."

"Terrible, really."

"Yeah."

"Awful."

"Thanks."

"What happened with you two?"

"I'm sure Cindy's told Sharon her thinking."

"She's said some things."

"Well, I don't have anything to add."

"Are you out dating?"

"It's been less than three months, Mike."

"Want word back to Cindy that you're lovin' and leavin' 'em?"

"It's over, isn't it? I don't care what gets back. How's Sharon?"

"We're getting married April twenty-ninth." He stopped. "Cindy's in the party. You understand."

"Sure."

"You know, it's funny," Michael said, sweeping an arm to the guests. "Seeing everyone here makes me realize you and I have never had a case together." He was looking at Philip as if he should be thankful as hell for that.

"That's true, Mike, we haven't."

"Who do you think would win?" Michael gave him a sly elbow.

Philip briefly considered putting this on the surface and just calling Michael the asshole he was. But with a word from Michael to his subordinates, Philip would have trouble making deals with the other ADAs. Until he got out, he owed his clients civility with this man.

"Gee, whiz, Mike," Philip answered, "I guess there's no way to tell till we get there."

The mayor and Congressman Cody had stopped to chat just behind Philip. Michael didn't want to be rude, but didn't mind, so he turned to find Sharon. She was already looking at him. Michael smiled primly at Philip. "Good seeing you, buddy." He squeezed Philip's shoulder, already past him toward the mayor.

"See you in court," Philip said softly.

"Better hope not," sang back Michael on his glide. Philip stirred his ice. Sharon went the long way around him.

Soon afterward, a woman tapped on a microphone with her nail a few times, and people started wandering to their tables to put food in their faces from big plates instead of small ones. Philip opened his name card and went to table sixteen. It was situated close to the hors d'oeuvres tables, far away from where the speeches would be made and the band would play. He was grateful for that, and again for the empty chair as he put his jacket over back and sat down. He recognized one of Sharon's distinctive bursts of laughter through the melee and, following it, located her and Michael at a table near the podium. Next to that table was the mayor's, at which in addition sat the district attorney, the chief defender (his own boss), the city's managing director, Judge Willison himself, and a congressman whose name Philip couldn't bring to mind.

The others assigned to his table were arriving in couples, looking him over and each other, while choosing seats. Philip didn't know any of them, they all apparently had civil practices. He joined the good-to-meet-you's but opted out as they settled down into law school one-upmanship. After a few tries, they left him out of it. Salads came and he ate his slowly.

Stamp, the client Michael had referred to, had called him that very day from Holmesburg Prison. Was he really going to be executed? he had asked, and started crying. Philip had told him no, of course he wasn't going to be, though of course he eventually was. There was the automatic appeal, he'd explained again, they had an excellent chance, excellent. Why not? If the man was going to die, why shouldn't he find out as late as possible?

Philip didn't believe in the death penalty, and he would do his thorough best to save Stamp on appeal. Still, his afterthought had been that it took ultimate gall to beg so sloppily about his own life, having taken so many others during a lifetime of heinous crime. But irony like that would be pretty thin soup to an episodic psychotic who liked lives ending right in his hands.

To applause and a standing ovation now, Judge Willison, slim and austere, nearing old age himself, got up from his chair and made his way to the stairs and onto the dais. He stood behind the podium.

"Ladies and gentlemen," he said in a resonant voice. "You are all so kind, so very kind, to be here tonight. And I thank you. You know, the law never provides to we its servants so much as it does when it affords us the opportunity to do good for others." The audience enthusiastically applauded its agreement. "Tonight, rest assured, there is a home filled with the elderly of our city who are most grateful to you, and who thank the legal community as a whole, and our business friends, for your support."

He waved and left the dais.

Dinner came and Philip ate his quietly, tuning out his table's animated conversation. But after dinner, as couples left for the dance floor, a group of Philip's colleagues from the defender spotted him. They wouldn't take no for an answer, so he danced a few numbers with one of their wives. He danced without looking around, the songs seeming to take forever to end, but when the woman wanted to dance still another, he made an excuse to return to his table.

His boss had greeted him on the floor and he'd made it a point to get in Judge Willison's line of vision. He'd spoken to four or more colleagues and even had a colloquy with Michael Leopold. He'd made his appearance, and could go now. At the edge of the dance floor he turned to a tap on his shoulder. A pair of equally beautiful women stood in front of him. The blond one had tapped him.

"Hi," Lisa said. He didn't seem to recognize her. "You don't remember me, do you?"

"I'm sorry."

"Don't be. My name's Lisa. You bought some paintings at the gallery I work in. You returned them."

"Oh, yes." He nodded now. "Thanks again for that," and she thought he meant more than just taking back the paintings. Lisa introduced him to Mindi, who extended her hand. Philip shook it briefly, and turned back to her. He seemed still in the haze she remembered from before.

"So, how is everything?" Lisa asked him lightly.

Philip smiled a bit too widely to fool anyone. "Just fine. How about with you?"

She laughed. "I'm fine, too," she said, gesturing to Mindi. "We came here with some friends tonight."

54

Lisa gave Mindi a sidelong look and Mindi said, "We have some extra seats at our table. Would you like to join us?" Lisa had wanted her to be the one to ask.

"I was just going to leave, actually," said Philip. He looked at Lisa and stepped back, saying gravely, then grinning, "This, I think, is the first acceptable moment to get out." He kept the grin on his face, but she thought his eyes were as lifeless as in the gallery.

"Oh," Lisa said. She shrugged. "I was hoping you would come over for a little." The music started again and the three of them went off the dance floor. "We're just hanging out at that table," she said. "Right over there," she said, pointing as they walked. They stopped near the first table off the floor.

"No, really," said Philip, "I can't." He added, "I'm supposed to meet someone."

"Oh, really? Why isn't she here?" Mindi gave her a warning glance, but for a second his smile seemed real.

"Because I like her too much for that. But thanks, really," he said. "Nice meeting you, Mindi. Good-bye," he said to Lisa. He turned away and went back to his table. They followed toward their own until they reached the hors d'oeuvres. They watched him put on his jacket from there. He was shaking hands and saying his good nights, and put his BlackBerry on his waist.

"He's not meeting anyone," Lisa said. She looked at Mindi and Mindi shook her head.

"Mindi, he keeps doing this to me."

"He thinks you feel sorry for him."

Lisa closed her mouth and crossed to his table.

"Listen. I'm not being persistent, so don't get a big head. I just want to know for informational reasons. Why won't you sit with us for a little? You're not talking to anyone. We won't take your money."

After a moment he said, "I don't like to depend on the kindness of strangers."

Lisa put her hand on the back of a chair. "Don't you realize how big a leap that is from being asked to come over and meet some people and laugh a little maybe?"

"But I'm right, aren't I?"

She looked down. "Yeah, a little. But so what? It's only because I like you."

"I appreciate it. I just can't, okay?"

"You've got that hot date to keep." She looked back up at him.

He didn't say anything. She turned around and walked back to Mindi.

When Philip hit the cold, he took deep breaths of it trying to get some feeling of being alive.

Inside, Lisa hated the woman without knowing her name and wondered what could have happened to destroy him so well.

There was a squeal from the dance floor where Michael Leopold was dipping the congressman's wife.

"It's survived plague and famine," Mindi said.

"Yeah," said Lisa bitingly, "and the trip from whatever planet she's from."

5
—
Cascadas

Freddy came into *Getting Feathers*'s small storefront office from the street, loosened his scarf, and immediately thought he was in the wrong place. Mindi's beautifully produced magazine couldn't come from this narrow and dingy, poorly lit hole-in-the-wall. From the very entrance to the back, all he could see among the several disheveled staff members were mismatched desks, ancient filing cabinets, buckling bookshelves, old computers, piles of periodicals leaning everywhere from tables, desks, and chairs. Framed glossy covers of the magazine hung on the walls, so this was the right place, but they hung askew from knots of wire.

Where was the British receptionist with her hair in a bun that such magazines were supposed to have, where was the espresso machine?

The small staff was even more disappointing, moving about in sensible shoes, skirting the junk, giving the place the feel of a thrift shop. Taking a tissue from his pocket as an excuse to stay his ground, he looked over heads for Mindi. For a moment while he pinched his nose he didn't see her, and thought perhaps she wasn't in today or had already left for lunch, but someone moved and there she was.

She was at a desk near the back of the room. Standing over her was a short gray-haired woman smoking a cigarette. He put away the tissue and approached. The people he went by leaned away to let him pass, or were bent over PCs or hunkered over their scribbling. A corned beef special sweated Russian dressing onto someone's mail. He passed a cigarette, lipstick on the filter, burning on a file cabinet without an apparent owner.

The short woman hunched over Mindi looked in profile to have very little neck. She seemed to breathe only through her cigarette, blowing out smoke and inhaling more while she made some point or listened to Mindi's response. He stopped in the space behind Mindi's desk and waited for them to finish. People excused themselves around him or didn't. Mindi finally turned away from a stream of smoke aimed at her eyes and saw him.

"Frederick," she said. "Hi," in her animated way.

"Hi," he said back. The woman next to her straightened and looked at him impatiently.

"Ms. Fineote," Mindi said, "this is Frederick Builder. Ms. Fineote is managing editor of the magazine."

"Nice to meet you," he said with a respectful smile. Ms. Fineote's shoulders may have relaxed a quarter inch and she said hello. Then she turned to Mindi again and lowered her voice. Freddy heard ". . . dear . . . appreciate your comments. I don't know . . . agree with . . . but I do appreciate them. I think we'll go with it, though."

"Of course," Mindi said.

Ms. Fineote walked away in her pointy shoes without another look at Freddy. She'd left her cigarette burning on the edge of Mindi's desk. Mindi put the cigarette out in an ashtray filled with other half-smoked and almost non-smoked Virginia Slims and stood.

"How are you?"

"Okay," he said. "I brought my stories."

"Well, let's see."

He had them in a manila envelope in the crook of his arm and he took it now in his hand. But instead of handing them to her he looked away as if to survey the place. The other workers milled slowly about like they were looking for places to die. They looked owned by their coffee, like they'd just woken up and come to work in what they'd slept in. There was no structure to the activity here, which always made him uncomfortable (at least the store had structure), and he wondered how they knew what to do. He looked back at her.

"It's funny," he said, not giving them to her yet. "I've picked up a few issues of *Getting Feathers,* and it's full of poems and stories with lots of italics, book ads, it's really . . . You'd never think . . ." He didn't finish but looked some more at the rickety furniture and the general ashy pall.

"I know," she said, spreading her arms to the place. "The magazine doesn't give us away, does it?"

"Not at all," he said, turning to her. "You're the only one that seems to fit with it. If you want to know the truth."

She looked down, and he wondered how she could be at once so demure yet completely provocative in black jeans and tight black turtleneck, no bra—the way she stood. She was saying something about what went on here, pointing . . . layout something was . . . somewhere, and her phone rang. She answered it and held up an apologetic finger to him.

He was holding the envelope tightly, feeling the weight of the stories inside. He had to give them to her, though. If he wouldn't do even that, he should just resign himself to his life in the store, designing merchandise displays. He could start wearing his Manager of the Month ribbons like the other Managers of the other Months, even lobby for the *big* award, hoping for the disgusting third-tier celebrity of a local weatherman.

Well, that's what he had to look forward to, wasn't it? To his face someday on Chanet's store bags and aftershave and on the front of the store? To signing detergent boxes in supermarkets for women with strollers and babies in Pampers? Shaking their varicose veins, instead of the firm soft hands of women who knew how to shake hands, women like Mindi who'd never settle for a department store manager, even—no, especially!—if he was Manager of the Year? Mindi hung up and he thrust the stories at her, then checked himself. "Well, here they are anyway," he said.

"I'll read them very carefully, Frederick, I promise," she said, taking the envelope. "Only, I'm not the last word, okay? It'll just be my opinion, for what it's worth."

"Sure, of course."

She put the stories in her desk drawer and while she had her back to him he unbuttoned his coat and brought out a single long-stemmed red rose. He held it out, presenting it to her when she turned again. "To thank you for your time," he said.

He saw her face flush and she jumbled some things on her crowded desk as she went for her coffee mug for the rose, and he was gratified.

"Thank you," she said, her fingers, soft and warm, brushing his for an instant, quickening his pulse as she took it. She put the cup on her desk with the flower resting against the wall so it didn't fall out.

"It's my lunch hour, Mindi," he said—she was still balancing the flower—"If you don't have plans, why don't we have a bite?"

She hesitated longer than he liked. "Let's," she said, turning back. "But is it okay if we make it a short one? I really have so much work to do." She pointed at her laptop, a document on-screen. "I have to finish this book review."

He helped her on with her coat and they left the office, turning south on Thirteenth. It had drizzled while he was inside because the pavement had water on it.

"It's great to get outside, isn't it?" she said. And the funny thing was, it was.

Cold drops of water beaded on cars and he ran his hand across one of the hoods to shove some at her, then thought it may have been a strange thing to do.

She kept turning her head to look at things as they walked, and he remembered that she'd always done that. It made you look, too. But Thirteenth was just pretty dilapidated this far north, there were just lots of rusty things, some street trees with trunks about as thick as your wrist, nothing much else. Now she had noticed a chalked hopscotch court that had lost its shape and was running into the cracks in the pavement. It might rain big and he tucked in his scarf.

"How about you, Mindi? Where's your novel?" he asked.

She turned around and walked backward a few steps. "Oh," she said, "I've published a number of them. But you couldn't know that then, could you?"

"Why couldn't I?" Her walking backward made him feel liked and especially familiar.

"Well, I don't usually tell people this, but . . . I write them under pen names. James Michener, Aleksandr Solzhenitsyn, Annie Proulx; perhaps you've heard of me." She turned forward again and Freddy laughed.

"Oh, I knew they were you, I did," said Freddy. "They're making your newest book into a movie, aren't they?"

She didn't turn around this time but became terribly divine instead, saying, "Yes, it's true. I'm playing all the parts myself, you know. Even the pets. Like De Niro."

"I see. That's very impressive. It must be very difficult." He wanted to be funny, too, but couldn't think of anything to say.

"It isn't as hard as it seems."

They turned the corner at Walnut. She pointed to a restaurant, Nick's Roast Beef. "Best roast beef sandwiches in the city if you're interested," she said. Freddy held the door for her.

"I'm interested," he said looking into her eyes. She went by him inside and said again, "Best ones in the city."

They were given a booth and they hung their coats on hooks while their ears and noses burned comfortably. "So tell me, Mr. Builder," Mindi said when they sat down, "what did you do before you became a writer of such renown?"

He answered, accepting the premise of present past. "I worked in a department store. It was unrewarding, demeaning work. I was an assistant buyer in china and glass at first. Then, before I quit, I was manager of the china department." He paused before adding, "So I guess I know what really counts."

"Well, how's the writing going then? How's the *novel* going?"

He hadn't actually started writing it yet, but he was putting down his ideas. In six months he could have it. Six months from today he would have it, he felt it so strongly with her across from him.

"It's going well," he said. "Slow, I guess, but sure."

"Well, don't get discouraged, and don't give up, even when it's slow and unsure. Giving up's what separates those who do it from those who don't."

"I think what I'm going to do is get some of my stories published first. Try and get my name out there a little so it's not a total shock when I come to people with a novel. Maybe in your magazine," he said without looking at her, "or one like it."

"Don't worry about that, Frederick. I mean, you're right, it's easier to get published if you're already published but what's most important—really it's the only important thing—is to have a quality piece of work. 'Oh, you have to know the business, blah, blah, blah,' lots of people will tell you that; it's just one point of view—you have to write a book. That's all you should be thinking about now. Then worry about publishing." She tilted the bowl of pickles to him and he took one out.

She said, "You know, except for those novels I've published under pen names, I haven't been able to get my own novels published, all the people I know. I get them read, but not published. I've written two and they sit on a shelf."

"Will you write another one?"

"Yeah."

The waiter came and Mindi asked if she could order for both of them. She ordered roast beefs "overboard," and Freddy told the waiter to bring them hot chocolate. The waiter returned in half a minute with the sandwiches, made at the end of the bar, and the chocolate. Mindi grinned at Freddy while the waiter set it all down.

"You're gonna die when you taste these," she said, lifting the top off the soggy bun. "See?" she said. "I had them dip the roll. It's going to drip all over your suit and ruin your tie and make your name plate all sticky, but you'll still thank me."

Freddy flinched. He hadn't removed his name tag? He'd gone to the magazine and was sitting here all this time, with it still on? He hated that tag, never wore it an instant longer than he had to, and only on the floor. Never out of the store. He had the name tag off in a single motion which Mindi interpreted as his joking fear for its safety.

"Yes, good idea," she said. "Keep it safe."

He felt his anger leap and glared at her without thinking.

"How is it?" she asked after a few minutes.

"Delicious," though he had quite lost his appetite, along with his nerve. He looked at the wall for some photographs but there were none, only one of those old-style table jukeboxes, so he flipped through the songs. Then he said, "How can you go on writing novels when they don't get published?"

She said, "I'll always write." She shrugged and tried to say it better. "It's the only thing that takes all of me."

Freddy nodded and bit his sandwich. He understood. Time disappeared and his discontent subsided when he was doing one thing only: arranging merchandise. Only then did he not have to think, things came to him, fell perfectly, implicitly into place, as he knew from the beginning without question they would. And the strain was the effort and concentration to keep up with it, that was the strain, to know what clues to leave so he could later find threads he had to abandon now as things rushed on, and the thing coming out to be so fucking intricate, so complicated, so right in every way that he didn't know how he could do it, how it was that everything he hated, feared, doubted, was, wanted—especially wanted—that dominated him, was accessible to him, and under his control for placing into some structure—Jesus!—some momentarily satisfactory structure, all of it, with no leftover nagging parts, so that it meant what—what?—what he wanted it to? Decided it would? It turned out to mean? He didn't know, but what it came together to say was, it would all work out, the irreconcilable would be reconciled, he had a destiny.

He bit his sandwich and chewed without tasting. Blissful for a moment, then just a stupid china display. Then anguished anxiety to keep it from falling. He put down the sandwich. But, all of it— couldn't he arrange it in words, too? Didn't he? Hadn't he in the stories he had picked from them all to give Mindi? *Yes,* he could turn himself around from the place from which he watched china displays come together, and instead of watching that, see a blank page, that fucking blank page. And if it seemed a little harder, counterintuitive, if he felt as much in him after as before, if he felt like he was jerking off and couldn't come and was finally getting sick of it, if it never, not even once, not even in college, came out of him the way stupid fucking china displays did every time, well it was because writing was more difficult, more worthwhile, it just *had* to feel that way, his writing was goddamn good!

"Jesus, Mindi. I hope you like my stories."

She was still hearing him say that, having now read his stories, pen still in hand, alone now at her desk in the office, everyone gone home hours ago. After he'd said it he had tried to retreat.

"I respect your opinion, you're an editor and," the rest of it, but, "Jesus, Frederick," she had wanted to whisper back with his same helplessness, "Jesus! Just what *am* I to you?" He'd looked sick when he said it. He had spoken, for God's sake, without even knowing it.

She'd snapped, "That's your job. To make me like them," and then apologized because what he'd had on his face had cut her. Because what he had on his face she was seeing more and more in the mirror.

After lunch she hadn't been able to do a thing about that book review. She'd read what she had written already on Bertram Kyle's new book, but it wouldn't sink in. "Jesus, Mindi, Jesus, Mindi, Jesus, Mindi," kept intruding. Finally, near the end of the day, she had taken out his envelope and slid the stories from it—she wanted to smile at their next meeting and say, "Whyever you're holding it, let out your breath, they're excellent," or whatever it was he needed to hear from her so much. "Yes, go, continue writing your novel," maybe that was it—but they weren't good, they weren't good at all.

They were all rags-to-riches melodramas, even where the rags were rich and the riches were spiritual, which wasn't always interesting but wasn't the problem. They were all driven by a protagonist's struggle against those keeping him down, which became a bit banal, but that wasn't what was wrong either. She believed now that these themes, the desire to transcend station, the perceived unfairness in not having done so, and a monumental resulting rage were what had to be the driving forces behind the display. Not exactly what she had thought, but not inconsistent. Here she was interpreting a china display, of all things, but there was no mistaking it in his writing.

His sudden angry look at Nick's now gave her pause. And something else bothered her, though she could not bring it to mind. But she dismissed the beginnings of any concern and returned to the stories.

The problems were twofold. First, his plot- and people-physics were bad. In each story, characters moved in circumstance by desire alone, not action taken, not talent and work, or risk taking. Characters didn't "go get," they just "got." These were fairy tales.

But okay, a writer could have his point of view and she could disagree with it—people did win the lottery, though it was boring to read about them. But beyond that that there were fundamental problems in craft that betrayed the struggle these stories had been to write. They were like buildings with their frames exposed in places to reveal twisted support systems. There never came a point where the story, good or bad, finally came under his control. And that was a failure of dedication.

The stories weren't finished.

She thumbed through her comments in red throughout their pages, more on the legal-size pages she'd stapled to them. Archeologists stumbling onto finds, poor girls "discovered" in malls, long lost uncles and money. Bank managers and literary careers. She could forgive the clichés, she was used to that and it didn't mean you couldn't develop. But even clichés had to work.

So what was she going to tell him? She put the stories back in the envelope and put it in her desk. The truth. Of course the truth. She had learned that lesson when she was ten years old. When she was ten, her mother had told her that when she played the flute, she heard *cascadas*—waterfalls. So Mindi had volunteered to play for the school assembly. When she did, the other children had jeered her and even her teacher had politely covered her mouth. Mindi still remembered the taste of her tears on her mother's neck, the smell of her mother's perfume afterward, when she told Mindi again that she *had* heard waterfalls, but she guessed that was because she was her mother. It would take a long time and hard work to make others hear them too. Her mother had told her that.

Mindi never candy-coated criticism.

She saw Frederick's face in her blur and thought, "Listen Frederick, this *is* passion we have, passion! You, too, Frederick. With passion like this a person will learn to work. And then you can do anything, right? Right?"

And when it got bad, as bad as it was tonight, she thought, "Why am I reviewing someone else's book, why isn't someone reviewing mine?" When it got this bad, and she envied Lisa and the Lisas who got to be excellent, she just looked at her laptop and cried. She opened a new document, hoping the action would start the flow. She sat there with her hands on the keys waiting for it to.

No.

No. The moment was going to last all night.

Mindi woke up and pushed the buttons on the phone.

"*Halo.*"

"*Papi?* It's Mindi. Did I wake you?"

"Hola, Mindi Quintana. No, don't worry . . . What time is it? One-thirty."

"*Papi*—"

"What's the matter, *hija*?"

". . . I'm sad."

"*¿Por qué?*"

"I don't know."

"Where are you?"

"At the office. I'm okay."

"I'm gonna come get you."

"No, *Papi*. Where's Mom?"

"She's here. She's sleeping."

"Would you wake her?"

"Sure."

"Mindi? . . . *Mindi.*"

"Hi, Mom."

"What's the matter?"

"Nothing."

"It's late, Mindi, what's wrong? . . . *Mindi.*"

"I wanted . . ."

"Daughter, what is it? We're asleep."

"I don't know."

"What is it?"

"I want us to get along better."

"We do get along. What are you talking about?"

"Mom—"

"What."

"I want us to love each other more."

"You are my daughter—"

"Please, let's try. Okay?"

"Halo, Mindi?"

"Hi, *Papi*."

"What did you say to your mother?"

"Why?"

"She's in the bathroom. Is she crying?"

"Is she?"

"What did you say?"

"It's between us, *Papi*. Okay?"

"What? . . . Wait, she . . . She says tell you . . . 'okay.' What about? *Hija* . . ."

"Good night, *Papi*."

"I'm coming to get you."

"I'll call Lisa, I promise. Please, I'm okay."

6

Portrait

The painting took hours but it felt to Lisa like one extended whoosh of peach, night purples, of red drops skittering across the canvas, wide black swaths, and silver. Her abstract portrait of Mindi came through her faster than she could paint, but she put a brush of deep violet here, raised the peach undercoat there, as reminders for when she caught up. All the while she saw Mindi in her mind's eye, spectacular against the background of the magazine's office where she'd picked her up earlier, but owing a debt to it greater than contrast.

In the car from the magazine to Mindi's apartment, Mindi had tried to buck up. At the curb, though, with the door open and Mindi about to get out, Lisa had asked again for honesty, and Mindi said the following, one foot on the pavement.

"I don't always feel like this, so don't worry. But sometimes I wonder. I mean, I know what I get from all of you. You and Des Moines. And Stuart. You're all so extraordinary. Sometimes—"

"What, Mindi? Tell me."

"Sometimes I wonder what you guys get back." There might have been an instant when, if Lisa had had the words, she could have begun them before Mindi ran from the car and keyed herself in. Throwing her red paint and bringing back her thick black and silver swaths, Mindi and the office pushed each other away, as far as contrast enabled. But they met at the back—because they *did* meet at the back—and there whipped each other around and were flung, with dull and shiny bits of each other, away into what they were. Lisa's canvas catching Mindi.

It was still dark when she finished, and she was so tired, but she waited for the sun, until the painting was dry enough, to sign it. She didn't sign it with her name, she inscribed it with other words. And stepped back. She saw Mindi's skin and blood, the deep hues of her ways, the vibrant widths and lines that described how she moved, the things Lisa hadn't had words for.

She put the painting in one of the frames she kept around and wrapped it in paper to protect it, careful to do it tightly enough that it wouldn't touch the paint. Rather than wait, she drove with the painting over to the house in West Philly where Mindi had her apartment. She keyed herself into the foyer and made her way to Mindi's on the third floor. It was very early and instead of waking her, she used another key and slipped the painting inside against the wall.

On the ride home, the joy of painting her friend became the sadness she'd felt with Mindi in the car. And fear crept in and ruined her depletion.

Mindi woke up and showered, then wandered into her living room toweling her hair. It always took a very long time for her hair to dry, and in the winter it couldn't be wet when she went out or it froze. She glanced out of the room at the arc of photographs on the far wall, and sat on the towel, in one of the off-white easy chairs separated by a low glass table. She pulled her hair together at the nape of her neck and brought it over the top of her head. She stood and brushed it downward until it was tangle-free.

She held her head up now, letting her hair fall to the sides, and looked at the vase for her parents on the square wooden base in the corner near the couch. She sat down again and looked toward the front door and saw the brown-papered square against the wall.

Mindi stood up, walked toward the front door, and read the note on the paper. "I see you like this. It should be dry now but be careful. Love, L."

She took the paper off carefully, then went to the wall to turn on the light. She came back and held the canvas in front of her.

The blues were so incredibly deep and electric, and the black, it glittered, and the silver streaks were wild. The red dots seemed to have been flung, as if from Lisa's fingertips, to the side. And there was movement in it, too, wide vital strokes, and not intricate. This was her to Lisa. This was her. It was highly abstract—this wasn't a likeness— but God, there was so much *life* in it.

Mindi saw the inscription in the lower right corner: *Truly Extraordinary.*

"Wow," she whispered, "wow," drawing it out, and then she couldn't see it anymore. She put the painting on the floor a moment, leaning it against the table. Then she stood and put it on the couch, going behind the glass table to look at it from there.

She had inspired this, something like this. She went to the couch again, stood on it, and removed the Van Gogh print centered above. She was going to hang the painting now—Lisa had threaded some strong wire through two eyehooks. But the painting was much heavier than the print when she picked it up again. She didn't want to risk it on the little nail sticking out of the wall, as much as she wanted it up, and the painting had to be hung higher anyway.

She had no heavier nails, nor a hammer. She'd buy them after work and hang it tonight. She took the painting with her back into the bedroom and dressed for work.

7

Christmas Streamers

"Uh, hey," Freddy said to the stock boy on the stepladder—the boy's twin brother held the ladder steady (Freddy shared the boys with Sporting Goods but couldn't really tell them apart)—"I told you how I wanted those streamers hung, and there you go hanging them the wrong way." He shook his head. "Pay attention: I want them hung high." He pointed up and the boys' eyes followed. "As high as possible, near the lights."

"Yes, sir," said the boy at the base of the ladder.

"But they're *Christmas* streamers," said his brother. "Don't you want the customers to see them?" The boy on the floor looked afraid. Freddy fixed a stare into the upper boy's eyes.

"No," he said, "I don't want the customers to see them. *I* don't want to see them. I just want you to use up our allotment of Christmas paraphernalia as unobtrusively as possible. If you have a problem with that, allow me to free up your days."

Again the boy on the ground answered for his brother. "It's no problem, sir. Near the lights," he repeated. The boy on the ladder dropped his brother a look he didn't acknowledge, fearing Freddy would intercept it.

The streamers were the traditional Chanet's Christmas streamers which pictured the Manager of the Year in bust every eight inches along their length. The picture always added a flowing white Santa Claus beard to the manager's face, and the word "Chanet's," in some weird wreathlike script, entwined lovingly in his hair like he was some sort of Greek god.

Each year as Christmas approached that picture could be found not just on the streamers, but on the large Christmas banners in each department, and not just there, but on the huge Christmas tarps outside the store, as well as on gift certificates, wrapping paper, lollipops, and a thousand tiny unexpected things that hurt Freddy physically whenever he noticed a new one.

But this year especially. This year the Manager of the Year was a balding rat-faced accountant of a man who, pictured in his conservative gray pinstripe, seemed about as capable of that beard as any of the various rodents he resembled, depending on his pose. And as he had little hair up top, "Chanet's" was forced to entwine lovingly instead with his scalp, penetrating the skin in what had to be a very painful way. Which helped explain, perhaps, why the manager seemed in danger of biting through his lip with his pointy teeth.

To the brothers, Freddy seemed to have entered one of his pre-display dazes. He was standing near the rosewood table, slack and staring, but not at anything in particular. And it was the quiet hour just after lunch, a not uncommon time for their boss to start changing things.

"You're gonna start all over, aren't you?" said the boy coming down the ladder. "You want us to strip it, right?"

Sometimes the boss had them strip a display he said had "died," whatever the fuck that meant (he'd just come out with, "It's dead," and they'd say, okay, they guessed it was). But sometimes he just told them to get lost and took it down himself.

"I'll do it," Freddy said from elsewhere. He began to circle the table plucking it clean, first of the glasses, next the plates, and so on. He plucked the glass from breakfast and placed it on the floor, moving to lunch. What a glorious year it must have been for the man on the streamers—pluck. With the media advertising and products bearing the bannered man's picture, he was easily one of the most recognized people in the tri-state area—pluck. He'd spent his year telling kids to "stay in school"—pluck—"eat your vegetables"—pluck—so they would grow big and strong, like the big strong runt of a razor-toothed little accountant—pluck. And be successful in business—pluck—like the gift-certificated sphincter of a management prodigy—pluck. And become possessed—pluck—of the social graces—pluck—like the lollipopped fucking creature from the plucking gray lagoon—fuck!—laughing his high-pitched giggle—damn!—and snorting God knows what into his throat.

The contents of the table completely on the floor, Freddy stopped his circling and breathed deeply for a moment. Then he went to the shelves on the wall behind the table and began stripping them.

Jesus. In just about a month some happy store fuck-up would be tapped, and the first wave in the yearlong tide of products with his picture on the packaging would wash astore. From that very day and for the next twelve months, anyone buying anything at Chanet's would have the manager's picture on the box; and if they had it wrapped, it would be on the paper, and in the center of the goddamn ribbon; and if they had it delivered, it would be on the truck; and if it was something they turned on and sound came out of it, or a picture came up on it, it would at prime times be the new manager's voice they heard or the manager's picture they saw.

He would scream and cry when he was picked, like the new Miss America—they always did—the rest of the employees clapping like idiots. And the story was of such local interest that normal programming would be interrupted for a moment of coverage.

The new Manager of the Year could look forward to travel to such meccas as New Jersey and Delaware and to the other exotic lands where Chanet's had branches.

And the pep rallies. "Use your fixtures productively," Freddy mimicked prospectively; he snatched a bowl from its base for punctuation. "Eat your fucking vegetables," he exhorted the abject floor managers in his mind; "Spread the division average!" he screamed at them, but only at the rally behind his eyes while he broke down the carcass in front of him.

Except for the étagère which he had not touched, there was no shelf that still held a plate, no base with its vase or bowl now, no desk or table with an inkwell or other unique piece. Except for the objects in the étagère, the entire contents of his display area were splayed about the perimeter of the carpeted floor. Freddy looked back to the étagère, and let it all happen from there again. As he waited for the images he knew would come, the thin underlayer of conscious thought went on.

He was an artist, burning out his engine in first gear was what it was, while for all of his putting of pedal to metal he got nowhere in the scheme of things. He heard floor managers trading customers-that-got-away, or discussing quota, their newest sales promotions, the new incentive program, their chocolate-pretzel problems, post-sale-wholesale-upsell product problems, and screamed silently at himself, "Shift!" *Shift!*—into second, third, fourth, fifth.

Fifth-gear people. They whizzed by him no differently than they did those properly in the store.

When he made it into high gear, he would know that and what to do: He would be witty for reporters, pensive when appropriate, insightful always, and clever sometimes. When people cared what he thought, he would think great things. When they came to *him,* he would know what to say. When there was no question of his stature, they would admire his work. He would say, "Call me Freddy," and they would call him Frederick anyway. He needed only an occasion to rise to.

He took a step, his foot finding a porcelain figurine on the rug, and the crunch brought him out of it. Back into the store.

It was as though the boys and their ladder had leapt from where they had been to where they stood now under the china department entrance. He looked at the remainder of his merchandise still lying on the floor, and then looked at the clock. An hour and a half had passed in five seconds. He wondered about customers.

The boys were hanging the two-sided Manager of the Year Christmas banner in the display area's mouth. The same boy—or maybe it was the other one—was tacking it to the ceiling. Freddy went over.

"Any customers?"

"A few, they went away, though," he was told cheerfully by the boy on the ladder.

Freddy looked at the face on the banner. "Pull that thing tighter so it doesn't hang so low," he said. He turned away and walked toward the stockroom.

Inside, Freddy picked up his inventory clipboard and stared at the shelves of boxed merchandise, ready to make notations if anyone came in. He knew he would have to go back out there in a few minutes and shelve his department because the slow hour was over. But the muse had run its course. It would take all he had just to put the stuff back on the nearest shelves and fixtures.

In a few hours, though, he would pick up Mindi, and the idea of it reanimated him. He'd waited four days after their lunch before calling her. That she'd mentioned a low-key, more platonic place for their meeting before he suggested drinks at Carolina's, a very *in* restaurant-bar in the city, he'd rendered harmless. Lawyers, stockbrokers and the like, even some of the store brass hung out at Carolina's and he was hoping one or two coworkers would be there.

He was somewhat ashamed now of the stories he'd chosen to give her. He'd included older ones, somehow thinking she'd like the ones best from closer to the time they'd been dating. But reading them over after giving them to her, they seemed immature to him. They hadn't before, so maybe he was being overly critical, but he was concerned about being judged by them, and had thought a lot about what to do. He'd decided to hear her out—she may have liked them—and if she was critical, he'd explain to her what he'd explained to himself. He also knew he'd made a couple of big mistakes with her at lunch and that he had to make it up to her. He had a surprise for her he thought would do that.

The workday finally ended and Freddy was in his car and out of the parking lot within minutes of his night assistant's arrival, and on his way to Mindi's magazine. He rarely drove to work. Besides the expense of parking, he didn't like to trust his car to the busy daytime traffic of the lots. On impulse, he turned into a carwash even though he'd had the Alfa washed just two days ago.

As he went through, the swirling brushes *b-thumped b-thumped* around him and finally just about shut out the light. He felt truly alone for a moment. Removed from the world in a life-tight compartment. His metabolism downshifted, his heart slowed, and he felt the difference from the pitch he kept himself at.

He had learned to keep himself still for others, but he was never really still, was he. He was like one of those acrobats spinning plates on sticks, forever watching and running between them. But the brushes lifted, the hot air forced beaded drops down the windshield, and the cold sunshine poured the world in again through the sparkling glass. He shifted into gear and accelerated with a squeal of tires and radio back onto the street.

He made it quickly to the magazine's office and pulled partially onto the pavement in front, the big, outdated cars from the surrounding neighborhood continuing around him. He saw Mindi see him through the window and begin to put on her coat. He made it inside while there was still one arm to help her with. She was wearing a sweater and jeans tucked into neat suede work boots.

He small-talked her out to the car while he studied her intently for a clue. Opening her door, he thought she looked worried, and he wondered whether he should explain the stories in the car, even before hearing what she had to say.

Inside, still undecided, he turned on the radio, pulling onto the street.

"Can I find a station?" Mindi asked.

"Sure."

As she flipped through the stations for a good song, his discomfiture was not lost on her, and she changed the look she'd put on to forecast the tenor of her remarks. First she wanted to let him know somehow she'd still be his friend, because she thought he might doubt it. Going by 95.7, there was a snippet of a spot advertising the circus coming to town. It was advertising in her magazine, too, and she could get free tickets. Spontaneously, she asked him if he wanted to go, giving him the date.

"It's a Sunday."

"Sounds great," he said happily. "Look forward to it." And he thought, how bad could they have been if she wanted him to take her to the circus?

He found a tight but makeable spot on Twentieth Street in front of the gourmet shop across from Carolina's. He beat down the image of the man spinning plates the circus had reconjured and turned off the ignition. Before they got out, Mindi gave him an envelope with the rest of the money for the vase. He put it in the glove compartment.

Inside Carolina's, Freddy said a word to the hostess, who led them through the happy hour crowd to just the spot at the end of the bar he'd imagined earlier, where everyone could see them, indicating the far seat to Mindi. The place was crowded with its good-looking upscale patrons, but unfortunately he didn't see any of the store execs.

But Mindi was having her usual effect. Eyes went to her in flagrant disregard of one of this set's most adhered-to game rules: Never let on that one thought someone else's girl was beautiful.

Freddy ordered his beer and Mindi her coffee and Kahlúa from the bartender who, as he set down their drinks, informed them he went by "Smitty." A guy in a beige cardigan and bone frames came and leaned into the bar next to Mindi. He asked Smitty, "What's mixin'?" and put his black American Express card next to Mindi's drink for his Louis XIII.

"Excuse me, miss," he said to Mindi, bending close to her, "my soul is a deep dark forest. Do you have a flashlight?" Right from the beer commercial. Right from it.

"Hey," Freddy said, leaning across the bar. "She's with me."

"Sorry, friend," the man said, "didn't see you there." He left his business card on the bar next to Mindi and wandered away.

Mindi picked up the card from the bar and handed it to Smitty. "Could you hold this for me?"

Smitty laughed and threw it away. He seemed fixing to chat but was called away.

Puffed up by his "She's with me," Freddy now said easily, "So what did you think?"

She squeezed his arm. "Okay, here it is: I think they need lots of work," she said. "I've made comments on the stories themselves, suggestions for revision, and I think if you work on them, and think hard about certain things, you can make them better." She took the envelope with his stories from her bag and gave it to him.

"Frederick," she added. "How many drafts do you do of a story?"

"Two, about," he said. "Two."

"You have to do more. Look at what I've written. Don't take it as gospel—you shouldn't take anything I say about your work, good or bad, as gospel, but think about it. Use the comments you agree with to do your revisions."

"Okay," Freddy said.

She wasn't sure she believed him.

"But what did you *think*?" he said.

"I think there are some basic things you need to look at." She hesitated, not wanting to get into detail or grade his papers for him. "Read my comments, I was very specific," she tried again. "And I think you should work on the stories first and *then* go back to the novel. You'll learn a lot that way and save time later. Just my opinion, though," she was careful to add.

Freddy was nodding and looking at the envelope.

There was something she should say, so she tried to, obliquely. "What you want to do—not just you, me, too—is very difficult, Frederick. I've tried to do it and let me tell you, difficult means *difficult*.

Let it wash over you. It's going to take hard work and several drafts to improve these stories, and much harder work to write your novel. You've really got to want it."

"I want it more than anything," he said.

"Well, you go for it then," she told him. "Work for it. Show me them again; I'll help you if I can."

"I will," he said solemnly and she thought she'd gotten through to him now.

Freddy had already decided to abandon the stories. There was nothing about them he felt attached to and he would study her comments to avoid doing the things she didn't like in his novel. What he'd heard in her words was that he should have worked harder on them, not that they couldn't be good. If they could be good, he didn't need to make them good. He'd spend his limited time on his novel rather than on work he considered unrepresentative of him now.

But he spoke carefully. "Thank you for reading my work," he told her, "and for your comments," he said gesturing to the stories. "I'll study them. And I want you to know, and I don't mean it as any kind of avoidance of what you say in there, that the stories I gave you were mostly written years ago. I hope I've grown a bit since then and that it will show in my revisions."

Mindi was impressed by this response, and very relieved. She started to answer positively but the hostess appeared and whispered something in Freddy's ear. He smiled and stood up. "Come on," he said to Mindi. "Take your drink."

"Where—"

"Shh, just follow me. It's a surprise." He led Mindi through the bar and into the peach-colored dining room where they followed the hostess to a table in the window. There was a fresh rose in the small table vase, and a bottle of champagne chilling at the side. He pulled out the chair he meant for her.

"In appreciation," he said. "I'm very glad that we've met again, and don't want it all to be work for you. So let's just relax and have dinner."

Mindi sat down and he took his seat across from her. He pulled the champagne from the bucket and put it on the table. He squeezed her hand tightly then released it, and she pulled it away and picked up her drink as he took up his napkin.

A moment later, Freddy smiled as the waiter poured their champagne. He tasted it, nodded it suitable, and the waiter poured Mindi's. He didn't need more tonight.

8
—
Stamp's Revenge

It was the prison chaplain's visit to Brian Stamp's cell that began the new trouble. For weeks now, the chaplain had kept Philip apprised of the escalating situation and he'd phoned last night with news of its culmination. Stamp would be charged with new crimes, so Philip had gone to see him at Holmesburg Prison this morning. He'd only just now returned to his office and opened his window, wanting the cold air.

On the eve of Stamp's sentencing, the prison chaplain had gone to his cell to assure him that despite the new triple-homicide conviction, Jesus still loved him. The decompensating psychopath had taken the chaplain by the throat and said to tell Jesus he didn't swing that way, and that if he ever saw the faggot in the yard, he'd tear his dick off for him and shove it up his ass.

Jesus, it seemed, had been following him prison to prison his whole goddamned life. The chaplain had protested that Jesus had *died* for Stamp, but Stamp explained that so had a lot of other people, plus one more in a minute if he didn't get the fuck out. The chaplain got the fuck out.

It was after this that Stamp began asking where Jesus was. "Everywhere," had been the general reply. Stamp took this to mean it was a smooth and dangerous dude he was dealing with. But that was okay, Stamp told Philip on the pay phone, because Stamp was pretty smooth and dangerous himself. Philip had figured that for Stamp's purposes, "everywhere" was about as helpful an answer as "nowhere," and had left it to the chaplain, through his network of religious prisoners, to keep him abreast of Stamp's hunt. That the chaplain did.

82

"Jesus!" Stamp would yell from his cell.

"Jesus!" would come back from the religious near and far.

"*Jesus!*" would come the exalted cry of the especially devoted prisoner in the cell across the corridor.

"I'm gonna find you, Jesus! I'm gonna find you!" Stamp would bellow from his cell.

"I've found him!" would come back the shouts.

"*I found him!*" would come the most zealous shout of all from across the corridor.

Through his sources, the chaplain learned that in the small hours of the night, Stamp and the man in the cell across were pushing their faces between the bars and whispering back and forth.

"Have you seen Jesus?" Stamp would whisper.

"I *have* seen him," the man in his raptures would respond.

"Where is he?"

"Look around you, man."

Stamp whirled every time. Prisoners staying awake for the show made their laughs snores, and whispered to those who couldn't see.

"Where is he? I'll take care of him," Stamp swore.

"He'll take care of *you.*"

"Tell me where is!"

"Everywhere."

One day, after about fifteen of these nights, and fifteen days under Stamp's interrogation as to the Lord's specific whereabouts, the prisoner got a queer bright light in his eyes. When next Stamp asked him where Jesus was, the prisoner calmly answered, "Here I am, my son."

Now, the more Stamp threatened and screamed at the prisoner, the more sweetly the prisoner smiled back at him. For days the prisoner sat cross-legged at his bars, serene in the face of Stamp's uncontained rage. Stamp would flail his arms through the bars, extending them wildly, as though this time they maybe would reach, while the prisoner replaced his rag bandanna with a fresh rag, or said simply, "I love you."

"You want my ass, don't you?" Stamp would scream through his tears of frustration.

"I want your soul," the prisoner would answer sadly and adjust his rag.

"What's *that*?" Stamp would shriek, rattling the bars.

Their exercise periods had coincided yesterday. The other prisoners had crowded around them in a circle in the yard.

"You Jesus?" the twitching Stamp asked in the tricky light of the outside.

"I am the Lord Jesus," the prisoner confirmed.

"You the fuck keeps saying you love me?"

"I love all men."

Stamp tore his dick off and shoved it up his ass.

A platoon of guards subdued Stamp, while the spectators were hustled back to their cells. The chaplain, rushing through in the direction of poor Jesus, heard their sympathetic laments.

"It's gonna take more'n three days this time, that's for damn sure!"

"Unh-unh, he's gonna be too scared to come back, it's the devil's world now."

"Well, if he does, it sure won't be as God's *son*."

Just before calling Philip last night, the chaplain had visited Stamp again. By then Stamp was in the prison mental ward for evaluation. Restrained in his bed by leather straps when the chaplain arrived, he looked about as secure as the chaplain felt. But with the knowledge that God was at his side, the chaplain said, "I came to tell you that despite what you've done, Je—you should have a nice evening."

Philip had finished with the chaplain and gone on alone to Stamp's cell. Stamp's immediately voiced but mostly gestured concern was whether what had transpired might have any unfavorable bearing on his appeal.

"No, no, of course it won't," Philip told him, because he thought it bettered his chances of getting out alive, and also because it was true. "But if you kill anyone else it certainly will," he'd added out of regard for his fellow man.

When Philip left, Stamp's parting words had been, "Next time bring brie. Fucks don't have no brie here. And Stoned Wheat Thins. You bring water wafers and I'll snap your neck for ya. Uh-huh huh."

In reassuring Stamp about the appeal and promising him brie, Philip had acted prudently toward survival. Why then, he wondered now at his office window, had he seen Stamp unrestrained in his cell? What it was, he felt sure, was that he'd hoped being at risk might bring with it some feeling.

Well, it hadn't. It left him dry-eyed. As had Stamp's new murder. As had the girl from the gallery when they passed on the street fifteen minutes ago, her eyes saying more than her perfunctory hello. As had the fact that the same hello was all he had to give back to her. As had his chief of division's response not ten minutes ago to Philip's refusal to handle Stamp's appeal.

"You will handle *Commonwealth v. Stamp,* or you're out. Think about it, see me in an hour."

Standing in front of his window, he noted that he didn't feel sad, or outraged, or determined—or even very cold in the winter blowing in against him. He felt dead, but had no doubt he could live quite easily to be old.

Philip yanked on the screen, but it wouldn't come up. He pulled at it, but it didn't budge. He stepped to his desk and took out his scissors, and made ready to rip open the screen with them. But he stopped. He didn't feel enough, his passionate yanking at the stuck screen had been false, he felt stupid with the scissors in his hand.

It struck him like a soft mallet what giving up really meant. Not throwing oneself out a window in some blaze, it was withering away.

He put the scissors down and sat in his chair for a few moments. Then he got up and made his way through the corridors to the office of his immediate superior.

"I'll do the appeal," he said into the open door, and turned back without awaiting response.

9

The Circus

It had taken most of his free time since dinner with Mindi at Carolina's, but Freddy completed the first two chapters of his novel by the day of the circus and had them printed out neatly to give her. He'd made some last-minute changes the night before, sprucing up the dialogue a bit with a thesaurus before going to bed.

Before beginning the chapters several days ago, he'd undertaken to review Mindi's story comments. The stories themselves were in places scarcely readable through Mindi's red ink, and her comments were often continued on the legal sheets she'd filled with her writing and stapled to each of them. He'd gone through two stories in detail but realized that they were irredeemable, and became even more ashamed than before that he'd showed them to her.

He did not know now what he could have been thinking. He was sure his other stories, some of them more recent—though one of the stories he'd given her had been his most recent—were much better; and he pulled them out, clean and without any red at all on them, and read them over, distinguishing them in his thoughts from the ones she'd read.

Now that he had the flavor of what she liked in a story and didn't—she'd given herself away a bit, writing some of the same things over and over, and sometimes with an emphasis that—he couldn't help it—made him very angry, he resolved to press ahead and not look back. He put the stories in his closet, deciding to come back to her comments and read the rest of them if he got stuck, or if he thought he was making the same mistakes, but he never did. In fact, he tried not to think of them at all.

After sprucing up the dialogue last night, he'd read the chapters carefully again, the way he'd read over the stories he hadn't given her, to assure himself they were different from the stories she'd read in the ways she would want them to be. He'd felt again a bit of pique, telling himself that if he'd already had a book behind him and was already well regarded, she'd probably have come to his stories with a quite different mind-set and had a quite different reaction, flawed as he had to admit those early stories were. But she probably read crap all day and expected only to read more of it.

Though pent up from the work, sleep, when it came, was smooth at first. He dreamt of the next morning, of taking the forty neat pages from his writing drawer in the kitchen. They were filled, the forty, with the sharp black fruit of his effort, their borders glittering white again, and he felt their heaviness as he fanned through them, catching words and phrases that were brilliant in his sleep.

But in the next dream, he arrived at his department to find Jill there, the salesgirl he'd fired. She'd smashed his display, swept it onto the floor, its broken pieces and shards lying between them. And she was twitching again, in excitement again, she was glowing again and had something to tell him.

"Mr. Builder," she began. There were knives at his feet, a set of good German ones.

"Shut up," he told her.

"Oh, Mr. Builder," she continued. The knives had ivory handles; he looked for the longest blade.

"Don't say it," he warned her.

"You, *you*—"

He bent for one, awoke and dropped off again, another dream coalescing. Mindi was atop the covers of his bed sitting Indian-style in a pair of his pajamas, her hair tousled by the night spent next to and under him. She thought he was still asleep under the blankets, but he was looking through slits. She had her red marker in her hand, and his manuscript on her knee, but she hardly used the pen except to mark spelling errors (he was a terrible speller; it had become a joke between them—and he was forever forgetting to spell-check) and the occasional mistakes in "point of view," "consistency," "motivation," that she'd penned on some long-ago stories.

He watched her react as she turned the pages: shock, and at appropriate intervals, laughter which she held in with her hand not to wake him. The curve of her waist showed, and some of her brown flat stomach and her bellybutton, where the pajama top separated in a wedge, the last button left open. And the cotton pajamas were somewhat sheer, so he could make out her perfect triangle. He could see the place where all the seams of the pajama bottoms met in a raised bit of hard cloth exactly where it began.

This time he awoke to daylight, depressed until he recalled their plans for the day.

The pages of his chapters were splayed on the floor, and he picked them up, putting them back in order. He put the sheaf on his night table, showered and dressed. Though it was still early—he wasn't to pick her up until eleven—he was just too restless to stay in the apartment. So he gathered his camera, his keys and his coat, and left.

In the car, he glanced at the dash clock, set his watch, and drove to the neighborhood where Mindi now lived, driving the streets there awhile to pass the time. She was standing on the porch as he pulled up on time, and she ran to the car from the cold, putting a nice sized canvas bag on the floor and getting in quickly.

"Why were you waiting outside?" he asked as she closed the door. "It's freezing."

"Doorbell's broken." She smiled at him and rubbed her arms through her coat, teeth chattering. He took off a glove and put the back of his hand to her cheek.

"My God, how long were you out there?" he said, putting the glove back on.

She just let her teeth chatter. Soon after they pulled away she conquered the chattering and said, "We've got pretty good seats." She brought the canvas bag onto her lap.

She opened it and peered in. "Let's see," she said, taking things out and naming them, as though cataloguing them for herself, but really to impress him with what she'd brought.

"Binoculars," she said, holding them in front of her. They were giant in her hand. "For me alone and not for you," she added to herself, but referring to him. "Hot chocolate," she said holding up a thermos. "But you can't have any," she said in just the same way, as though ticking it off. "The tickets," she said, holding up the envelope. "Both for me." Then she looked at him, surprised. "What are you doing here?" and laughed beautifully, undoing him.

She put the bag on the floor, then pulled her black hair over her shoulder, giving it a twist, and let it drop on her jeans, leaning back again.

He couldn't believe she was in his car.

"I brought a camera," he said lamely.

"Small potatoes," she replied and bent for the hot chocolate. She unscrewed the cup and poured some in, then held it out to him. "Know how to get to the Civic Center?"

"Sure do." He took off a glove with his teeth and took the cup, but now he had his glove in his mouth and no way to take it out. He was about to let it drop but she took it away, giggling helplessly.

And he smiled despite himself. Smiled despite everything.

At a light, seeming happily warmed up, she asked, handing him the cup again, "What do you think about when you're building a display?"

"I don't think. They're done," he said and took a sip, hoping they were finished with that.

"But when you 'wake up,' is there ever any touch-up needed? Anything you missed or that just isn't quite right?"

"No," he said. "But when a customer buys something important, the whole thing falls apart. I let it go for a while—I don't care about it, really—but after a while," he admitted, chuckling falsely, "it really starts to bother me." He shrugged, as much to himself. "Then I'm changing everything." The light turned and he started through, handing back the cup.

"Interesting," she said. And then, "You should think about doing design work for museums."

"Design work for museums," he repeated, hanging his head exaggeratedly.

She laughed. "Seriously," she told him. "You'd be very sought after once they saw what you can do. It's really a gift."

He adjusted the rearview mirror though it was fine. "No, it's not. It's meaningless."

"What do you mean, meaningless?"

"Nobody respects it."

Mindi poured in more hot chocolate and pulled a wad of napkins from the bag. "They would in a museum setting," she said, "or in an interior design setting."

Freddy was silent. She handed him a napkin.

She said, "I've been to a lot of museums and my father's a builder. I used to go with him all the time to meet interior designers and space planners. They sure consider what they do artistic."

He balled up his napkin and she held out her hand for it.

"Don't say nobody respects it, Frederick," she tried again. "Creating a different world in a department store can't be easy. Think what you could do elsewhere."

"I appreciate that, Mindi. I do—" He stopped. Museum worker? Interior designer? He could count on no fingers how many of *them* he'd ever heard of. What could she think of him if she thought he was aiming for that?

"It was a friend of mine, a set designer, who told me to go to your department in the first place. You could meet him if you want. I'm sure he'd like to meet you."

Set designers. "High-paying job, set designing?" he heard himself say.

"No, it pays next to nothing, if that's what it's about." He glanced over to see if she had said it in anger, but she seemed more disappointed. She was sipping the chocolate.

"No, that's not what it's about," Freddy assured her. "That was a quip. Look, all I'm saying," he said solemnly, knowing what he'd say next wasn't true, "is that writing's the same for me as it is for you." He added, "It's what I want."

"And all I'm saying is, it would be nice to be as articulate as you are, in anything. You should value it more."

"Okay, Mindi, thank you," he said, hoping giving in would end it. "I really don't want to talk about the store, though." He said, brightening and shifting gears, "Guess what. I've been hard at work and I've finished the first two chapters of my novel. They're in the backseat."

Mindi was taken aback. "What about the stories? Aren't you going to rewrite them?"

"Yes, I am, sure," he said quickly. "Of course I am. I've got one done completely. I went all through your comments and really absorbed them. I've got to be honest, it was really dumb of me to give you those old stories. They're immature. I'm reading your comments and thinking, 'Right, right, right, of course she's right,' and thinking, 'Damn, I should have showed her something from this century.'"

"So why'd you give me those?" She took a sip and made to give him the cup again. He held up his hand. He was concentrating very hard on what he was saying, careful not to make a mistake. She sipped the chocolate herself.

"I thought you'd like to see the ones from college. The one about the archeologist was the one I was thinking about that night we met."

"It was?" she asked, looking at him over the cup.

"Mm-hmm. But I should have read them over first, I haven't looked at them in years. And I am going to fix them, the rest of them, but I'm really excited about the novel, which, you'll see, is much more representative of what I can do now."

She seemed to be considering all this.

91

"Well, these chapters in the back; they're from this century, right?"

"This week," he told her grinning over. "Can I have some more hot chocolate?" She poured from the thermos and handed him the cup.

They turned into the Civic Center lot and parked. Getting out, she shook the cup of its last drops and leaned into the car to put the thermos in the bag. She put the binoculars on their lanyard around her neck, as Freddy reached into the back for the envelope. He closed his door and went round to her.

"These are them. Chapters one and two."

She looked at him questioningly, but asked no question. He leaned inside the car, putting them in her bag and she closed the door.

Inside they finally found their row, smelling the hay and the animals as they made their way down the aisle to their seats. The circus was already in progress, clowns piling out of tiny cars, others on stilts. Next to Mindi was a man with a paunch and a little girl about six sat on his lap. The little girl kept staring at Mindi's hair and she whispered something to the man, who laughed. "My granddaughter wants to know if she can have hair as long as yours when she grows up. Her parents keep it short," he confided.

"Of course you can, honey," Mindi said to the little girl, and by the middle of the third act the girl was on Mindi's lap, watching the circus through her binoculars.

After a while, Mindi said something softly to the girl, who nodded her head and took the binoculars from around her neck. She leaned over to Freddy, poking his shoulder and saying, "Wanna look at the binoculars?"

Mindi winked and Freddy took them silently, holding them up to his eyes. He tried not to sob. From the moment the little girl had sat down on Mindi's lap, until the instant the girl poked him, he'd been lost in imagining the little girl as theirs. He and Mindi had brought her to the circus because it was her birthday and that was what she wanted. The idea that he was ridiculous was foreign, it was not even an idea. Her father was a success, a provider, a personage, he had books and business and warm scarves for his overcoat, he went to Europe with her mother and they missed her and came home; and he loved his little girl, his lovely wife, their little family. And he doubted nothing, not his wife's love or respect, not himself, he was torn apart by nothing.

He'd felt such warmth and peace, and cessation of anguish, that when the little girl poked him he was brought back too quickly, and the truth he was unprepared to avoid was so enormously in relief and was so painful, he had almost sobbed.

But now he was coming back to himself, he was regaining perspective and realizing again that there was no reason he could not be that man, that Mindi was right beside him, that if he hadn't had what it took for her, he would never have had her before, and that he was breaking her down, overcoming the resistance he felt from her now, and that one day soon, one day soon she would see him, he would show her, and then he could—"

"Mister." The girl was poking him again.

He took down the binoculars. "Yes, sweetheart," he said, looking at her kindly.

"The bear is there. Can I have them back?"

"Of course," and he gave her the binoculars.

"Mindi," he inclined his head to her to say. "Let's go get her some cotton candy."

So they got up, Freddy asking the man and the girl to watch their things, and taking his camera along. They made their way down the aisle, up the stairs, and through to the concession area, where Freddy took Mindi's arm to guide her through the crowd.

"Cute kid," he told her. "You'll be a great mom."

"My legs were falling asleep," she complained. "Maybe when we get back, she'll sit with her grandfather for a while."

At the stand, he gave Mindi a ten, tied his shoe, and let her order the cotton candy and soda. While she was waiting, he got the attention of the woman behind them in line and pointed to his camera, then pointed to Mindi and himself. The woman, understanding, nodded and he handed her the camera. Freddy held up a finger so she'd wait for the right moment. The woman smiled and nodded again and stepped back a few paces.

Mindi turned around with her purchases and Freddy grabbed her, planting a kiss on her lips.

Surprised, and so not to spill the soda, she pressed her arms to his sides, and the instant after he saw the flash, turned her face away from the kiss. He let go of her, slipped behind, and put his arms around her, deliberately covering her breasts with his forearms while he smiled out over her shoulder. He knew she was wearing no bra—he could feel the way her breasts moved, and their pressure on his arms. He was instantly hard, and almost pressed against her to let her know. The flash went off and he let go of her again, retrieving the camera from the woman.

Mindi had moved away from the stand and was just looking at him as he came back to her. "Why did you do that?"

He shrugged. "Just impulse, I guess. Sorry if I—"

"Look, Frederick," she interrupted, "I really don't appreciate someone just . . . kissing me without . . . not knowing if I want him to or not."

"Mindi," he said abashedly, "we're at the circus. I was just . . . I don't know—having a good time. In the spirit, okay?"

She waved the cotton candy. "I'm sorry if I've given you the wrong impression, I've probably—"

"Now wait a minute. I don't think we need to define things right now."

"I think maybe we do." She handed him the cotton candy.

"Come on, Mindi," he said, throwing his arms wide, "you know, like Mardi Gras. Grab a woman, plant one on her."

"Picture for the folks back home," she said. She nodded at the camera.

He held his arms out in a gesture of sincerity. "I mean it, I'm really sorry. All right?" She put the straw in her mouth and sipped the soda.

She kept her eyes on his face and he was careful his expression did not waver.

"I'm sorry," he said again.

"Okay."

They heard cheering from inside and started walking back to their section.

"Hurry," he said after a minute, speeding up, "we don't want the cotton candy to go bad," and coaxed a small smile from her. Then he stopped them again. He and a middle-middle, who had his small boy with him, had recognized each other. The man's son was dressed in a tiny gray pinstripe embroidered with *Manager of the Year* in red yarn on the pockets.

Freddy introduced Mindi, letting the man infer what he would about their relationship. The man must have been impressed, because he let go of his son's hand. Mindi deftly retrieved him before he was swallowed up. Then Freddy started them off again at a trot.

By the time they got back to their seats they were both a little flushed and out of breath. They gave the cotton candy to the girl, who kept pulling some off for them.

Freddy was careful to laugh at the funny acts and gasp at the scary ones, and not to give back the binoculars too fast. The fear that he had ruined everything eventually passed. But though he looked in its direction, he could not pay attention to the circus and the acts cascaded by.

Once, Mindi dropped her soda, grabbed his arm and looked at him with such an instant expression of fear that he thought something had wounded her. There was a collective "*ahhh,*" and he looked back to see the knife still between an unpopped balloon and the leg of the thrower's assistant.

After the circus, in the car, they had good conversation again. About which acts they'd liked best: he named the knife thrower because it came to mind first. About a friend of Mindi's who was a mummer and who'd traveled with a circus for a year playing banjo.

About Lisa and a painting she'd just sold for eight hundred dollars. He parked in front of Mindi's apartment and she gathered up her bag with the binoculars and the thermos and the envelope with his chapters inside. He got out and went with her to the steps, thinking that if he'd been a little more reserved before, he might have ended this day with a kiss on the porch. At the steps, she turned around.

"The circus was fun," she said. "I'll read your chapters carefully." He thought she meant it on both counts. After the business at the candy stand she'd become relaxed again, and they'd had a good time. She'd grabbed his arm when she'd been startled.

Freddy glanced at the pavement. "I have an idea," he said. They stood separated by a crack in the concrete. He looked back up and grinned. "Why don't we spend Christmas Eve together? I could cook us dinner."

Mindi said, "I'm spending Christmas Eve with my parents." She shifted her shoulder to get the strap of the bag farther up.

"Oh, of course."

"What about your family?" And then she remembered about his parents, her face showed it. He looked away for an instant, milking it.

"Sorry," she said immediately, "I . . ."

"It's okay. I've got a few people in Detroit. They're getting together. If I didn't have to work Christmas Eve, I'd have probably gone. We're closing early, though, that's why I asked."

'Well, look . . . why don't you give me your phone number?" she said. "At least I can wish you a Merry Christmas." The bag slipped down again so she put it on the ground while she took her keys from her coat.

"All right." He had a pen in his coat. He crouched next to the bag and wrote the number inside on the envelope. He picked up the bag and handed it to her.

"Well, bye," she said, taking it and starting up the steps.

He watched her into the building and got into his car, thinking about where he could go to develop the film.

10

Miss America

Today was the principals' meeting for Jamison's chocolate termination "by committee," so Freddy was on an early train into the city for the unveiling of the plan. The bar for its success was especially high, according to Jamison, because this year's termination had been a huge hit at the upper-middle-management Christmas party. Helpless tears of laughter had flowed, Jamison kept reiterating; they had coughed their drinks at each other.

"Someone even aspirated an ice cube!"

This year's termination was in the same tier with Jamison's own chocolate molecule termination. But the one *they* were planning by committee, when Freddy learned what *his* part would be, well, he would see what a friend he had in Robert L. Jamison. It would make him a star.

"Oh," Jamison would say, stopping by to clap his back some more, "you're going places, pal. You're gonna be one of us soon." He'd aim his finger-gun at Freddy and fire. "Bet on it."

In the week and a half since he'd seen Mindi last, Freddy had thought often of kissing her cheek at the station after drinks at Murphy's Twelfth Street, and of squeezing her hand at Carolina's as the waiter poured their champagne, and most of all of Mindi grabbing his arm at the circus (which he invested with particular meaning).

They were trophies to him, the indisputable proof of the accomplishments they represented. He held them out in front of him wherever he went, marveling at them. He carried them with him in the store like a crucifix against Jamison's friendship. They lined the shelves of his newest display, and he walked around them in his imagination to see them from every angle.

But one.

When at Carolina's he had let go of her hand—from the angle he ignored—she had removed it quickly on a pretense calculated not to offend. The kisses at the station and at the circus she hadn't participated in. He knew of the angle from which he would see this. But he built his display on his own terms, and on his terms, that angle of view was blocked.

So it was on the ride into town, his head against the cold window. On Christmas Eve she had indeed called and wished him a Merry Christmas from dinner at her parents' home. He'd countered by suggesting Club Brasil as a good place to talk over the chapters when she was ready. She'd agreed in a general way and when he'd pressed, just a tad, saying a Salvadoran band would be playing on the twenty-ninth, she'd agreed in particular to tonight. She'd need to make it an early night, though; the new year's first issue was going to print—and he could certainly understand that. In his china display, they were already lost in the exotic beat of whatever music Salvadoran bands played.

From the station, Freddy walked the south side of Market to Chanet's. He passed Murphy's, the regulars not yet in line, and since the street was empty at this hour of panhandling drug dealers, their Rolexes and marijuana did not cross his mind.

At the employee entrance, Freddy rapped. The guard inside looked up from his paper, put aside his steamy cuppa, and rose from his used-to-be-a-bar-stool to key open the door. Freddy inside, the guard grunted his "morning" and got back on his stool, paper folded over one pant leg, the one darkened by ink over time, the cup again resting in its worn ring on the other. The paper dropped as the guard leaned over to use the black store phone, and Freddy was past him.

Freddy took the escalator to his floor and, reaching his department, strode through the display area without turning on the lights, and into the stockroom. He did not like seeing his displays without normal lighting, for instead of the cohesive whole, the pieces seemed silhouettes of children suffering horrible body deformities. Strange-shaped heads, or absent limbs, huge lower bodies with no heads at all. But turning on the lights might provoke a visit from some needy floor manager or a cruising middle-middle.

Inside he went left, feeling in the dark for the edge of his little desk and switching on the lamp atop it. In the small illumination, he grinned back at himself from over Mindi's shoulder, the two of them in their little silver frame in the corner of the desk. The sister frame, on his bedside nightstand, held the picture at the circus that documented their kiss.

By habit and without looking, really, he went back to the door and hung his coat on the hook there, hearing an unfamiliar rustling of paper as he did. He removed his coat to look and hanging punctured on the hook was a note. He took the note to his desk and read that he was *late* for the principals' meeting, which, the note purported to remind him, had been moved up half an hour weeks ago. The hired actors were cooling their talented heels at high rates, along with the important in-store participants, and Freddy was to proceed forthwith to the basement auditorium where they were all waiting (he knew not patiently) for him. He rushed from the stockroom—he would not let himself run—because the note was signed with a threatening "Mr. Jamison."

Hurrying across the display floor, he bumped the étagère hard and the whole thing tilted, the pieces began to slide, and Freddy only just grabbed it in time, steadying it and placing it back on all fours. He hurried on, took the escalator quickly, bounding the steps at times, at other times stopping and cursing himself for doing it, and got to the auditorium doors, pausing to straighten his tie, pat his hair, and slow his breathing.

He entered at the back and stood in the center aisle, looking at the stage on which stood Bobby Jamison. Freddy automatically scanned the section reserved for floor managers, situated behind middle-management and in front of buyers and untouchables, and looked for an empty seat. It shocked him while he did that the auditorium had in it not just several managers and hired actors, but seemingly all the store's employees.

He was still standing at the back, had not taken a step, when Jamison spoke into the microphone. "Here he is"—and to Freddy it seemed Jamison was pointing at him—"our Manager of the Year, 2006."

All turned to look over their shoulders and a thunderous applause and stomping of feet shook the floor. Freddy's knees threatened to buckle. He half turned, pleading with God and destiny, but neither was behind him. Uppers, who did not fear individuating themselves from the masses, left their seats at the front and came toward Freddy to clap him on the back, even as the thereby emancipated untouchables flooded the aisle behind him, cutting off his retreat. He was pushed and dragged through the parting crowd as Jamison started the "speech, speech" chant, which was taken up immediately and rocked the place.

Freddy noticed for the first time that television crews, reporters with pads, and photographers had emerged from the wings, and saw the sudden gesture with which Jamison whipped the tarp from the huge brass face on the stage that would join the others on Chanet's storefront. Freddy's eyes were wide as they pulled him frontward by his arms, pushed him forward from behind. He stumbled along, falling, grabbed up again.

At the stage, Jamison was handed Freddy's arms and, with help, dragged him up. The edge of the stage ran the course of his body, clicking home between each pair of ribs, for he had made himself dead weight. But he was quickly thrust up on the stage, where they steadied him, and he stood on his own, swaying over knees that failed and recovered for him repeatedly.

"Congratulations, buddy," Jamison said, putting his arm around him and smiling wide for the crowd and cameras. Then, with great fanfare, he slapped some aftershave on Freddy's cheeks, from a bottle with Freddy's personnel photo on the label, and pointed to the traditional case of it for the Manager of the Year to take home. With more solemn ceremony, he pinned a blue ribbon on Freddy's lapel. Freddy burst into tears and last year's manager gave him two dozen roses.

The ceremony was suddenly over and stock boys and girls gushed around him onstage, setting up tables, casting reverent glances, bringing out coffee and Danish. His coworkers mobbed him, clutching at him, clapping his back, patting his head, pumping his arms. Reporters pushed through everywhere for sound bites, punching him in the head with their microphones.

"Say something to the youth of Philadelphia!"

"Who in retail history inspired you?"

"How 'bout a picture with the Christmas beard?"

Freddy fought past them all and rushed through the stage door out of the auditorium, fleeing around corridors and banging through a men's room door halfway round the building. He scrubbed the aftershave from his face and slammed into a stall. He tore the blue ribbon off and flushed it and flushed it, and flushed and flushed and flushed until he was sure it had to be deep in the sewers below, mixing with the shit where it belonged.

He threw up in the bowl but felt no sickness leave him. He banged down the toilet top and sat down, violated, beaten, and robbed, a girl raped on prom night, left bleeding and ruined on the side of the road.

He was Manager of the Year, Manager of the Year, *Manager of the Year!*

He wept bitterly on the toilet. Bus placards, newspaper ads, store brands, bags and boxes, gift certificates and billboards were waiting outside for him. Everywhere he went, everyone would know! He was Manager of the Year!

He was the greatest manager—*in retail!*

11

Getting Feathers

Freddy left Chanet's from the men's room, employees turning in ones and twos to clap respectfully as he passed, and in Consumer Electronics to point to the hundred television sets in which he held roses, the blue ribbon already back on his lapel. He pushed through the revolving door out into the sun.

Waiting at the light to cross Market Street, he realized he still wore his name tag and chuckled, feeling strangely calm now. He hadn't returned to his department to retrieve his overcoat and he knew on some level that it was cold, but it didn't bother him. Removing his name tag, he dropped it in the street as he crossed.

He walked the north side of Market looking for a dark place to hide in. He wanted a serious bar for men who'd lost everything, one the street was too bright to look at from inside. Next to a shoe repair shop he found a suitable dive, a basement remove down a smelly stairs from the purposeful street bustle. He couldn't see down into the place, but a buzzer panel hung from its wiring in the doorway and the street-level sliver of window was opaque with dirt. So he went down and took a place at the bar, among the few down-and-outs already along it at intervals.

Feeling still oddly dull, he drank the first three beers he ordered, after that ordering another whenever the barman gave him an annoyed look. These beers—he must have ordered twelve more throughout the day—he traded for a drunk's empty mug or poured out in the john. He wanted to drink, he *wanted* to get blood poisoning, but he saw Mindi in the ale and held off.

The ruse played through his mind. They'd already chosen him when they took him to lunch, and lied so he wouldn't expect it. And the principals' meeting. Jamison's visits to add texture and nuance. He laughed weakly again. Swallowed a mouthful of beer. He forced his mind blank.

Evidence that his obscurity was fading began in the afternoon. Coming back from the bathroom and peering up the stairs, he saw a bus go by with his face on its side. Then he was recognized in the bar by a patron who looked like he couldn't be counted on to know World War II had ended.

At five, the bartender switched on the early news and he was the second story. He saw the top of his head as the crowd moved him to the stage, the camera getting him full as he was dragged over the edge. His ribs ached extra as he watched, and then he couldn't watch.

He watched the bartender instead, who got a funny look on his face like he might be smelling gas before revelation struck. Freddy turned away but the men along the bar were all looking at him.

"That's you," said the barkeep for all of them.

Freddy shook his head.

But the barkeep still had the TV to compare him to and said, "Yes, you are. Same suit."

So Freddy removed his tie and jacket. He balled them up and threw them in the bathroom trash. Before he left the bar he mussed up his hair and he walked looking down to the station.

Riding the train, he assiduously avoided anyone's look, but aside from that, was still stupid from the shock. Didn't remember having a thought all day at the bar, had an additional none now. At his stop, he detrained mechanically and walked home. Lay in bed, stared at the ceiling. Showered when it was time, dressed in the mirror, and called Mindi saying nothing except that he was on his way.

Mindi buzzed him in from the cold. Her door was open when he got to her floor and she was standing in the doorway. She greeted him and he took a sluggish step inside, and another to the left when he saw he needed to if she was going to close the door.

"I'll hang it up," she said holding out her hand for his jacket.

She didn't know he was Manager of the Year or she would have said something about it. He noticed with that that he had started thinking again and gave her his jacket. While she went with it to the closet, he stood and took in her apartment. He looked straight through to the sitting area at the back, clutching at its detail to order his jumbled thoughts.

There were curved-legged end tables on the back wall as bookends to an off-white couch. Fronting each table, almost touching the couch (did they touch?), were similarly upholstered armchairs. On each of the little tables was a simple antique-looking lamp with a milk-glass shade. Through the shades came a soft light that made him want to sit in the room. Over the couch hung a painting, an abstract of some sort, of silvery gray streaks, night purples, black swaths, a deep sort-of-rose color under all of it, and peppered, it seemed, but he could not yet see with what.

He brought his gaze back from the living room. On the wall to his left, curving down sharply, and back up again closer to him, was an arc of black and white photographs, each behind glass cut to size and attached to the wall by a means not apparent. The frameless picture nearest him—it ended the arc at a point higher than it began—was the only one he could see clearly: a little girl on a swing, her tiny hands holding the thick ropes, her hair in a bun and her eyes widest, at the top of her own arc. The photo captured that wonderful, terrible instant of motionlessness before the swing fell again.

Mindi came back and led him through to the living room. He saw, passing them, that the photos were all of the same child at different stages of flight to her breathless instant, and that the arc on the wall described the path of the swing. He turned his head to the opposite wall, against which were two bookcases. Books filled them and he saw more, and magazines, piled on the floor in front, and then he was with Mindi in the living room.

"Are you okay, Frederick?" she asked.

"Yeah."

She indicated the couch for him, and he could not help sinking further when she herself sat in one of the armchairs. He said yes to her offer of coffee and she went into the kitchen. He noticed for the first time that in the corner created by the meeting of the painting and photograph walls, his vase sat atop a lacquered base. She came back with mugs for them, but he never touched his.

"Is she rising or falling?" Mindi asked with a smile.

"Who?" Freddy asked.

"The girl in the photos," she answered. "I saw you notice them."

He looked briefly again but without interest. "She's rising," he said.

"Stuart did that. It's amazing, but everyone knows she's supposed to be rising. Do you know *how* you know she's rising?"

He looked again. "Yes."

"You do? Sure you do," she said with friendly doubt. "I've asked him a thousand times, but he won't tell me. How do you know?"

He just knew. It was display crap.

He said, "They made me Manager of the Year today," without emotion.

Mindi started a smile but his face and flattened affect brought back their discussions and warned it away.

"Congratulations," she said anyway. "People respond to what you do. That's wonderful."

"No," he said distantly, "it's far from that."

Mindi was explaining that Lisa had done the painting over his shoulder, the one he'd noticed before. He locked his hands behind his head and it took all his resources to strike an expression of normalcy. They were going to Club Brasil, he told himself, out for the night of dancing he'd looked forward to forever. But he couldn't wait until then. He couldn't wait. His attention wouldn't surround her words. In the middle of one of her sentences he held up his hand.

"Did you read the chapters?"

She was silent for a moment before shifting herself toward him. She put her elbows on her knees and her chin in her hands, and looked up at him, considering her response. She had spoken without alacrity about his stories at Carolina's, simply giving him her written comments. And he abandoned them, writing these chapters instead, which reading made her doubt he'd considered her comments very seriously. He needed to hear it from her straight.

"Frederick," she began, "I told you I was going to be honest."

Freddy began a descent into darkness that, this time, she steeled herself against. She straightened and continued softly.

"I don't see the differences you do from the stories you gave me. I think you're heading down the same problematic paths."

She started going into detail but he only caught snippets. Wasn't she seeing him? Didn't she know not to do this? ". . . another one of your unexplained-success stories . . . too quickly . . . to show it . . . You describe that nicely but . . . not realistic, no justification . . . winning the lottery . . . By the middle of your second chapter . . . no trigger, no action . . ."

She was shaking his knee. "Okay, you've got a lawyer who wants out of the profession. *Why?* And why should we care? You expect us to know, but we don't. So he's got a small-time practice, no big cases, you keep telling us that, but what's a small-time practice look like? You've got him going to court and leaving from court—but no court." She stopped here.

"Here's the thing, Frederick. I wrote the same things in my story comments that I've written again here. You're gonna have to do the research—the work necessary to convince us."

She went and got the chapters, bringing them back with the envelope and sitting down. She handed them over, stapled by chapter now, several legal-size pages behind each. He flipped through the first few pages of the chapter on top, and they were covered in red. He put them on the couch and closed his eyes.

"Please understand, Frederick," she said, watching him. "I owe you the truth. I wouldn't be doing you any favor by holding back."

Freddy lifted his head and opened his eyes, tears tickling his lids, which he did nothing to hide and which startled Mindi and made her stand.

"Can I fix them . . . is there some—"

"Frederick," she said kindly, but concerned and frustrated, too, that her words could cause this. She knew there were other causes also, and her face flushed with her sympathy for him. "Of course, if you work, you can improve . . ."

"Can I do it?"

It made her sit down again and shake her head. He was asking flat-out questions but didn't want the answers. She did this for a *living* and wasn't going to say she heard waterfalls. She felt his anguish, which made her own eyes well up as she cast about for response. Her tears only started with her decision to answer him honestly.

"I spent a lot of time reading your stories," she said, wiping them away, "and commenting on them. And you abandoned them, right?— *I* think, because they were very hard to fix. You've got so much *desire,* Frederick, but you're not doing the work."

Exasperated, she went on. "It's all over these chapters. And you know it, too, because you recognize the problems and try to skirt them. What do lawyers actually do? I don't know what they do but I have to feel like you do."

Freddy had closed his eyes and hung his head. He started slowly shaking it.

She looked at him, pained again. "But try, let me see them again."

He sniffed sarcastically.

"Just stop expecting it to come out of you like your displays." She lowered her head to see if his eyes were open, and to look at him if they were, and sat up when she saw they weren't.

"That's my opinion, Frederick, but, please, understand, someone else might feel differently. I'm not the last word."

Now he looked up at her. "You are to me."

She stared at him. "But that's not fair," she said. He said nothing.

"It's not fair," she said again. "Why are you making me so important? How do you think I feel? I'm trying to be your friend, but you manipulate me. Why?"

He shrugged. "You know why."

She put her hand to her forehead. "But I can't get you out of your store. I can't get myself out of mine!"

"No," he said, as though to himself and not in response to anything going on.

He looked over at Mindi again. He saw that her mascara was running and from her expression that she cared about him. He thought of the pictures of them on his nightstand and stockroom desk, of taking her hand at Carolina's, remembered again how she'd grabbed his arm at the circus, startled and immediately thinking that he could protect her, and he tried to believe that she would love him if he could only figure out how to make her. He was in her *apartment*. She was right there. Right there!

He reached down slowly, he felt in a dream, his eyes never leaving her face, and he touched her leg. He moved his hand lightly about two inches over it, caressing it.

Though she remained still, Mindi shook inside. Freddy leaned his head toward hers and closed his eyes to kiss her. She closed her eyes and stood slowly, Freddy's hand trailing from her leg as she straightened.

His mind screamed, *Don't stand, please don't,* even as she shook her head and said very quietly, "Frederick," but firmly, "no," and stepped away.

And looking into the space where she'd been he saw himself for true. The kisses, the writing, his failure, his future, all of his display lies. He was Manager of the Year, yet he would never again build a display, he felt the ability leave him. Reality's parts had cooled, fused together, and were no longer susceptible of his arrangement. Its new razor edge cut him open and left him in agony, and need.

Of Mindi! Who stood with her back to him, facing the vase in the corner. The vase that *he'd* sold her, that *he'd* let her lay away. His arms actually ached for pressure in the places Mindi's would be if she would only put them around him, and he crossed them over his chest, holding them there himself.

He went to her. She heard him coming and turned around. He touched her arm tentatively.

"Mindi." He paused, there was no other way to put it. "Please." He moved his hand to lightly stroke the side of her breast.

"I can't," she whispered. "I can't change how things are. I can't change how I feel about you, Frederick. I'm your friend, always, but I can't be more. I can't *do* more." He didn't move his hand. "You're a man with a sense of beauty, Frederick, you have an ability to create it. Those china displays are art. Anybody could see that if they took the time, but not you. I can see it. Why not you?" She put her hand to her forehead, the charms on her bracelet dangling down.

It was stark. He would never gather her hair in his hand while they embraced on a street corner. Passersby would never gawk and see it was he who'd earned her. They would never rush home to take their daughter to the circus. He didn't have what it took.

Now Mindi's eyes went suddenly wide. She'd taken her hand from her forehead and was staring at her wrist. At her bracelet. He saw the thought forming on her face and knew what it was. He saw her on the floor of Murphy's searching for the bracelet, but it did not move him now.

"Frederick," she said in dumb disbelief. "You told me my bracelet was missing while I was still coming back to the table. I was too far away. You wouldn't have noticed. You already had it." She was nodding now, convinced. "You let me go through all that while all the time you had it." She breathed in sharply and brought her hand to her mouth.

The sheer magnitude of his decimation watched him, made him give a short laugh. Mindi backed away from his hand, and the absence of the warmth of her breast through the soft jersey sweater made his fingers feel ice in the air. He took a step toward her, his arm still outstretched.

"That's so mean," she whispered quickly through her fingers. And then, seeing Freddy, her look changed to one of despair for him.

"Frederick," she said. A tear fell on his outstretched cuff. He brought his arm back now and rubbed the tear into the fabric, turning it the deep blue of his ribbon. She—pitied—him.

"Leave."

His punch caught Mindi square in the face, shattering her cheek-bone, and knocked her back into the vase on its base. A few drops of her blood sailed toward the wall and the couch, and the vase fell on the rug. It did not break. Freddy stood a split second as Mindi, dazed, not all there, tried to get to her feet. The base spun-wobbled and finally fell on the vase, shattering it.

The crash brought Mindi back a ways so that she started a sound that might have become a scream had Freddy let it. But he bent and punched her in her face again, this time breaking her jaw and her front teeth—his hand—and she was unconscious.

He looked down at her, her face so broken, shards from the vase sticking out from her cheek. He felt the line he had crossed, the line of acceptable behavior that, without knowing where it was, he'd always known he was far behind. Now he had leapt over it into some free zone where his longing was rage and poured forth from him in a whoosh of savage kicks, elbows, punches. And at its culmination, he stood over Mindi with a foot on each of her shoulders, reached down, wound her hair into his good right hand and jerked her up sharply, twice, breaking her neck.

Letting her head fall back, he noticed that one of her breasts was exposed. A rip in her sweater reached to her navel. He bent down and touched her breast, so warm, and fondled, then kissed it, brushing his lip against her nipple that was, at last, erect for him. He stood, and the painting on the wall beckoned him at eye level. He went to it and looked at it closely. He felt the roughly brushed-on life tone with his hand, was stirred by the sensuous dark purple, found out by the red dots, moved by the shining silver streaks.

He turned around, exhausted as never before. His hand throbbed dully. He collected his jacket from the closet, passing books and a little girl with her eyes as wide as they could be. He left Mindi's apartment and the building and emerged on the quiet winter street.

The sky was clear, there was a frozen crunchy snow on the ground, clear ice in places that made the walking hazardous. But he walked staring straight ahead, instead of safely down, until he was next to his car.

It was 9:14.

Mindi had died six minutes ago, at 9:08.

At 9:08, the mayor's daughter signaled her orgasm, and a relieved and fatigued first assistant district attorney congratulated himself on a virtuoso performance. The unsated mayor's daughter wanted an encore.

Philip, at that moment, was at home at his computer. He was working on a brief and was squeezing his head in his hands. He tried to squeeze hard enough that "sudden and accidental," from a statute at issue, would come to include gradually and on purpose.

Lisa was at the Borgia Café, a small restaurant that played jazz and served coffees and liquors. She laughed at a table with friends—other painters and Stuart, a poet, a banjo player. Someone asked after Mindi and Lisa told them about Freddy—"They made him Manager of the Year today, I saw it on the news." They read the poet's new poem, passed around some sketches, and listened to the music.

Judge Gunther Willison III, covered by a blanket, slept on his easy chair in front of the TV. He had drifted off during the Big Picture. He awoke to a commercial for Bounty paper towels and got up to turn off the television.

Bobby Jamison and his date drank white wine. They touched their glasses in toast. The couple traded exaggerated glances and raised their eyebrows in silent laughter at the strange-looking crowd and the poem being read at the table next to them.

The chocolate manager they'd planned to fire by committee had been smoking in his kitchen when he left for the 7-Eleven to discuss a night job with the manager, at 7:34. It was 8:16 when he returned to find his house on fire and them carrying out his son Joshua, who was burned in the third degree.

"Over seventy-four percent of his body," said the admitting physician, at 8:53.

"No, seventy-*two* percent of his body," corrected the specialist at 9:04.

"He's dead," said the attending physician at 9:07.

"He's *not* dead," noticed a weeping chocolate manager at 9:07, "he's breathing in my ear."

"Oops, sorry," the attending, "I thought the machine beeped."

"That's my watch, it must be 9:07," the admitting.

"What time is it?" croaked Joshua from semiconsciousness.

"Wait a second, wait a second . . . 9:08!"

It was time for Freddy to snap someone's neck.

12

The Defender

The last day of December did a mean pivot in the direction of the new year; it sent an icy wind into Philip while he waited for his bus.

His parents had wanted Cindy and him to come out to Oregon. (He hadn't told them yet, it would only lend specificity to their general hysteria.) But he had declined their kind invitation pleading his caseload. Their New Year's card had arrived yesterday with two others. The three colorful, almost square envelopes lay between an unsolicited Chanet's store catalog and a to-the-resident supermarket flyer. They were somewhat soothing to see: most of his mail came in longer, rectangular envelopes, his name peering out from behind glassine windows, along with one or another of the hyphenated numbers by which he was known to the important computers in his life. There was no possibility that one was from Cindy. He had simply opened the cards in the order he found them on his floor.

His parents' had been on top. On their stamp, a bird winged swiftly through the blue.

"Happy New Year to our son, THE LAWYER, and lovely daughter, also a lawyer. We love you and are always thinking of you. Love, Mom and Dadd."

"Dadd" had personally penned under the typing, "P.S. Isn't it time you kids started a retirement account? It sneaks up fast. Think about it." The card had been cracked and bent from the typewriter. When Philip put it down it curled up and rolled away.

The second card's stamp was a soothing sunset over water. This one was handwritten. "Happy New Year," it began, "We love you."

And the flowing feminine signature, "Metropolitan Bank." The postscript: "Come in, why don't you: We've a plan for your retirement security." How thoughtful. He tried to stamp feeling back into his feet, thinking why not put his folks and his bank directly in touch and eliminate the middle man.

The last card had been addressed carefully in graceful calligraphy. The stamp just said "LOVE." The card itself was handmade from red cardboard, and an array of daisies with white petals had been drawn on its face. Inside, a delicate white lace had been sewn to the border. "Christmas cheer to you and yours," was handwritten inside. "A joyous New Year filled with happy, dancing days," it said. "Stamp."

The postscript: "Don't forget my brie."

The bus made its wide turn onto the street and skidded in the slush toward the cars stopped perpendicular at the intersection. A single look of terror kicked car to car like a chorus line. The bus recovered its traction and continued its turn, finally stopping in front of Philip and the others. It opened its doors.

It was even colder, if possible, inside. The metal vertical and horizontal railings had grabbed the winter and stored it in concentrated form for release on human contact. There were no empty seats except for a few near a stuck-open window. For a change, due to the record-tying cold, those standing stood together. They huddled close in the back over the engine.

He had received one more New Year's message. It had arrived for him a few days ago at the defender, an invitation really. From Lisa, the girl from the gallery. He still had it in his coat, and he took it out to read again.

"Some friends are throwing a party at the Warsaw Café on New Year's Eve," read the note in pertinent part. "I hope you'll come. (If you don't have another hot date.) I'm leaving your name at the door. Happy New Year, if you can't."

He thought he should go tonight, and that he might.

The bus hit downtown. When his stop was next, he moved through the people to the front and stood next to the bus driver. "How ya doin'?" he said to the man, who didn't answer.

"I hear you," Philip said softly.

It made Philip want to tell the gallery girl, "Don't send me invitations. Don't stick me with your needles. You don't know what I'd feel if I could." But no, she was right to. She was kind to. And he didn't want to be like the bus driver. Maybe, maybe he would go to the party. If he drank, danced, and felt this year finish, maybe he could start another one tomorrow.

The doors opened and Philip mumbled, "Catch ya later," out of habit, going down.

"Take it light, pal," came the driver's response.

Philip hit pavement and the twenty-floor office building he worked in stretched up directly in front of him. Located at Broad and Chestnut, the building was conveniently situated close both to City Hall, where most criminal trials were held, and the DA's office. Thus, files and evidence left behind in the often mad rush to court could be quickly retrieved without seriously pissing off a judge. And plea bargaining sessions with prosecutors were easily set up. It was even common for the attorneys to drop in on each other without appointments.

The brass plaque riveted to the cornerstone still said SOLYD CONSTRUCTION CO., dating from the building's construction by Solyd, though the day was lost when it needed the entire twenty floors for its own offices. Today the plaque drew his eye for a reason it hadn't yesterday, and if he could have felt sadness, and not just the occasion for it, he would have.

Inside the building, he used the back of his tie to push in the greasy elevator button. He had to use his hand, though, to dig it out again. Other people were deposited into the building now through the revolving doors and asked how long ago he'd pushed the button.

"Half a second."

"Shit." And they settled into dazes to wait the five or so minutes the old elevator took no matter where in the building it was when you sent for it.

This floor contained not just this dank lobby, it also housed a branch of that thoughtful bank. He wondered, what if he went into the bank and tried to wish it a Happy New Year in return? Would he be regarded strangely? Would feet hover over silent alarms until he either pulled a gun or slobbered harmlessly? Or would a lovely woman, the owner of the sprawling feminine signature, produce herself, curved as her writing—"Hello, I'm Metro, Metro Bank"— and extend her hand demurely to receive his reciprocal good cheer? He thought not.

The next three floors, which from the pitch of its grinding the elevator was still nowhere near, were still occupied by Solyd. It had rented out the floors down from twenty slowly at first, one by one, as the company had gotten sick, then sicker. Today, as it continually reorganized under the Bankruptcy Act, as it, more aptly, convulsed and contorted trying to satisfy its requirements, it chewed off floors like limbs. But the weight as the company fell in on itself seemed to crush it quicker still. Until, one day soon, Philip thought they would all hear the crash as Solyd's remaining assets fell through the ceiling into that sentimental bank below, to which they were pledged as collateral. Hopefully, onto the head of "Metro, Metro Bank," while she signed her sexy signature onto cards.

But perhaps Solyd's poor founder, who several years ago had tried to bribe a city official for a contract to save his company (and who just the night before last, had had his daughter murdered for him), would by then have started walking around the house naked, chuckling. Today's papers had no picture of the dead girl, though her lineage was fully set forth. But under the fatter than usual headline there had been two of the man they were already calling "the China Manager." Side by side were his police mug shot and his Chanet's "personnel portrait," as it was captioned. The personnel portrait could be found again on A-14 and 15, the two pages Chanet's had purchased to introduce its new Manager of the Year.

Well, the four floors above Solyd were rented by an accounting firm with its own problems. Three of the firm's principals had gone to prison with the dead girl's dad. They had doctored Solyd's books to hide the bribe. The accounting firm had been forced to sublet its top floor and was down to three itself.

So floor eight had been available when the University of Pennsylvania needed space on short notice. It was now equipped as the university's animal experimentation lab or, as they called it, "Employees Only." There had been a small but bothersome student body segment for whom no ratio of blind beagles to sighted cosmetic consumers, no fraction expressing screaming beagles in terms of pretty black lashes, no correlation between beagles with eyes and blind mascara wearers could make important enough the important-enough relationship between blinded screaming beagles and safe and waterproof makeup. Students at the law school sued to have the lab kicked off campus.

Occasionally some horrible dog sound—a whimper-bark-yelp-scream—found its way through closed windows or cracks in the floor into the defender, and keyboards would stop clacking. People paused in their activity to let their eyes well and say, "Those poor dogs," before replacing their running mascara and taking up where they left off.

The elevator arrived and those waiting got on. The passengers left Solyd behind, the accounting firm, the beagle works. They stopped on nine, the floor just below the defender's office. On that floor was a bail bond company that had jumped at the chance to locate under the Office of the Public Defender. To capitalize optimally, it had changed its name to the Office of the Public Debenture, hoping the defender's often illiterate clientele would compare their little pieces of paper with the lobby directory downstairs and find their way to its offices instead. A probably shady import-export company was directly above the defender's floor, and an acting school was on twelve. After that Philip didn't know.

The elevator stopped for Philip at ten. He turned right at the end of the hallway, and followed straight to a pair of double doors with OFFICE OF THE PUBLIC DEFENDER divided between them in gold block. He entered and waved his fingers at the admin in the reception area, filled a Styrofoam cup with coffee from the machine on her file cabinet, and walked, sipping it, through the winding inner corridors. To his own office three-quarters of the way back. Closed his door. It was still before nine, and sat in one of the chairs with slatted backs that fronted his desk, instead of going around to his chair.

He spread out his paper to read while he drank his coffee, and noticed the file on his desk. He opened it to see what new case he'd been assigned and his newspaper hissed to the floor. He paid no attention because his new case was the China Manager's.

Why? Why in the world was Chanet's new Manager of the Year in need of a public defender? And why him? After all, this case would be big and the big cases were snatched up before they made it to his office.

This was the Manager of the Year who was accused of murder here. This was the daughter of a still well-known criminal who'd been killed. Obviously, his superiors had reviewed the evidence, found it overwhelming, and didn't want to be publicly embarrassed by a conviction.

Just what was the evidence? He retrieved the front section from the floor and read the article again. This early the file would have next to nothing in it, and the paper was almost always a better source of background anyway. Then he looked through the file carefully. It had the arrest warrant and complaint, which he'd expected. But it also had the number forty-eight and number forty-nine police report forms with their preliminary crime scene and witness information. That was strange because you usually had to wait till the discovery phase of a trial to get them, unless you had contacts and could get them unofficially. It confirmed his suspicion that his higher-ups had taken an interest before passing the case along.

Soon he had pieced together a rough picture. A neighbor had called the police, in her words, "after the Big Picture," in their words, at twenty-three hundred hours. She had heard "bumping noises" next door "during, you know, the Bounty paper towel commercial"— which it turned out had been shown two hours before her call at 9:08.

After the show, the lady said, she'd started thinking about the noises again, which hadn't sounded "quite right," and called the police. Police had arrived to find Quintana's door locked and the girl not answering. After quickly ascertaining that there was no other key or pass key, they kicked down her door. Quintana hadn't minded. She was dead on the floor at the back of the apartment. She had been brutally beaten, according to the medical examiner, by a left-handed someone who'd made his efforts superfluous by breaking her neck.

The China Manager—Builder, Philip corrected himself—was left-handed, which left hand, to make things easy, had been unset, blue, and broken at his arrest.

A friend of Quintana's, a Lisa Bianchi, had told police that Quintana had planned to have drinks with Builder that night at Club Brasil, but in the paper was quoted as saying, "She wasn't dating anyone at the moment." Restaurant workers, including a few who knew Quintana, never saw the couple. There had been no reservation in either name. What else? Quintana's kitchen calendar had an entry for the twenty-ninth: "Drinks F." Builder's prints were in her apartment, and some hair of his medium brown color was found near the body. Nothing visible under her nails, but blood and other evidence had been collected for scientific analysis.

Builder had been arraigned last night at police headquarters, a building called the Roundhouse. A phone call and Philip found out he'd missed him, that he'd already been transported back to Holmesburg Prison in Northeast Philly. Another, and he made arrangements to interview Builder there that afternoon. A few more inside and he was talking to the PD who'd covered the Roundhouse the night before last and handled Builder's arraignment. The woman gave him an informal rundown of the evidence, which added nothing significant.

Philip closed the file and slipped it in his briefcase. Rising, he drained the coffee, now cold, that he'd forgotten while on the phone. He left his paper where it was, partially on the floor, front section on the desk, and chucked the cup at a wastebasket that it floated nowhere near. On his way out he got a taxi voucher at reception. He would visit the crime scene, he always did that.

He thought, riding the elevator down, that he smelled the fear of beagles in there earlier. And deeper in the vertical corridor, he thought he heard them screaming.

13

Holmesburg Prison

Later that day, Philip was brought through sliding barred gates, connecting corridors, and corresponding frisks that he knew when to expect through experience. He opened his jacket and lifted his arms, he spread his legs by rote, and the equally perfunctory hands slid over him, not really checking.

They passed him through detectors anyhow, waiting on the other side. He was taken along the last corridor by a pair of guards, one very short and the other tall, that for years had been kept together as a team, probably for laughs. They'd been nicknamed "Short" and "Long" way before Philip came on the scene.

At the door through which lay Visitation, they frisked him, Long high and Short low, and as their fingers flew over his chest and buttocks, he instinctively didn't say, "Oh, fellas." He had said, "Oh, fellas," once when he was green. They'd told him they got that all fuckin' day and gave his balls a squeeze. Now he was a steady customer and knew better. They finished their frisk and he didn't say, "Hey, you missed the submachine gun." He just waited until they unlocked the door and took him into the large room.

"PD," said Long to the two guards at the table in front.

One of them opened his eyes and shifted in his chair. "Who for?"

"Frederick Builder."

"The China Manager?" asked Short. There was a general perking up among the four.

"Yeah."

"I got 'im," said Long. He took his cap off languidly and brought some sweaty hair to his scalp with the bill.

"We kin both go," Short told him, and they started slowly away.

Visitation was about as big as a ballroom, though no one was dressed for a ball. There were four little rooms set in the wall behind the guards' table, which Philip checked by habit for occupancy. All four doors were closed, lights off, through wire-threaded glass. He looked at the guards again, thinking they must be new since he didn't recognize them. They were blazing examples of the custodial art—eyes peeled, one's to the back of his lids, the other's to a muscular female-in-bathing-suit centerfold. He turned away from them.

The room stank of sweat and baby shit. At small tables, prisoners in gray prison whites sat across from lawyers and mothers, girlfriends and infants. Most everyone seemed about an inch from tears, except the lawyers—they looked bored—and the babies, who were crying. Besides the two at the front, three more guards moved around the room. They stopped here and there to listen without hiding it to a prisoner's conversation. Mostly, though, they found suitable places to put a foot up on a chair, or lean against a wall, and watch the girls get their guys off.

The sex wasn't exactly hidden here. There wasn't time or self-esteem enough for that. A woman with a shoe on her guy's table had one leg on the ground. The other played barefoot in his groin above a pair of lowered prison pants. Each of them held a baby, though the man was fast losing interest in his, his *coo coo*'s becoming *ahh ahh*'s. Another young lady had her fella straddled in his chair. Not even one of her feet was on the ground, her heels touching behind the back of the chair, her elbows on the table behind her for support. Their movement revealed what her skirt hid. The woman caught Philip looking and winked. He smiled slightly back: he'd defended her for pretty much what she was doing now.

"Bam!" said the man under her. She raised her eyebrows at Philip. "Bam! Bam!" said the man.

"Yeah, baby, pow," the woman said, leaning back for her cigarettes and letting his convulsion shake one loose from the pack for her.

Short and Long were back with Freddy in tow. It may have been the new plaster cast, the clean prison whites, or the lack of resolution in the background provided by Short and Long, but Frederick Builder struck Philip as a man in control. Stiff-backed and face set, he looked as starched as his garb. His eyes moved around the room slowly, and he seemed unsurprised, satisfied, if Philip had it right, that all eyes were upon him. That people stopped fucking when he entered a room, even that didn't faze him.

The guards were taking their time, shooting the shit with his client. They took especial care with his injured arm as they removed the cuff from the cast. Philip took a seat at the nearest table. They'd punch Freddy's good arm, tell him, "Kill one for the Gipper," and bring him over any four to six hours now. Philip removed a clean legal pad from his briefcase, and an office interview form. Took a pen from his jacket pocket and, to make sure it worked, wrote "For the Gipper" on the pad. He thought about the party tonight. He would blow a noise-maker till his eyes bulged, he would scare off this old year with that shrill noise—when a flash of white next to him took his eyes to the right. Freddy was looking down at him, Short's hair, and Long's chest and head behind him over either shoulder.

"I think we can spare 'em a room, can't we?"

"Hmmm," said Short as though considering. "Yeah, I think we could."

The rooms in the front wall were supposedly reserved for client-lawyer discussions like this one, but they might as well have had signs, WHITE-COLLAR CRIMINALS OR WELL-KNOWN ATTORNEYS ONLY. None of Philip's clients had ever rated a room before, certainly he hadn't. The guards were smiling at him expectantly, waiting for some expression of gratitude. He pointed to his throat and shook his head—"Speechless." They were satisfied and sauntered ahead with Freddy.

Philip didn't hurry. He closed his briefcase, gathered his things and followed. He did look once, despite himself, to see if the other attorneys had noticed where he was headed, but only met the hooker's look again.

Inside the small room, Freddy had already taken a seat behind the rickety desk. There was another, smaller chair in front of the desk, and that was the only furniture. The walls of the room were the immaculate white of his client's cast and clothing. Philip put his things down on the desk in front of Freddy.

"I'll just be outside the door. Knock when you're done," said Long.

The guards went out and Philip helped them close the door. The old sweat, new sweat, crying babies, coming convicts were cut off. Philip felt a separation from everything, in limbo in this little white room. He turned and walked back to Freddy.

"If you don't mind," he said in the new quiet, "why don't you sit over there." He indicated the little chair. He was here to interview Builder, not the other way around. Freddy moved around.

"At your arraignment, you asked the court to appoint an attorney to represent you," Philip said. "I'm him." He took one of his cards from his briefcase and handed it to Freddy. Freddy held out his good arm to shake. "Frederick Builder," he said.

"—to meet you," said Philip. He found Freddy's handshake warm and dry. "Mr. Builder—"

"Frederick," Freddy said.

"Frederick. I can't help wondering if you fully appreciate your situation."

Freddy gave him a worried look. "I fully appreciate it," he said. "Believe me."

"Because out there, you seemed to regard this as theater or something akin to it. A dream. I just want to be sure you're not in some kind of shock. You understand you've been arrested—"

"For murder. Yes. I spent all yesterday pinching myself."

"Okay." Philip leaned back as much as he could in the hardback chair. "Then what I'd like to do first is to get some preliminaries out of the way." He began the standard spiel, forcing inflection into the chain of words. "To begin with, anything you say to me is strictly confidential. I can't use it any way to hurt you, even if I wanted to, and the courts can't either. So I'll expect you to be completely honest with me. All right?"

"No matter what I say, it won't get me into trouble?"

"That's right. Even if you were to tell me you committed the murder, it would go no further."

Many attorneys did this differently these days—they didn't want a confession that would technically preclude putting their client on the stand to lie about his alibi. More attorneys solicited the confession, and didn't let technicality get in the way of their defense.

Freddy nodded. Philip went on from the script.

"Next. Henceforth you are to make no statements whatsoever to the police, anyone from the district attorney's office, to any guards or prisoners that you may become familiar with, or to the press, regarding your case. No matter how unimportant you think the comment may be, no matter what they threaten, promise, offer, if I'm not there, you've got nothing to say."

"Why not the press?"

"Because the press will misquote you, or quote you accurately, whichever is more exciting. And because you don't know what could be damaging to say. The press is going to be a factor in your case, and so has to be handled with extreme care."

"I can handle myself. I'm probably just a bit more intelligent than your regular nigger."

Philip blinked. "Keep the slurs to yourself. If you don't mind. And if you ever say 'nigger' within earshot of a reporter, you can forget any possibility of sympathetic press coverage."

"I know that. All I mean is, I can handle the press. I know what to say."

Philip tried to keep his distaste from his voice. "Do you remember what you said to the arresting officers when they asked you about your hand?"

"Yes," said Freddy. "All I said was I fell down the steps."

"Yeah. That's all you said. So, you know how many times a woman gets beaten to death and it causes a male friend, way across town, to take clumsy on the stairs? It's amazing—sometimes in a fall so violent, traces of her skin and blood get deposited under his nails." Philip leaned forward. "Christ, semen in the dead girl, semen in the suspect's underwear: 'I fell down the stairs and it got me excited.' Do you know how often?"

Freddy shook his head.

"Well, I do, and so do judges. And so do reporters. Did the cops ask you before or after you were Mirandized, read your rights?"

"After."

"Well, see, you're stuck with that then. And what if it turns out your injury is inconsistent with a fall down the steps? You listen to me: I'll be the smart one."

Freddy's legs were crossed so that the back of one knee touched the top of the other. He uncrossed them and put both feet on the ground.

"Okay."

"We'll get back to the press later. But I think I've got you listening now. I don't think any of this really has hit home with you yet, despite what you say. I watched you playing the crowd out there. There are TV cameras now, but there won't be this time next year while you're sitting in prison all alone. Until it hits you as real, I just don't want you to mess yourself up."

"I'll be careful. But you're wrong. It has hit home. I'm—" He stopped and crossed his legs again.

"Go on."

"I am in control, that's all. My mind's clear—I'll tell you the truth. I don't feel like I'm dreaming, I feel like I've woken up from a dream."

"How did you break your hand?"

"Yes," Freddy answered.

"You killed her then."

"I freaked."

"You're not allowed to freak." It'd come out before he could stop it.

"Hey, look! You said to tell you the truth—"

"I know."

"—If you don't want to defend me then get me someone who can!"

"I'll defend you. That's my role," Philip said.

They eyed each other for a moment, then Freddy said, "I loved her, you know."

"Okay," said Philip. Fine. He turned the pages of the office form past the section for biographical information to "Facts of the Arrest," subheading, "Background."

"I'd like you to tell me how this all happened. Don't start with the night of the incident. I want to hear about your relationship with Mindi Quintana, from its very beginning. And everything else of importance that's been happening in your life along with her."

Freddy sighed and brought a six-year-old night into the prison. He painted it for Philip in such detail that Philip imagined its purple-black onto the walls of the room, and was surprised along with Freddy by Mindi on her porch. Listening minutely, he moved Freddy from that night and into an account of his two months with Mindi in college, carefully eliciting details, which he made note of and circled back to at intervals to see if he could elicit again. A crude tool for gauging if Freddy was lying but about all he had, and as honed by him over time, better than blunt.

From there he moved Freddy to his years at Chanet's, where there were Managers of the Month, and of the Year, Tweed restaurants and chocolate managers, and where Freddy's superior, Bobby Jamison, carried a pearl cigarette holder. He then focused Freddy on the recent reunion with Mindi. Here, as a claimed romance unfolded, he began to feel lied to. He heard about dates that didn't sound like dates, but let Freddy continue; about a desire to publish him in her magazine that didn't make sense, but he did not interrupt.

And while he listened, Freddy's one-word response to "How did you break your hand?" kept coming back to him. Where was the remorse if he'd loved her as he claimed? Where was that anguish that someone he *loved* had died by his own hand? Philip had seen that anguish, he knew that remorse; it often made society's punishment seem beside the point.

Now Freddy came to the day of the murder and Philip felt the rage.

"They promised not to make me Manager of the Year. Then they did." Freddy's face was red. He shook, livid. He slammed his hand down on the table.

"What did you do?"

"I went to a bar."

"You got drunk."

"I had two or three beers and poured them out all day." Freddy's forehead was damp. He dabbed it with his good arm, calming himself. "I needed her. You understand? I needed her." Philip did not sympathize and Freddy seemed to sense it. "You wouldn't understand." And he did not reassure him. "You wouldn't understand . . . first-gear self-satisfied . . ."

"Go on," Philip said.

"I went to Mindi's. We talked about my book. She liked it. She knew people, and told me she wanted to—"

"So you killed her," Philip cut him off.

"It didn't happen like that. Let me finish." But he'd lost his thread.

"Did she rebuff you sexually?"

"No, of course not."

"So you've slept with her. Lately, I mean."

"Of course."

"No, you haven't. Her friend said she wasn't dating anyone. You wanted a relationship. She didn't."

"I know what her friend said, I've read the papers. She's incorrect."

"No. You're lying to me."

"I have pictures of us at the circus. Kissing! Embracing and kissing."

"I don't care. Why would she lie to her friend?" Freddy didn't answer.

"See? It doesn't wash. If I didn't know you killed her, and if you hadn't told me so much of the truth, maybe I wouldn't know the rest. But the jig's up. You're Manager of the Year. It was—these are your words—your 'worst fear realized.' You go to a bar, but you don't get drunk. You need comfort, Mindi, so you can't take the chance. You go to see her and—"

"That's not what happened!"

"Freddy!" said Philip. "Give me a break. Fool the world, but tell me the truth. I don't want to find it out at trial and you don't want me to." He leaned across the desk. "If I'm going to weave you a defense around what the prosecution's got, I've got to know what that might be. You're going to have to decide whether to accept a deal, if one's offered, and if not, whether to plead guilty or go to trial. If you want me to advise you, I've got to know." He sat back in the chair. "That's the last energy I'm expending on you. I've got fifteen more minutes to talk today, then I'm going to proceed on whatever you tell me now, true or false."

Freddy stood and bent over him. "You want to know? Okay. I loved her. I needed her. I had plans for us, she ruined them. She knew how much I cared about her, and she couldn't just give me a little bit, couldn't come around just a little and give me a chance. For six years I thought about her, and that's what I get in return? Six years—and then she was here. And I started taking her out. And she was reading my stuff. She *knew* people. It would have been so easy for her to help me. So easy, and after all the attention I was showing her. But in the end, she refused. She refused!"

"Is that all she refused you?"

"You know it's not. She didn't refuse to let me take her out. She let me spend my fucking money on her. Led me on, let me *think* she wanted to be with me. But when I really needed her—in the one moment that I *really* needed her, she chose to back away. Okay? She says, 'You're a man with a sense of beauty. You have the ability to create it,' and all she means is I can make people buy china?—"

Seeming to catch on finally that Philip had purposely provoked this rant, Freddy halted unfinished, straightened, sat down and crossed his legs.

Now Philip had what he'd wanted. Now that he did, he realized why he'd pushed for it. It had not only to do with Freddy's defense. It was that Freddy had killed a woman and Philip hadn't. Where Freddy had exploded, he had imploded. He'd wanted to find the difference between them.

The biggest was that Freddy hadn't loved Mindi. She was a blue ribbon as surely as the one he despised, but she represented something he wanted. She had never been real, except maybe for the few months in college. Not during the six years of imagining, nor after, when she was flesh and blood before him, then bloody flesh before him, did he possess her with a life, purpose, or meaning of her own. So it wasn't love that had moved him to kill her, but lack of it that had allowed him to.

"None of this," said Freddy, "is my official position for court. It's confidential like you said. What I want to say to others, what I want the press to think is my business."

"I said we'll get back to the press." He took Freddy's file and his notes out of the briefcase. "Let's talk about what the prosecution's got on you to date. Normally we wouldn't have too good an idea yet. At this stage, usually all that's in the file is the complaint—which merely sets out the charges against you. We also happen to have the police reports. The medical examiner's report, witness statements—except those in the reports we already have—investigatory and scientific findings will take awhile. We won't get them till after your formal arraignment, which I'll get to. But the papers have done a job, and I spoke to the PD who covered your preliminary arraignment. She gave me a breakdown of what she thinks they've got so far."

He turned to his notes. "From what the medical examiner could determine at the scene, Mindi Quintana sustained a brutal beating by a left-handed man. But it was breaking her neck that killed her." He looked up from the pages. "You're left handed. Your left hand was newly broken at the time of arrest." He looked back down. "I've had left-handed, right-handed attributions before and they're tenuous. Sometimes you can really eat into them." He flipped over a page. "We've got the Bianchi girl's statement that Mindi planned to go out for drinks with you that night. There's the stuff in the papers, and probably a lot she could add, about your relationship or lack thereof. Plus, we've got an entry on Mindi's calendar for December twenty-ninth that says 'Drinks F.' To make a long story short," he said, his eyes again on Freddy, "we might be able to keep much of what the friend has to say out of evidence under something called the hearsay rule. Now, I don't want to get into a long explanation of what that is, and the law in the area is somewhat unsettled at the moment anyhow. The bottom line, though, is that the court might exclude the friend's statement about your plans for the evening. But the calendar will come in."

His rundown of the evidence was partly to get himself thinking about it; he did not restrain his analysis and took notes on what he said.

"Moving on. There was no sign of forced entry into the apartment. The implication is that Mindi knew her killer and opened the door for him. Still, the police had to break down the door. In so doing they may have destroyed evidence of a break-in they'd have discovered otherwise." He wrote it down. "Well, that's our argument anyhow. That she knew her killer, however, is also supported by the fact that the only struggle was at the back of the apartment in the living room. And of course there's the extra cup of coffee."

He went on.

"Fingerprints were removed. Some from the living room, none from any particularly incriminating object. None, except hers, from the coffee cups. Some of the prints are yours, which places you there at the very least."

"I've been there before. A number of times," Freddy offered.

"Well, yes, that's our obvious argument. And it works. But some hair was found, too. Of your medium-brown color. Apparently there was more of it than would be expected under normal, nonviolent circumstances. I believe the word my colleague used was 'tuft,' though that could just be how the ADA characterized it for the court."

"My hair's been thinning."

Philip looked at the full head of hair. "That's helpful, too." He thought of something a colleague had told him once. If he remembered correctly, hair that is pulled out has a live root, or maybe it was a whole root, as opposed to hair that falls out on its own. He made a note to check it.

"You sound optimistic."

"No. You did it and the investigation is ongoing. It may well be that more evidence will turn up against you. And the scientific findings, DNA and such, could be the ballgame. Under any scenario, we're fighting an uphill battle with Mindi's plans for the night and your broken hand. By the way, was she dressed already for the night out?"

Freddy nodded.

"Well, that's not good, either. Let's go on. The prosecution will move the court at some point to order a sample of your hair for comparison." He jotted down to pull a form answer to such a motion and the accompanying brief. "We'll lose that one," he said.

"What if I'm convicted?"

Philip chucked the file back in his briefcase. "Depends of what. If the jury comes back in the first degree, you'd receive a mandatory life sentence. There are no aggravators here that I know of so death isn't

132

in the picture. The life sentence is without parole, though, meaning the only road to release would be through commutation of your sentence by the governor. That's very rare and happens only after many years.

"On the other hand, it was a frenzied beating. The jury might decide you intended to beat her but not to kill her. In that case they'd come back with a verdict of murder in the third degree, which is a felony of the first degree. The bottom line there is a maximum sentence of not more than twenty years' imprisonment, and you could get less. Probably would because you're employed, have no criminal record, and used no weapon. Under the sentencing guidelines, a guy like you would normally—and remember, I'm by no means guaranteeing this—be put in what's called the minimum range. Plus you're white. You'd probably draw, for third degree, between six and ten years. With good behavior you'd serve less than whatever your sentence was.

"We need a lot more of the scientific and medical picture, but even with a broken neck, we might get a third-degree verdict. First-degree murder requires proof that you specifically intended to take the life. The fact that you made a date arguably indicates you didn't go there with that intent. That alone isn't enough since the premeditative element can take place an instant before the killing act. And if you're still not leveling with me, they might have more on intent. But the point is—the trick is, rather, to negate the intent to kill: Whoever killed her didn't necessarily yank her neck up. He could have kicked her in the head or thrown her against the wall, or she could have fallen during the beating and broken it. And if the prosecution can prove her head was purposefully yanked up, we argue that it wasn't necessarily done with the intention of killing her. Are you following me? This is complicated, I know."

"I'm following."

Philip rubbed his eyes. "I can tell you too that whatever the additional evidence, there's another factor. If the jury likes you, feels sorry for you, or dislikes the victim, it'll help them come back in the third degree."

"What do you predict?"

"I don't make predictions. Anyway, it's much too early and I don't know nearly enough. We don't know what the evidence will be once it's fully developed. We don't know if the prosecution will offer a deal. I would say that the facts as I know them so far might support a third-degree characterization. Here's what happens: The DA will charge murder generally and will argue first degree. It's the jury's right to reject that and come back with a verdict in a lower degree. It can also acquit you, of course."

Freddy nodded. He put a finger in his cast to scratch.

"The other possible verdict, besides acquittal, is voluntary manslaughter, which is a felony of the second degree and carries a maximum sentence of ten years. For that, the jury would have to find that you were provoked in some legally adequate way by the victim. Tough under the circumstances, but it can be a sympathy verdict. Again, with good behavior your actual time served would be less than your sentence."

He paused and Freddy asked, "What about second-degree murder?"

"That's 'felony murder' and only applies when the homicide occurs during the commission of another crime, a felony. So barring the unforeseen, it's not in the picture."

"Okay."

"All right, I told you I wanted to get back to the press. You've read the papers."

Freddy nodded quickly. "I have."

"Big news, Frederick. Your case is big news. They've got a nick-name for you already. The China Manager. It's catchy. The victim's father, Henry Quintana, was a symbol of corruption in Philly a few years back. The crimes of the father may have inured slightly to your benefit so far. There's a hint in the speculation that maybe this very

pretty Latin American woman, whose father may have links to organized crime, drew you in, had her way with you, then wanted to spit you out. Symmetry is satisfying, as you would know, so maybe, maybe there's the feeling that the acorn doesn't fall far from the tree or, even deeper, that the girl got just what her father deserved. You, the new Manager of the Year, symbol to the youth of Philadelphia. White, yuppified, no record—"

"I'm not Manager of the Year anymore. They stripped me of it."

"My point is, Freddy, my point is, there will be a war in the media over you, with the DA's office trying to make you worse than you are and me trying to make you better. But what we really want to do is have the press go away. We want the publicity to die down so that the ADA can deal and so the judge can rule favorably on the white-guy-with-no-record's motions, without a backlash. That means when reporters get to you, and they will, you have no comment on the advice of your attorney and refer them to me. I've got your word on that?"

"Yes."

"Fine. Your preliminary hearing is listed for the tenth at ten-thirty. That's to determine if there's enough evidence to hold you for trial. So you know what to expect, the prosecutor will be assigned by then, he'll put on witnesses, and we'll get a better idea of what they've got and how it looks on stage. Your job is to listen carefully and write down anything you hear that you know isn't the case, or that we can attack."

"Okay."

"Now, after the preliminary hearing, we've got the formal arraignment at which time your trial will be listed and we'll be given a trial date. It's after the formal that we'll start getting copies of everything, reports, scientific findings, statements, et cetera, whatever the DA's got against you. A pretrial conference will be scheduled, which we'll talk about down the road, and then there's the trial. This is the general way things run, just so you have some idea."

Freddy nodded his understanding.

"Now, they denied bail at your arraignment and I'll renew your petition at the prelim, but I don't think we'll get it. If we do, it'll be a bundle."

"How much?"

"Two hundred thousand at least. That's an example of what the press can do for you. You'd need ten percent for a bail bond. Can you raise that kind of money?"

"If I could raise money I'd have hired . . ."

"Right. They'll probably move you to City Hall on the eighth or ninth. Have you got a suit?" He had asked automatically because often his clients didn't.

"The lapels are all frayed from the pinholes."

Philip didn't care enough to ask. "If you'll sign your keys out to me, I'll pick one up for you." He put the rest of the papers in his briefcase and closed it.

"Can you pick up something else for me while you're there?"

"Sure, what?"

"In the kitchen. The middle drawer to the right of the sink. I have my writing in there. If you could have about ten copies made of everything, I'll reimburse you."

"All right. I'll bring them with your suit. Why the copies?"

"There might be some interest."

"I told you. You've got to keep your profile low."

"Please, just—"

"Sure. It's up to you, Freddy." Philip stood. "We need to get into more detail so I'll be seeing you again shortly. And I have to get more history from you. Work, family, education, and the like. I'll arrange a call tomorrow for that." He extended his hand. Freddy shook it. Philip went to the door and knocked. Long slid his head in.

"Hey, China Manager. You got some reporters out here wanna talk to you."

"Since when you let reporters in?" Philip asked.

Long ignored him.

"No reporters," Philip told the guard. "Keep them away from him." Long looked to Freddy for confirmation.

"What he said," said Freddy.

"See you before the prelim," said Philip and went out. Half a dozen reporters accosted him, jostling each other and raising their voices to get their questions heard. Behind the group two men held television cameras, red lights on indicating filming, and another snapped photos.

Philip answered no question and said, "I have a statement. I have a statement," until they quieted down. "I'm taking no questions; my client isn't either. Mr. Builder is innocent of the charges against him. Mr. Builder is an upstanding young man, a budding writer, an outstanding, longtime employee of Chanet's Department Store. He has no criminal record. He is wrongfully accused of this dreadful crime, as will be shown." He walked on, hoping to draw them away from the room. Only two followed, though, with their additional attempts, the others waiting for Freddy to come out. A few seconds later he did and the reporters dogging Philip scooted back. Philip watched as Freddy was led through the group.

"I loved her, I'm innocent, that's all," said Freddy. He was a fine shade of downtrodden-yet-determined.

Philip could not help but notice the envy with which he himself was being regarded by the other attorneys. They "unh-huh"ed their small-time dealers, "right"ed their rapists and three-time losers, and looked at him with wishing eyes. A lawyer from the defender vigorously gestured him to take advantage of the photo session and shook his head disgustedly when Philip stayed where he was. Philip caught his client's eye and held a finger to his lips. Several minutes, connecting corridors and sliding gates later, he was back in the winter.

14

New Year's Eve

Lisa sat alone near the back of the Warsaw at a table they'd set up for her away from the New Year's Eve diners. She held a cigarette in the same hand as her wine, the glass cool against her cheek as she exhaled the smoke.

Her name had been on Mindi's calendar for lunch today. And they'd found her number and address on the phone list in Mindi's kitchen. When Lisa returned from the Borgia, she'd heard her phone ringing through the door to her apartment while keying it open. Thinking it was Mindi—who else would it be at two in the morning?—she'd left the door ajar, hurrying to the phone and answering with, "I'll call you back from my cell, Mind, let me lock up."

But the voice on the phone simply asked if she was Lisa Bianchi, and then transferred her call when she said she was. She had become afraid. Another voice came on and identified itself as a police voice. Did she know a Mindi Quintana?

"Yes," she said, adding an instant prayer to God, but the voice regretted to inform her—even as she begged, it regretted to inform her—that a woman they knew to be Mindi had been murdered in her apartment, that she'd been beaten to death.

Lisa swallowed more wine and brought the cigarette to her mouth again, drawing smoke deep inside. She removed a strand of hair from her mouth, and let it out.

The voice—she did not think of it as connected to a person—said they needed her to answer some questions. Mindi's parents couldn't

138

be reached, did she know where they were? Connecticut. Did she have cell phone numbers? No. Did she feel able to identify Mindi officially at the morgue? She couldn't answer, could not say anything, even when asked repeatedly if she was all right, and the voice just kept talking, telling her to be calm, until in a few moments a policeman was next to her taking the phone from her hand.

A black-bearded thickly built man wearing a tuxedo came to her table now and sat down next to her. He was Rico, the Warsaw's owner, and he put his arm around her. She, Mindi, and he had organized the party that would have been held here tonight. Lisa had arrived at four today and he'd been taking care of her since, getting up when he had to attend to business.

"I talked to Des Moines and Sarah. Everybody's still coming," he said. A peal of laughter rang out from across the room. He stood up again. "I'm closing."

"You can't make them leave, Rico," she said vaguely. "They're still eating." There was something else, too. He knew it and sat back down. She shook her head. "They were going to make her father go." She took out another cigarette, then put it on the table. It rolled off.

He brought her close. "It's okay, Lisa. Just go ahead." So she did, they came out of her silently again until her eyes ached and her sinuses burned.

"She was all broken."

"I know she was."

She pulled her head away.

"I told the police about him."

"You're how they got him. Did you see the papers?"

"News," she breathed.

"They have him," he repeated.

"They put her back in the wall."

Rico was making circles on her back with the flat of his hand, but it didn't feel like he was doing them on her. They had reached Mindi's parents later in New Haven. Lisa thought of their faces at the airport.

Tomorrow was their anniversary. She started to shake again and felt Rico's fingers push under her hair. After a moment he leaned back and said a quiet few words to a passing waiter. The waiter went table to table, politely reminding the remaining diners that the restaurant was closing in twenty minutes, as planned, for the New Year's Eve party.

Soon the restaurant was empty of customers and Rico left Lisa again to put the SORRY, WE'RE CLOSED sign on the front door. She watched him lock the door and go to the piano a moment to speak to the singer and the three men with instruments. Then he called the wait staff together into a group of black pants and white shirts and spoke with them.

Lisa poured more wine and let her vision thread through the narrow restaurant, past the staff and band members packing, through the window to the sidewalk trees outside strung with lights. Not for the first time she thought of Philip. She thought of him in the gallery with his wife, and then alone at that old-age home dinner; and thinking somehow that he would understand, she hoped again he would come.

Friends began arriving in twos and threes looking dazed. They went to Lisa's table and each other's, smoked cigarettes and lit new ones, while waiters unobtrusively moved gin and vodka, whiskey and rum, cognac, to a table they'd set up to one side. They all drank heavily, mixer pitchers staying near their original levels.

After a while, she noticed Des Moines, Mindi's fair-skinned writer from Wisconsin, sitting next to her, red faced, pushing his fingers back through his hair. Mindi had published him for the first time and he'd moved here two years ago when a local theater accepted his play for production. He and Mindi had dated for a while.

Seeing Lisa was watching him, he pulled his hand from his head and said, "Stuart's blitzed. He thinks it's his fault for sending her to Chanet's."

Lisa looked over to where Stuart was standing with Cari and Don, two of the dance instructors from the ballet school near *Getting Feathers*. She caught his eye and mouthed, "Come here."

People from the gallery, *Getting Feathers*, friends, people some-body had brought along someplace once or had dated, who had stuck and become part of the group, they were all here. Lisa had never counted and didn't now but she guessed there were about twenty people at the core, like Des Moines and Rico, Craig and Anika from Mindi's magazine, Sidney, Stuart, Cari and Don. More at the fringes like Frank and Sal from Murphy's, Tom, the gallery's lawyer, even Ms. Fineote.

As it neared midnight, the notion descended that it was New Year's Eve. No one talked about it—it seemed horribly wrong to leave Mindi behind in an old year, almost like they were abandoning her—but the fact was acknowledged with pained looks at watches.

Soon Lisa got up and went to the front of the restaurant. She stood next to Des Moines while Anika was telling him how Mindi had had a fat lip when she interviewed for the job at *Getting Feathers*.

"Yeah," Lisa heard herself say. "Sidney hit her with a Frisbee." Then she laughed.

Someone whispered that it was almost twelve o'clock and Lisa stopped laughing. "How long?" she asked. A few seconds.

She turned to Des Moines. "I don't know how to say good-bye to her—"

A dull cheer came from the city. Horns honked outside. For a moment there was silence inside. Lisa turned to the window. "Good-bye," she said. And then everyone was shouting, "*Good-bye—good-bye—good-bye.*"

Philip faced Lisa in the window. There was the glare from the street-lights and he could barely make out that it was her. He heard shouting from inside, though the city had already told him it was 2006. He saw her say something, but could not read what it was and could not see her expression. He waved slightly and realized she didn't see him at all. The cheers around him lingered and died, but she stayed in the window and the yelling continued from inside.

He felt no different in the new year.

He hurried to the door, as he had hurried to the window weeks before—but this time he would force himself through—and pulled it to go in. But it was locked. He pulled it again anyway, then leaned against it and thought about knocking. He thought about going back to the window and rapping.

But now he was thinking it was good the door was locked. He would have pushed himself through, but then what? He'd be a downer, even embarrass her, he wasn't sure now he could hold up his social end.

He passed by the window again, looking in, and she seemed to be looking at him. But he continued away.

15

Morton's

Michael Leopold and Sharon, his fiancée, were dining at Morton's Steakhouse, a Philadelphia power corner where about the only thing thicker than the steak was the interest in who was eating it. Appointed in wood and brass, it was frequented by the city's business and legal elite who went there for reasons that included eating as only an afterthought.

Michael and Sharon were here tonight to conduct an informal poll. Drinks in front of them, steak and salmon on the way, they had settled back in the heavy chairs to munch sesame sticks and see who came over. No one had just yet, but Sharon picked up her glass and leaned forward happily. Michael met her halfway.

"To your big case," she toasted.

"The Manager," he said and they touched crystal.

A week ago on New Year's Day, Michael had received a call at the office. He had telephoned Sharon afterward and whispered the following emphatically: "I got it! I got it! I got the China Manager!"

To which Sharon had whispered back just as emphatically, if a bit drunkenly, "You don't have to whisper! If they're bugging the phone, it won't help. If they're not, I had your office soundproofed last year for your birthday, remember? So you'd stop whispering, remember?"

He'd laughed. "Where've you been?"

"Out benefacting, where else? Patronizing the arts. After, a bar. I know you got the case, dear. Daddy interceded with Larry fully hours ago. I'm going to throw up now, bye. I hope you'll stop moping around."

Yes, Michael had been almost despondent when Larry Fullbody, the district attorney, assigned the case around him to Emmanuel Fitzer. Fitz was good, but junior to Michael, and giving him the case had been an intentional slap. But since the mayor's suggestion that he rethink the matter, and Larry's call to Michael, having rethought it, Michael had been floating on air. His name was as good as household. He had a gorgeous, classy victim whose criminal daddy's trial was still within memory. He had her artsy, wild friends, who wrote and painted, sung and played, danced and fucked their way into the local papers, mourning their way into them now.

Girls like Mindi Quintana didn't get killed every day, and she wasn't even the big draw. Chanet's had been choosing Managers of the Year in Philadelphia for ninety-five years! Shit, if Builder hadn't killed the girl December twenty-ninth, Sharon's dad would have given him the key to the city on New Year's Day.

Sharon was adjusting the fuselage of a brooch Congressman Cody's wife had insisted she borrow. He thought, watching her, that if he'd known in advance that the Manager of the Year was going to kill someone—and there was nothing he could do to stop it, of course—he'd have gone up to him, tapped him on the shoulder, and said, "Uh, Mr. Builder? Please, if you're going to kill her, can I ask you one thing? Would you, could you see your way clear to doing it the very day they pick you?" He had hung up with Sharon sure beyond doubt that someone upstairs, besides her father, was looking out for him.

Sharon had said to him several times this week almost exactly the same words that she said now, gesturing with her drink.

"Remember. Daddy put himself on the line for you. You'd better convert this one."

"Bet on it," he said tightly. He leaned over and whispered inches from her face, "This guy don't hail from the ghetto/barrio, baby. I've seen his yearbook picture and he ain't holding a number in it. It don't say, 'Someday Imma killa cop like my daddy done,' underneath. He *has* a yearbook picture. This is the Manager of the Year here. He's not just middle class, they've crowned him Mr. Middleclass."

Sharon smiled lovingly. "You're so cute when you're trying to put someone away."

"And he's thrown it in their faces. Folks read the papers, and every day it's another murder. And every day it's the same blank stare above a different dirty shirt. But on December thirty-first, folks woke up and saw his white face and thought, 'Now that's a trifle peculiar.' The headline registered and they realized, this time next year, he would have been wearing the Chanet's Christmas beard. This was the guy they *wished* was banging their daughter instead of the kid working on the car. This was the guy they'd been yelling at their son to grow up and be. Sharon, think about it. Oh, they're going to blame him. They're going to hate him for having everything and killing that girl. I'm going to make them."

"Oh, sweetheart." Her eyes glistened. "I want to marry you. I want to have your parties."

"No deals. He's going down." He crushed a breadstick between his teeth and pointed the stump at her. "Do you know that jackass Fitz was thinking of letting him cop to third degree? There wouldn't have even been a trial."

"No trial?"

Michael laughed. "Don't be afraid, Fitz can't hurt us. It's my case now."

"What if the defense says he's crazy, what then?"

He shrugged. "They'd have their shrinks, I'd have mine. Insanity's a real tough row."

"There'd still be a trial, though."

"Of course, honey, I told you." He stirred his drink. "No, I'll get him on one. Three at worst. I can make a case for premeditation jurors'll buy." He stopped stirring. "They'd have to really like him, or hate her, to come back any different."

"What if they like him a lot?"

"They won't." But he knew what she meant and drained his scotch and soda. There had been a sinister thread of coverage from the start that he'd vowed to snip. A nascent view expressed in some articles and television news reports that Builder might not have done it, but more frightening, that if he did, the girl might have brought it on herself.

While perhaps four-fifths of the coverage had Quintana maturely attempting to limit their relationship, the fifth left the door open to some malintent, some betrayal on her part. Perhaps because she was so beautiful, perhaps because her father was who he was. And the lovers' quarrel angle, the suggestion of triangles and such made copy, sold papers.

In the past few days, the papers in general had emphasized that the Manager of the Year was also a would-be writer. A few articles, not many, had cast him as a tortured, talented soul, driven to murder by—what? His passion? The creative spirit? His greater soul? It wasn't clear.

A big case was what Michael needed, yes, to be sure. But what he didn't need and couldn't afford was to lose one, or to win one if the public was going to come down on the other side.

He reminded himself not to be paranoid. The great majority of the coverage, especially of him personally, had been even better than he'd hoped. He was, according to one favorite editorial, "The city's white knight come to slay the evil China Dragon." He was sought after and quoted often, perhaps more so because Philip and his client were largely keeping mum.

Sharon was kicking him under the table. Approaching their table was Sam McDonald, the preeminent defense attorney in the state. "But I don't own a fast food chain and I don't have a farm," he'd say at least ten times a trial, linking himself with an American institution and a childhood memory.

Michael and Sharon straightened and became absorbed in each other. They laughed, captivated by one another as Sam came nearer.

Sam was fat with a full distinguished head of white hair and a bushy mustache, and he was squeezing his way between tables to reach them. He slapped Michael's shoulder and looked down the front of Sharon's dress. Sharon leaned forward to make it easier for him.

"Been reading good things about you, son," Sam said by way of greeting.

"Sam," said Michael, having looked up with surprise. "Why, thank you."

Michael introduced Sharon, who told Sam that her father spoke of him often. Sam called Sharon's father a good man.

"And it seems from what I've been reading, you've got another good man right here," Sam said. To Michael, "Might see about taking the case away from that young PD, things go on like this."

Sam said it jokingly but Michael knew better. "Defended Quintana's daddy, you know. Met the daughter, too. Bet her daddy'd stop sending me Christmas cards"—he winked—"bu-h-h-t everyone gets a defense in this great country of ours."

It was a fantastic omen. Sam would never consider a case he didn't believe to have at least regional potential. Sam was fingering his suspenders.

"Know anything about him, our young defender?"

"He's nothing, Sam, nil," Michael said with conviction.

"Tissue paper," added Sharon.

"It'd be great if you took him over," Michael said. "I tell you, this could be really big."

Sam nodded. "Know it could. Let's see how the prelim plays."

"All right. It sure would be a pleasure to work with you though."

Sam put his hand on Michael's shoulder again. "Now, in the meantime," he said to him, winking loudly at Sharon, "don't you be putting us defense guys out of business." He chuckled deeply, moving away toward his table. They laughed good-naturedly behind him until he was safely seated.

"Can a good prosecutor really put—"

"No."

"What if he takes the case, Michael? He's good. What if he wins?"

"He won't win. The evidence is damning as hell. Even if he did get him off, that's all he would've done, not proved him innocent. I'd be the young kid who fought the good fight against a pretty famous trial attorney, and I'd recover. It's worth the chance."

"But won't he turn the press against you?"

"No. He doesn't care what position the press takes, as long as it's interested. He's not running for anything except clients. In fact, if he can get a guilty guy off, it's better for business than getting off an innocent one. And Sam likes me. I think he might even go out of his way to help me with the press."

Michael struck Sharon suddenly as admirable. She thought of the scrapbook they'd started, the one at her place with all "his" articles in it, and covered his hand with her own.

She said, "'His moral outrage reflects our own with precision,'" and gave his hand a quick squeeze (*Philadelphia Inquirer*, page A-32, January 6).

"'A talented young prosecutor,'" he told her warmly. "'Perhaps our city's next district attorney'" (*Philadelphia Daily News*, page 17, January 8).

"*New York Times* or bust!" she said but her hand jerked and she shot him a subtle look of excited warning. The senator she'd been keeping tabs on was coming over with his wife, on their way out.

Michael asked "who?" with his eyebrows without turning to look.

"Santorum," Sharon said softly, happily, sweeping away some crumbs by his arm and smoothing the tablecloth.

16

The Reporter

The guard through his sleep heard a dull ping against the granite floor and awoke. Opening his eyes, he just caught sight of the nickel rolling under his chair, front legs up, back against the stone wall. The wall had been cool and delicious against the back of his head while he slept. The rest of the place dripped of too much paid-for heat made more oppressive by the smell of caged men. The bit of cool had been enough and he jerked his head in the direction the nickel had come, giving hard looks cell to cell for the prisoner who'd thrown it.

A lanky man watching from the freedom side of the barred door to this holding area chuckled at the guard's hard looks. Manny Sykes was that type.

The guard's glare shot to him directly, which the man took with equanimity. Scuffed browns, wash 'n' wear suit, thin, expressive lips in an overlong face. He gave back fish-mouthed mock concern.

"Sorry to wake you, buddy," he crooned, eyes big and sorry indeed. Then he grinned.

"It's fuckin' three in the morning, whadya want?"

"Heard the China Manager's here for his prelim." The man shrugged a bony shoulder. "I want a word with him."

"No."

"You owe me."

"No fuckin' reporters in holding. You'll get your crack with the others."

The two were deep in the ground under the courtrooms and offices of City Hall. An imposing building in the "General Grant" style, City Hall smacked of having a dungeon, which was just what this lockup seemed like with its rock floor and walls, drops of water running down them in crooked paths like tears or cockroaches. One naked bulb in front of the middle cell.

A drop of water fell from the ceiling directly onto the center of Manny's bald spot and trickled down the back of his head. Cold on his tiptop at center point.

"I want my crack before the others." He took out a ball of hanky and dabbed the back of his stringy neck. "You owe me," he repeated. "I've still got those quotes. I'll use them again and attribute them this time."

The guard clenched his teeth and got up off the chair. Eight months ago this knee-jerk had got him laughing and telling how a couple fellows over the Roundhouse had pushed some wrong computer switch and walked the wrong guy. The guard had realized quick enough he'd let his down and begged the reporter not to burn his two buddies, but the guy wouldn't budge. Said he wouldn't use the guard's name, though, but that he owed him one.

"Okay." The guard approached the door. "But let's get it straight while you're outside. My name don't come into it, anyone asks you got let in. And we're square. Right? You don't never bring them quotes up again."

"Uh-huh," said Manny.

The guard keyed the door and slid it open. "Right?" he repeated.

"Yeah, right," said Manny, sliding past him a head taller.

The guard gripped him by his elbow and led him back past the cells, each with a suit hanging inside on a crossbar for court. Freddy's black box was the last one on the right. The guard unholstered his leaded flashlight. He let it drop in his hand so it rapped Manny's shin.

"Sorry."

Flicked it on, shone the powerful beam into the cell onto the body atop the cot. Freddy's cell had a cool wall of granite on the cot side, which made it the most comfortable, and Freddy's back was against it. That he was given this cell was testament to his status. It had been explained to the guard that Freddy would be in contact with the press, so to treat him cordially. The guard had kept away instead. The flashlight beam traveled to Freddy's face and the two saw that he had a hand up already to block it.

"What's your name?"

Manny gave it.

"I'll talk to him." Freddy had read Sykes's *Bulletin* stories on his case.

The guard chose another key and scratched back the rusting door.

"How about some light?" said Manny.

"Gotta turn 'em all on to turn one of 'em on. Your eyes'll get used to it. Just scream or somethin' if you get in trouble. Or throw a nickel at me, you know I'll come runnin'." He threw shut the door.

Freddy swung his legs off the cot. "There's a chair just in front of you."

Manny moved his hand around slowly for the chair. His eyes were starting to adjust and he saw its outline. He pulled it back and sat down.

"Yeah, keep your distance," Freddy said.

"No, it's not that," said Manny, looking up from massaging his shin. He was seeing better now. He stood, bringing the chair closer to Freddy, and sat again.

Freddy rubbed his eyes and took his hands away. "Why should I talk to you?"

"Because I'll tell it fairly," Manny said without hesitating. "And I don't want to just write an article. I want your interview. It's a chance for you to get your side out."

Freddy was silent. He hoped Sykes could see the curve in his posture, that he'd put his head in his hands. This man had come to see *him*. But the last thing Freddy wanted, for the moment, was to seem to be dealing from strength. "What kind of things would you want to know?"

Manny took out his pad. "Did you kill her?"

Freddy looked up quickly. "No. She was everything to me. But somebody did and he's out there."

"Then where were you that night?"

Freddy started to answer immediately then stopped. He shook his head. "I can't. My attorney told me not to answer anyone's questions about that night. It could all be twisted at trial, any little mistake I make. I'm not supposed to talk to reporters at all. Look, don't ask me anything about that night, okay?"

"Sure, sure," he said. He'd get back to it. "You must know that if you had seemed proud to be Manager of the Year, instead of telling your true feelings, it would be harder to think that you did it. Nobody kills on the happiest day of his life. Why'd you speak out?"

Freddy leaned forward and rested his chin on his fists. "A few reasons, I suppose. Maybe one is, I'm not a lawyer—or a reporter— and I didn't think about that. But the main one is, I didn't do it. And, it's just that place, its whole value system, and—I don't know—glori-fication of the meaningless, the perks, the bullshit, Store Symbol, awards, Christ, nothingness."

"I know all about Chanet's," said Manny. "And I know about you. I do my homework. Spoke to a Robert Jamison, senior upper-middle?"

"Well, if you spoke to Jamison, you know what I mean."

"Sure, but there're Bobby Jamisons everywhere."

Freddy sighed. "Well, that's why I told the truth. I never bought in. I always dreaded being Manager of the Year and I wasn't going to act otherwise. Can I go off the record?"

"Yes, you're off."

"All right. That's why I didn't go out with Mindi that night. I called her, told her I was sick, but really I was too depressed. I didn't fall down the steps. I punched a wall. I told the cops I fell because, I thought, who would believe I punched a wall?"

Manny laughed. "Who would believe you fell down the steps?"

Freddy's look was instantly pained. "I know. But I wanted to say it, even just off the record."

Manny moved his chair up to the cot. "Why?"

"I just want to tell someone. I want you to believe me, I guess."

"Why?"

"Stop asking why, okay? I don't know why. You just sit here and everybody's writing things and saying things about you. And maybe you're going to prison for something you didn't do. And your lawyer tells you not to talk to anybody, just to read all the lies and shut up. I'll be honest. I've read your pieces on me. You and a couple others have at least tried to be fair. That's the only reason I let you in here." He hung his head a moment and then shook it slowly. "I hate this place."

Freddy felt rather than saw Manny shift in his chair. He'd done his homework, too, and had bided his time before pushing that button. When Manny said, "Shit," Freddy rejoiced and shook his head some more.

"This place is a pisshole, Frederick. A prison is a filthy fucking warehouse that nobody ever came out better from than when they went in. Only worse, every single time worse. It's revenge—which is fine, but just fucking call it that. And that's what I mostly write about. I've got a book on the state prison system, my reporting is centered on that subject, and judicial, sometimes governmental, corruption, excesses, et cetera. They've got people on the paper to balance me out and I make no apologies. Now, that's off the record. I can tell you this: I don't know if you killed her. I do know you're on someone's agenda for a full-court press on facts that so far read to me like no more than a third-degree kill."

"Michael Leopold."

Manny began pacing the cell. "Tell me your story. I promise to be fair. I want to follow you through the system, do interviews at each stage of your case. You're intelligent, articulate, close enough in circumstance to those who need to read about your experiences for them to listen. I recognized that immediately. And you're sensitive to your surroundings. They'll have to empathize."

"I can't, I just can't. I have to think about myself. My lawyer says, in my case, the press . . . the press could be a deciding factor. This is an article for you—"

"No, it's more."

"—but for me it's my life!"

"Okay, I know. I know. Okay, let's see. Okay. Look. Frederick, look at me." Freddy looked. "We'll go article by article. This is what I propose. You give me interviews at every phase, total access to you and to your lawyer. Okay? And we'll go article by article. The first piece you feel you're treated unfairly in, you stop talking to me."

Freddy hesitated, rubbing his temples.

"Hey," said Manny, "the cement's still soft out there. You said I've treated you fairly so far."

"All right, then," Freddy said, looking up. "If I get fried in any of your articles, you can forget my cooperation and my lawyer's. I'm trusting you."

"Done." Manny came over with his hand outstretched. Freddy shook it. Manny sat in his chair again and took out his tape recorder. "I'd like to record this if you don't mind."

"You can take notes, but no recorder."

Manny nodded.

"The writing angle," Manny said.

"Here," said Freddy. He took a folder from a stack of them under the cot. "These are some of the stories I've written. The two on top have been accepted for publication." He handed the folder to Manny. "Mindi was helping me. She was going to publish one in *Getting Feathers*." He got off the cot and stood over Manny, who gave him the file back. "This one," Freddy said, putting the story about the archeologist on top and handing back the file. "It still needed work, though, it's an older one." He went back to the cot. "I've got nothing else to do in here except pursue this," he said by way of explanation. "It's that or go nuts. So if you want to publish excerpts of any of these, feel free. Or you might know people at magazines who'd be interested."

"Okay," said Manny. "Have you published anything before the two in here?" He tapped the folder.

"Sure, but under pen names. Aleksandr Solzhenitsyn, James Michener."

That one broke Manny up. He jotted it down. "Solzhenitsyn," he repeated. He finished writing and looked over at Freddy again, appraising him. "Let's get to it. Were you platonic? That's what the Bianchi girl says."

"We were friends, too, but we were much more than that."

"What's that mean? Were you lovers?"

Instead of answering, Freddy leaned over again and fished in a box under his bed. He pulled out a thin photograph envelope. He said, handing the envelope to Manny, "These are pictures of us." Manny removed the two photos and took them over to the bars. He held the first one out toward the light from the corridor. It showed Freddy with his arms around Mindi, she was holding cotton candy to his side. Then he did the same with the second, Freddy kissing Mindi in front of the candy stand. "That's what we were," Freddy said quietly from the cot, "that's what."

"Can I print these?"

Freddy was already holding the negatives. It was like arranging china.

"I've got the negatives here somewhere. They're all I have left, though."

"I'll take good care of them," Manny assured him, coming to the cot.

"Okay."

He did some rummaging and gave him the negatives.

"Have you shown these to your lawyer?"

"No," Freddy lied. "I guess I should."

"You must," said Manny. "They could be very helpful. The Bianchi woman is saying you and Mindi were platonic but that you wanted a relationship. Leopold's maintaining that's your motive."

"I'll show him. Thanks."

"They don't mean you didn't kill her," Manny said. He sat down on the cot. "They just mean Quintana didn't keep her friend in the know. You're jilted instead of unrequited."

Freddy started to protest, but stopped and began nodding, in a way that said he knew Manny was right and it depressed him.

Manny looked down at his pad and continued. "All right, Mindi Quintana," and looked up for a moment. "Doesn't surprise me, by the way, her not confiding in her friend. I covered her father's trial and that's a pretty clannish lot. Beautiful girl, by the way," back in the pad.

"Thank you," said Freddy.

"So, tell me the story of Mindi Quintana."

Freddy moved so that his back was against the cool wall again. He relaxed against it, enjoying the contrast to the overly heated cell while he listened to himself answer the reporter's question, and his next and next, until he was sure the sun must be up though it was dim as ever where they were.

He sensed the reactions his answers engendered and knew they didn't depend on Sykes's belief in their truthfulness. In fact, Freddy was sure that much of what he said Sykes didn't believe at all. Freddy didn't need him to.

Because despite the dispassionate questioning, the crime Sykes had already written about was the alleged passionate one of a lover, a roar of revenge against beauty's rejection, the rebellion of an artist in corporate-American bondage. The buds of it all were in his stories so far. They were there in his hinting that Mindi was promiscuous. In his repetitious allusion to her father's criminality. In the unquestioning acceptance of Freddy as budding writer. In his rendering of Chanet's and the sympathetic credence given Freddy's hatred of the store.

"To feel that much!" seemed to seep from the pauses in Freddy's reconstructions, as Manny pointed and Freddy watered the buds. "Enough to kill her!" It obviously fascinated him. It fascinated them both.

And Manny would have had to admit, had he been privy to Freddy's thinking, that he did see his stories in epic terms, and that when he didn't, he figured out how to. It was how he made sense of things, how he knew he'd gotten them right. It was when the elements fell into place, and he knew he'd seen all the way through. It was how he had gained a readership and professional acclaim. How he got to the truth, since all truth was epic.

For both of them now, as they talked through the night, the anti-hero emerged further and was a type of tragic hero nonetheless. The type Manny appreciated and wrote about, and the type, without realizing it before, Freddy had known how to be.

He remembered thinking in his displays that when he made it into gear he would know what to do. That he would be witty for reporters, pensive when appropriate, insightful always, and clever sometimes—and he was. That when people cared what he thought, he would think great things—and it was true. That when they came to *him,* he would know what to say—and he did. That when there was no question of his stature, they would admire his work. And he was sure now they would. He would be accepted as a writer now. He was sure of it.

Two weeks ago, Manfred R. Sykes would have sneered at a man forced to live his life in a department store. Now he was squinting in the dark hoping Freddy wouldn't throw him out.

17

A Zealous Defense

The spectator section was full, and the reporter and sketch artist overflow had settled into the otherwise empty jury box. There were no television cameras, as Willison never allowed them pretrial. Philip sat at the defense table, Freddy next to him in a good suit. Between that table and the jury box was the prosecution table at which sat Michael Leopold. The door to Judge Willison's chambers opened and a bailiff came out. He stepped smartly to the side and a beat later, Judge Willison himself presented into the courtroom.

Philip closed a folder and slid it aside. Stately in black robe, the judge peered ponderously into the spectator section until the bailiff closed the door. Then he climbed the massive bench that took up most of the front wall and strode to the farthest of the three high-backed chairs along its length. The bailiff stayed at attention, silver badge sparkling in a sky of blue uniform, resembling a marine in proud demeanor.

"All rise," he barked, as the judge leaned down the bench for a water-filled coffee pitcher. "The court is now in session, Honorable Gunther W. Willison, III, presiding."

All stood pursuant to the "all rise," but the court officials, Philip, and the press only halfway. Long years had bled substance from the gesture of respect. Michael Leopold slouched upward, too, until Philip committed a hand to the back of his own chair to support weight he would never quite place on his feet. Then Michael uprighted to ramrod. He wanted to impress Judge Willison with the contrast he made to Philip. But the judge had spilled the pitcher while

158

eyes were on the bailiff and was rather preoccupied with a sudden puddle in his lap. The cloth of his robe, he was pleased to be reminded, was water resistant.

When he finally spoke, it was with baronial gravitas.

"You may be seated."

The bailiff announced the case.

"Mr. Prosecutor," said the judge, waving vaguely before him. "Would you set forth the charges and begin your presentation?"

Michael stood and breathed deeply. "Certainly, your honor." He shuffled some papers so the press could get set for him, and began.

"May it please the court, my name is Michael Leopold, first assistant district attorney. Your honor, the Commonwealth will show that on the twenty-ninth of December, in the year of our Lord 2005, one Mindi Quintana, a beautiful young woman of especially lovely spirit, was willfully, intentionally, purposefully—savagely, brutally, relentlessly—beaten, till her very life was nearly thrashed from her body, and that she was then killed, her neck premeditatedly broken; this in violation of Criminal Code title eighteen, section 2502. And the Commonwealth will make a prima facie showing that it is defendant"—he pointed at Freddy—"one Frederick Builder," he shook that finger, "who committed said homicide, and should be held for trial on the charge thereunder of"—he paused—"homicide in the first degree." He bowed his head.

The judge heard these remarks with his elbows on the bench and his fingers rubbing his temples. He stopped rubbing now and rolled his eyes up to Michael. "Did you really just say, 'In the year of our Lord,' Mr. Prosecutor?" he asked.

Michael did not respond. Obviously he had said it, but he did not think it warranted the amusement now twitching on Willison's face.

"Well?" asked the judge, "did you say 'In the year of our Lord' or not?"

"Yes, your honor, I did."

"Of course you did, of course, we all heard you," the judge said.

The small grin disappeared. "I don't like that kind of thing, Mr. Prosecutor," he snapped. Michael moved not a digit but the judge raised his eyebrows to indicate response was called for.

"Oh," Michael said. "Your honor," he added, inspiring assorted chuckles behind him in the gallery.

"Proceed," Willison said.

"The Commonwealth will show through reliable witness testimony and incontrovertible evidence probative of and relevant to the various issues of fact and law at han—"

Willison began gaveling Michael to silence. He said, "Off the record," and the court reporter's hands, which had flowed until then like water over smooth black stones, stopped. Time in the courtroom stopped with them. Willison regarded Michael from his bench as if he were a peculiar fuzz.

"Look, counselor," he said, "the upshot is this. For our Lord's sake," he deadpanned, "do not use flowery, poetic constructions in my courtroom. Do not use esoteric legal patois in presenting your case. I do not like it, am not impressed by it, and I will not have it."

Michael kept his demeanor. Any trial lawyer who couldn't take a little of a judge's rough stuff was in the wrong line.

Willison informed the court reporter they were back on the record and bade Michael proceed.

"Your honor," said Michael, choosing his words, "we've got enough to hold him over."

"Call your first witness."

"The People call Lisa Bianchi."

Philip turned to see the girl stand in the gallery and, realizing who she was, froze. He felt all strength leave his body as Freddy whispered just one word in his ear: "Bitch."

Philip asked himself quiet questions. How was he going to do this? How was he going to stand it when she saw him? What should he do? What would he find himself doing? He followed her progress to the stand. She seemed so scared, she walked so tentatively. He wanted to go over to her, to comfort her, hold her away from this experience. He needed to protect her from this sonuvabitch next to him, from this sonuvabitch inside of him. And then she saw him, and his wall went up before he felt an added thing.

She looked at him as she stepped up to the stand and as her face went so much whiter, he said softly to himself, "Everyone gets defended."

She put a hand over her mouth and one on the Bible that had "Courtroom #675" in marker on its closed cover. He looked at that instead of her. Did she swear that the testimony she would give before this court would be truthful to the best of her knowledge and recollection?

"I do." Lisa's voice shook.

Michael was approaching the stand. He handed Lisa a handkerchief. He was quick and painless with the preliminaries of name, address, and work, then moved right into substance.

"Ms. Bianchi," he began. "Lisa," he said more softly. "Did you know Mindi Quintana?"

"Yes," Lisa said. She was staring at a point on the floor in Philip's direction.

"How long had you known her?" Michael asked.

"Since second grade."

"Would you describe to his honor your relationship with her?"

Lisa slowly turned and looked up at Willison. She shrugged slightly.

"She was my best friend."

"By your 'best friend,' would that encompass your discussing very personal matters? Boyfriends, would-be boyfriends—your love lives, that is?"

"Yes," Lisa whispered.

"I'm sorry, Ms. Bianchi, would you mind speaking up? Did you discuss—"

"Yes," Lisa answered more loudly, and tears fell, as Philip guessed Michael knew they would.

"Did Mindi ever mention the name Frederick Builder to you?"

Philip stood. "Objection." He felt the eyes of the judge hard on him, and the beams of unchecked hatred from friends and family behind him. He felt the irritation of the spectators who wanted to watch the show uninterrupted. It was his job not to let them. "That calls for hearsay, your honor. And the entire line is irrelevant."

"Your honor," Michael said, "I'm laying a foundation for questions that are inarguably relevant, questions I will come to quickly. As to hearsay, this goes to the victim's state of mind."

"How?" asked the judge.

"Our theory, your honor, in part, is that Ms. Quintana was going to make very clear to defendant that night that their relationship was purely platonic. We can establish that her state of mind was such that she would have rejected the advances, sexual and emotional, made by defendant, and that the beating and murder followed. This line will also establish, as to state of mind, that Quintana would have admitted Builder to her apartment without a struggle."

"Overruled. Continue."

Michael turned and smiled toward Philip. Philip took his seat. "That was crucial. She's in for the prelim," he whispered to Freddy.

"Nice job," Freddy whispered back. Philip let the bench form a wall that momentarily filled his vision.

"You may answer the question," Michael said.

"Could you repeat it please?"

"Would the court direct Ms. Bianchi to speak up?" Philip heard himself say.

"Yes," said Willison. "You'll have to keep your voice up, miss. Speak as though it were to someone at the back."

"You may answer," said Michael without repeating the question and Philip knew he'd got him.

"I've forgotten the question," Lisa said angrily, and her confusion increased appreciably. She didn't cry but she was trembling a bit and it looked due to Michael's insensitivity.

"I'm sorry, Miss Bianchi. Take a moment and try to be calm. I'll go as slow as you like." To Michael's credit, he gave her some breathing time. He might want her crying—on his terms—but he needed her oriented. "Did Mindi Quintana ever mention the name Frederick Builder?"

"Yes."

"In what regard?"

"Objection, your honor." Philip stood. "First, I object again, this time to the entire line as calling for hearsay. Second, the question is vague. One would expect there to be many instances and 'regards' in which a woman would mention a boyfriend to a friend of hers. What specifically does Mr. Leopold want to know?"

"That's a speech, judge! They were not boyfriend and girlfriend," Michael said.

Willison was high above it. "Overruled, counsel, as to hearsay. Sustained as being vague. Next question, Mr. Prosecutor."

"I'll narrow it." Michael walked to the stand. "Miss Bianchi, did Quintana—Mindi Quintana—ever discuss her relationship with the defendant with you?"

"Yes. It was platonic."

"Thank you."

"Objection, move to strike." Philip rose. "Is that what she said, or what the witness concluded from what she said? Either way—"

"It's what she said!" Lisa cried. "She told me that! She said—"

"You weren't asked a question, Lisa," Philip said. He should have addressed himself to the judge but Willison did not admonish him.

"Miss Bianchi," Michael said. "Did Mindi elaborate at all on the status of her relationship with the defendant?" He looked tersely at Philip, getting at whatever he had cut off.

"Objection."

"Overruled."

"Answer," Michael said. Another demeanor slip.

"Yes." She was looking at Philip desperately, who had not retaken his seat. She was shaking and confused and, in spite of it all, it seemed, looking to *him* for guidance. He looked away and sat down.

"Miss Bianchi," Michael said, "I'm asking the questions just now."

"Yes, sir." She turned to him.

"What more did she say?"

"When?" objected Philip.

"What more did she say when she said they were platonic," Michael said angrily.

"She said that he wanted to be more than friends, that she had tried to let him know that she was interested in being his friend, but that he just kept trying. She was going to tell him flat out."

"Did you speak to Mindi on the day she was murdered?"

"Yes, I did."

"Did she tell you what her plans were for that evening?"

"Objection," said Philip, standing. "Again, your honor, calling for hearsay."

"Overruled. The PD's continuing objection to this line of questioning on hearsay grounds is noted for the record. Now will you please stop objecting to every question? You may answer, miss."

"I asked her to go out with some friends to the Borgia Café, and she said she was going to Club Brasil with Frederick Builder."

"Brasil being a club at Second and Chestnut streets?"

"Yes."

"Did she say where they were going to meet?"

"He was supposed to pick her up. I don't know what time."

"What other bad news did Mindi have for Mr. Builder that night?"

"Hearsay, leading," said Philip from his chair.

"Still state of mind," said Michael.

"Overruled," said the judge.

"He'd given Mindi something to read. Some stories or something to read, and she was going to tell him she didn't think they showed a lot of talent. Actually, that he needed to work on them harder or something. She thought it was going to hurt him—but she thought she owed it to him to tell the truth. He was talking about quitting his job." She looked at Philip. "She told me that."

"Thank you, Miss Bianchi," Michael said. "Nothing further, your honor."

"Cross," said the judge as Michael sat down.

Philip stood but came no closer. He looked down at the counsel table at his legal pad labeled "X" for cross-examination.

"You say that Miss Quintana told you that she and Mr. Builder were platonic, correct?"

"Yes," she whispered.

"Speak up please, miss," said the judge.

"And that you discussed each other's love lives as a matter of course?"

"Correct."

"How many times did Miss Quintana discuss Frederick with you?"

"Just a few. Three, maybe. You see, if he were important it would have been more."

"Or perhaps it was that, for whatever reason, she didn't share all her feelings about him with you." He said it forcefully.

"We were like sisters!"

And the judge broke in on his own. "Counselor," he said to Philip, "this is a preliminary hearing, not a trial. I would add that the young lady is understandably quite upset. And I would ask you to keep that in mind, though I am not restricting your questioning at this time."

"Thank you, your honor. I would just like to say," and he looked at Lisa, "that the preliminary hearing is a proceeding of vital importance to my client, and as much diligence is required of me here as at trial."

"Continue," said Willison.

"Did she tell you that she accompanied Mr. Builder for drinks to Murphy's Twelfth Street Tavern at Twelfth and Market?"

"Yes. I was—"

"I'm sorry, Miss Bianchi," Philip said. "The question calls for a yes or no."

"Okay."

"Did Miss Quintana relate to you that just a week after drinks, she had lunch with Freddy in center city? At Nick's Roast Beef in center city?"

"No."

"Then she probably didn't tell you that she accepted a rose—"

"Objection!" Michael stood. "There's nothing in the record about any rose, or any lunch, for that matter. I move this all be stricken."

Philip stepped closer to the bench. "I have an employee of Nick's who knew Miss Quintana, and has told us that she and my client ate lunch together there. I've got coworkers of Mindi's that saw her accept a rose and leave with my client for that lunch. If Mr. Leopold likes, I can establish their various dates first—"

"Not dates," Michael cut in.

"No, she never told me about the lunch or the rose. But so—"

"Did she tell you that just one week later they had dinner together, complete with champagne, in the window at Carolina's, a rather intimate restaurant on Twenty-first Street?"

"As friends."

"Yes or no?"

"Yes." He saw her eyes fill.

"And that just a couple Sundays later they went to the circus, with tickets *she* obtained?"

"Yes."

Philip went back behind the defense table and searched through a file. Then he went to Michael's table.

"Your honor," he said facing the bench, "may I show the witness two photographs?" He held them in front of Michael's face for a second and then walked them to the bench. "They were taken at the circus and the prosecutor already has copies. My client won't be testifying today but I have the sworn statement of the circus counterman who saw these pictures being taken in front of his stand."

"Objection," said Michael. "And where's the statement?"

"Let me see them," said Willison, "and the statement." Philip brought the photos to the bench and gave them to the bailiff who handed them up. He retrieved the statement and gave copies to the bailiff and to Michael. Willison motioned over one of his clerks who climbed the bench and stood next to him. They studied the photos and the statement until Willison motioned the clerk off the bench. There was a long pause and much temple rubbing before the judge said, "She can look at them."

Philip took the photos and approached the stand. "Lisa," he said quietly. "I'm going to show you two photographs." He handed her the first one.

"Have you seen this before?"

"No."

"What does it show?"

"It shows a man kissing Mindi."

"What man?"

"Batman." Her eyes flashed. "Who do you think? Him," she said, pointing at Freddy. She stared Freddy down. Freddy showed no malice. Then she stared back into Philip's face.

"Indicating my client, your honor."

"Yes," said the judge.

"And the second," said Philip handing it to her.

"Him with his arms around her."

Philip turned to Lisa again and laid the question down hard, the way he had to for impact, because she wasn't going to be allowed to answer it. "Do they look like buddies or lovers to you in these photographs?"

"Objection."

"I'll withdraw the question." He took back the photographs from her and moved their admission into evidence.

"They were friends. Not even," Lisa said.

"You weren't asked a question," warned the judge, not unkindly.

"Now you say you spoke to Miss Quintana on the day of her death, and she said she was having dinner with Frederick Builder," said Philip.

167

"Yes."

"What time did you speak with her?"

"About five-thirty. At Murphy's."

"So you would have no idea whether, in fact, that date was canceled by Mr. Builder later that evening, would you?"

Lisa was silent.

"Would you?" he repeated.

"She would have come to the Borgia."

"Nor did you actually see them together that night."

"No—but she had plans with him."

"To your knowledge, were there many young men who wanted to date Mindi, but whom she turned away?"

"There were some."

"How many in the last year? That you know of."

"I don't know."

"More than ten?"

Michael objected from his seat. "She said she doesn't know."

"Overruled."

"Yes," said Lisa.

"More than twenty?"

Lisa nodded.

"Would you answer out loud for the record, Lisa?"

"Probably."

"Were any of them upset when she refused them or broke off with them?"

"Some."

"So even if Mr. Builder, forgetting the dates and the pictures for a moment, were just a friend who wanted more, he'd have had quite a bit of disappointed company, wouldn't he?"

Her eyes were liquid fire. "Some," she said.

"Twenty disappointed men, your honor. Nothing further," said Philip.

"I have some redirect, your honor," Michael stood to say. Judge Willison waved him to proceed.

"Of those other disappointed suitors, did Mindi mention any that were problems, who bothered her, or threatened her?"

"No."

"Did she mention that she had dinner plans with any of them for the night she was killed?"

"No, she did not."

"Or had bad news to tell any of them that night?"

"No."

"You wouldn't know, would you, if any of *them* had fibers from her rug in their suit?"

"Objection! That's wholly improper—"

"Sustained. Watch it, Mr. Prosecutor, don't do that again."

"I apologize, your honor. That's all I have."

"Nothing," said Philip.

"You may step down, miss," said Judge Willison.

"I want to say something—" Lisa began.

"That will be all. Thank you," said Judge Willison.

Lisa didn't get up. Philip wanted to tell her to, she was going to get herself in trouble.

"Miss—" said Willison sharply.

Lisa stood and stepped from the witness stand. She hesitated, then crossed the floor to the spectator section without looking at Philip again.

Philip turned as she passed and saw her go to Mindi's parents. He recognized Henry Quintana, a short dark man with one arm around a wife who stared vacantly, and the other around Lisa whom he pulled close as if she were his own daughter, perhaps imagining that she was.

Philip went through the remainder of the prelim in a daze, but one that left what was machine and logic in him unencumbered. The witnesses cascaded by.

Michael called the neighbor, who testified to the thuds and glass breaking and the Bounty paper towel commercial, and Michael introduced an affidavit pinpointing the time of the commercial at 9:08.

Next, he called the policemen first on the scene who testified to the time of the call from dispatch, their time of arrival, the circumstances leading up to their finding the body, and the details of Mindi's body as found. Most notably, they testified to their conclusion of a unforced entry.

Philip cross-examined but did not get the officers to admit that in breaking down the door, they might have destroyed evidence of a forced entry. He did get one to angrily explain that they had been trying to save a life. He did get that one to repeat that there had been two coffee cups on the table.

The arresting officers were called next to testify to the circumstances of the arrest. They testified to Freddy's injured hand. One testified that Freddy stated he'd been to the apartment six or eight times all told, which was the first Philip heard they were locked into that. On cross he painted Michael disingenuous for not bringing out his client's fall down the steps, and had one officer repeat Freddy's exact words when told Mindi had been murdered:

"Who would do such a thing? Who would do such a thing?"

The medical examiner repeated that Mindi was dead at the scene, the obvious victim of a terrible beating culminating in homicide with the breaking of her neck. He testified from the autopsy report to the various contusions, concussions, abrasions, cuts, breaks, and traumas he'd found, as if proud he'd discovered the difficult ones. And he made his left-handed attribution, basing it on the heavy preponderance of injury to the corresponding side of the face and body, coupled, he explained, with the angle of blows, knuckle impressions, and the position of the body against the wall. On cross, Philip could not shake the ME but felt confident he'd find an expert to say the killer could have been right-handed.

A police chemist testified to his comparison of the "clump" of hair found in Mindi's apartment with strands in one of Freddy's suits. The suit was the one investigators noticed had fibers in it similar to those of Mindi's rug. A police hair and fiber expert testified it was Freddy's hair in the apartment if it was Freddy's hair in Freddy's suit, though she would need a court-ordered sample from Freddy himself to make the definitive comparison.

The rug fibers were from a rug of the same color as Mindi's, and were otherwise similar, but more definitive analysis was not yet completed. And on the sleeve of the same suit, three broken strands of Mindi's hair had wound themselves round a button.

Philip elicited that force, struggle, murder were not the only ways that hair got on the floor, or round a button, or fibers in a suit, especially when one was in love. Michael called no blood expert, but Philip brought out through several of Michael's witnesses that there was no blood on Freddy's suit, and none on any of his shoes or other clothing except traces of his own type, not Mindi's, on a shirt collar. And that there was no blood in Mindi's apartment that was of Freddy's type. They had found nothing of Freddy, or anyone else, under Mindi's nails.

The fingerprint expert testified that Freddy's prints had been lifted from just two spots in Mindi's apartment. On the living room table where they were clustered within six square inches, indicating they had been placed there on the same occasion, and on the broken vase near the body. This suggested he had been in the apartment only once, contradicting Freddy's statement to police.

On cross: If Mindi had dusted recently she might have destroyed Freddy's prints from prior visits, yes. There were some sets of unidentified prints, yes. Yes, Lisa Bianchi's prints were also in the apartment, and those of other friends, too. And yes, if Freddy had sold Mindi the vase, his prints might still have been on it.

The emergency room physician who'd set Freddy's hand called it a fresh break. For Michael the fracture was not inconsistent with a punching injury. For Philip it was not inconsistent with a fall down the stairs. For Michael, the pain would have driven most to seek immediate medical attention. For Philip, one might have hoped it a lesser injury and waited till morning.

Michael offered Mindi's calendar through a Lucia Fineote, her employer, who identified Mindi's writing, and Judge Willison accepted it into evidence.

Finally, Michael summed up with a simply worded, though obsequious, argument maintaining the prosecution had met its burden, and Philip with his argument that it had not.

The judge ordered Freddy held for trial. Philip argued for bail and Michael against it. Some back-and-forth and bail was set at half a million dollars.

"Few surprises evidence-wise," Philip told Freddy as the courtroom cleared. "Except for the rug fibers, Mindi's hair, and your six to eight times in her apartment. We watched, we listened, and we saw what we could do with Lisa Bianchi's testimony."

"There's the calendar to back her up." Freddy handed over his notes.

Philip nodded. "But I think we learned a lot today."

The guards came to take Freddy back to holding. Philip took his time gathering his things and the courtroom cleared. Everything didn't fit in the litigation case he'd brought but he didn't have the patience to repack it. He put the rest under his arm like a newspaper. And stood still a moment. Then he put everything down again and sat on the table, his feet on a chair.

He was sitting that way in the empty courtroom when he heard, "I was wondering why you didn't show up New Year's Eve." He focused his eyes. Lisa had come back into the courtroom. He lifted his chin from his fists.

"I'm sorry. Really—"

"Save it." She came farther into the courtroom, her arms crossed over her chest. "You were a sap in the gallery," she said. "You didn't know your wife was shitting on you. And on New Year's Eve I kept waiting for you to come—you of all people—because I thought you would understand a—a—how *I* was hurting."

"I didn't know who she was until you took the stand. I'm sorry," he said again.

"It's not right," she said, her hands fists at her sides now. "You made it seem like I wouldn't know what was going on between them. And you know that's not true."

"I'm going to have to do things like that." She deserved to have it straight. "Don't expect anything different," he said.

"You're not supposed to make things seem different than they really are." She came closer. She seemed to be begging him.

"Yes, I am."

She gripped the back of the chair he had his feet on. "No, you're supposed to tell the truth."

"You are. You're the witness. I'm just supposed not to lie." She didn't say anything. "This is my job," he told her sharply. He sounded like every asshole he had ever known.

"That's not even good in the abstract. And we're talking about my friend, more like my sister. You *met* her."

He pulled over his briefcase and undid the catch. "I know that."

"How can you defend her murderer?" she asked grabbing his arm.

He looked up from the case. "My client is pleading not guilty, Lisa. To the victim's friends and family the accused is always the murderer. But sometimes he's not—"

"But this time he is."

"—and if I didn't defend him, I couldn't defend anyone." He pulled away his arm.

"Did you see her parents?"

He opened the case. "Of course I did."

"Their lives are over. Only they've got to wait twenty or thirty years until it's official."

He pulled the loose files over. He stuffed them in, bending them— he wished they could break—and forced the damn thing shut again. He snapped the catch.

"Wait, I'll introduce you," she said, "they're right outside." She half turned as though to go to the doors.

"Don't do that."

She faced him again. "Do you think I would? I wouldn't do that to them."

They stayed where they were, glaring at each other. "If he's innocent, the murderer's still out there." This, knowing he killed her. "You can't know that he did it, you can't, just because of how horrible a crime it was and how sorely you feel her loss. We've got to protect him against that. We have to protect you against that when a horrible murder happens and you happen to be a suspect. And somebody's best friend thinks it was you."

"Well, thanks loads. Thanks for the civics lesson. That's just what I need right now is a civics lesson."

"Everyone gets a defense."

"But don't ask me to like it. And don't ask me to like you."

"I asked you not to."

Her eyes were dry and clear now. And they were hard. And it was better for her like that.

"You liked me, too. When I tapped you at the old-age thing and you turned around, you saw Mindi first, and then me. You stayed looking at me." She started to walk to the doors again. "Or maybe it was because you knew somehow you weren't going to want to remember her."

She stopped at the doors but did not turn around. She spoke very quietly, he had to strain to hear her. "How dare you talk to me without any emotion? How dare you not pull it up when I tried to help you?"

Something stabbed at him and he stood up immediately. She pushed out the doors.

"How dare you?" echoing from the hall with the outside commotion.

He caught a glimpse of the parents standing against the wall, reporters getting nowhere with them, and reporters around Michael not having the same problem. And then the door muffled everything. He sat back down.

18

Politics and Justice

Philip was dreaming that Stamp had hidden in a prison laundry cart hoping to be wheeled to freedom, but that he'd neglected to cover himself with any of the dirty sheets and towels inside and was discovered forthwith. He killed his discoverer and hid him in the cart and, having learned from his mistake, covered him with the sheets and towels. Dressed in the laundry attendant's uniform, he got close enough to the windpipes in the way of his release to crush them.

Now, the counter arrow lit and the small tone sounded and Stamp proceeded to the unoccupied teller window. He'd lost one of his three teeth in the Jesus incident, so his smile wasn't quite as dazzling when he yanked out the UZI from his coat and held it hard against the glass.

"Okay, lady, you start forkin' the dough or I'm gonna blow you apart! You got me?"

The woman laughed behind her bulletproof glass.

"This here's an *UZI* lady!" He lifted the magazine. "You think that little bit of glass is gonna save you from this?" It was Stamp's turn to laugh.

The lady slapped the counter, laughing like a loon.

"Lady, listen," Stamp said, waving the UZI, "I swear ta God, this is your last chance." Tears streamed down her face, she was pointing at him unabashedly.

"I'm warnin' ya, lady!" She held up her finger and teased him by twirling it in the air as in prelude to pushing an alarm button.

"Okay! I told you!" He held up the magazine again and pointed to the UZI pictured inside. "I'm sending away for this baby, and I'll be back!" He whirled to find the bank security guard with his pistol drawn. Philip woke up in the blackness of his room and mood.

He pulled his arm out from under the pillow and stared at the hands glowing faintly on his watch. Four-thirty. "Just let me sleep." He pushed his face back into the pillow but was up with finality. He got out of bed.

He sat back down and tried to figure out how long until seven forty-five, when he normally got up for work. But his mind wasn't working so he figured it out on his watch. Four hours. He decided to cook breakfast and stood again. But because he usually slept to the last possible minute, he had no breakfast food in the refrigerator. In fact, there was nothing downstairs, he was remembering, but condiments, foods to put on other foods. So he moved in the dark to the chair near his bedroom door, and lifted the ball of clothing on it.

He climbed into the old jeans he usually had time for only on weekends—their big comfort made him sleepy again—and a sweatshirt, too large, the way he liked it. Sat on the chair to tug on hiking boots over the socks he'd worn to sleep. He fished in the closet until he felt his spare overcoat, its lining drooped out a little in back, and pulled it on.

His bedroom was cold but now he was warm and he hugged himself tight in his comfortable clothing. He lumbered downstairs to the door, undid the deadlock. The cold metal stuck to his thumb, warned him of the outside, so he buttoned his coat. Pulled gloves from his pockets, putting them on before stepping out. Into his West Philly neighborhood as he seldom saw it on this side of the night. Still and clear as the cold. He breathed deeply through his nose, and was awake now more than in name, from the inside out.

He stood on the top step of four down to the sidewalk, and examined the street in both directions. A car's engine turned over easily down the block. He watched the exhaust rise like pipe smoke and dissipate under the streetlights, plunked down the four steps. And began the four blocks to the 7-Eleven.

He bought eggs, juice, bread, milk, and coffee. A real breakfast. And a paper. He folded it under his arm as he did during the day when his arm would be weighted against it by his briefcase. The paper fell twice on the way back. He finally put down the bag and put it on top of the food.

Home again, he cooked some up. He cleaned a plate and sat down to eat. He half stood to flick on the television. Unfolded the paper between his orange juice and coffee, his plate and the TV. He saw the headline and the photograph and swallowed his mouthful hard. Switched off the television.

"You'd better read this," Sharon said, walking into the bedroom. For an extra five a week the paperboy knocked. She switched on the light. She did not take the time to walk to Michael's side but kneed her way over the bed instead and shook his shoulder. He woke to the front page and Manfred Sykes's byline in his face.

"You're mentioned," she said. Not as the surprise winner of a Congressional Medal of Honor is what he gathered by her tone.

"Fuckin' Sykes and his black helicopters. Got me driving one, I bet."

He seized the paper.

POLITICS AND JUSTICE, VINEGAR AND WATER
by Manfred R. Sykes
First in a series

This series is the result of The Bulletin's *investigation into the effect of politics on the dispensing of criminal justice in Philadelphia courts. Dozens of interviews were conducted, many on condition of anonymity, with attorneys of the District Attorney's Office and the Office of the Public Defender, and with attorneys in private practice, judges, police and prison officials, inmates, and representatives of inmate organizations.*

In addition to reporting based on these interviews, a single case will be followed through the courts and through the more elusive regime of behind-the-scenes maneuvering and deal making. The case will be that of Frederick Builder, "The China Manager," as he has been dubbed in the press. Builder is charged with the beating death of Mindi Quintana of West Philadelphia on December 29, the same day he was named Chanet's Department Store's Manager of the Year.

Frederick Builder spends his time these days in a Holmesburg Prison cell writing his novel and preparing for trial on the charge of murder. But he, like many awaiting criminal adjudication in Philadelphia, fears more than conviction based on the evidence against him. He fears that the system charged with providing him a fair and impartial trial will fail to do so.

The Bulletin has uncovered a threat to courtroom justice more severe perhaps than that revealed in recent police and judicial corruption scandals. This threat inheres in the political aspirations of courtroom actors and in the career-related pressures to perform that can put questions of justice, of even a defendant's guilt or innocence, on the judicial back burner.

The result in a press-worthy case can range from familiar courtroom and press conference theatrics to, according to many observers and participants, overzealous charging of defendants by prosecutors, and failures by lawyers on both sides to reach plea agreements that might cut short coveted media exposure.

In his prison cell, Builder looks up sadly from his writing and speaks with a gesture of resignation. "I always thought heavy press coverage guaranteed people fair trials. Nothing could be further from the truth. Michael Leopold wants to be president. Packaging me as a monster and getting a conviction, why, that's white paint on his house. I wish the press would just go away." Leopold is prosecuting the case against Builder.

In cases the press does not cover, the result is often just as calamitous for the criminal defendant.

Says Felix Sheadhit, professor of criminal procedure at the Temple University Law Center, "Court dockets are horrendous, attorney caseloads are staggering, conviction records are all important to career advancement, which is all important to political advancement for those so inclined. Plea bargains are worked out in batches in City Hall toilets and over lunch at Pickles. Defendants are pressured to sign on, never knowing if they've been traded for or traded away."

Thus, the extent to which political and career concerns influence how courtroom actors try cases normally goes unexamined by the public. Yet, not surprisingly, it quickly becomes a key worry of those accused of crime.

And there is basis, in the Builder case, for the claim that Leopold, who is engaged to Mayor Filbert's daughter, Sharon, is making political advantage of the attention attendant the "China Manager." At a recent press conference on the subject of the Builder case—such meetings are convened weekly by Leopold—this reporter initiated the following exchange:

"Are you planning to run for office?"

Leopold: "I have many ideas for Philadelphia. If called upon, I would think about it, surely. First I need to rid this city of a beast."

"There's been speculation that you're planning a bid for City Council or DA. Are you ruling it out?"

Leopold: "It's true, I'm being pressured to run. And I've received lots of mail, especially from the ward where the poor Quintana girl was so brutally slain. We're exploring the possibility."

Leopold's stated position has been that Builder and his alleged victim, Mindi Quintana, were merely acquaintances. Builder has steadfastly maintained that he and Quintana were dating. Two photographs in Leopold's possession—

(See MANAGER, on A-12)

The two attorneys finished the front page and before turning to the jump on page twelve, stared a moment at the photograph of Freddy and Mindi kissing at the circus.

"Shit," they both said.

Freddy was reading page A-12 in his Holmesburg Prison cell. He finished and read the companion story on him alone that included his interview. The stories left him thoughtful, talented, and in pain. Who could ask for anything more?

He read again the quoted appraisal of one of his short stories by a creative writing professor Sykes knew at the University of Pennsylvania. "His writing betrays a malleable talent, a piercing awareness of the vicissitudes of successful endeavor, and not a little good comic sense. In 'The Archeologist,' for example, Builder's main character quite literally 'trips' over his fabulous find, not in some far-off land on some dreary dig, but in his own backyard!" Freddy kissed the paper. He had known in the store that it happened this way, reporters writing about you, finding the worth in your work while you slept.

His job now was to reflect the new reality. To be the Frederick Builder they thought they would see when they shone their beams on him. What Manny and the professor had found in his story was in it, he was sure. He had just finally got them to the point where they were willing to see it.

Philip was cognizant of how cleverly Freddy had dealt with Manny Sykes. He'd convinced him of the romantic nature of his involvement with Mindi. Indeed, everyone would be convinced who looked at the photos within the context of this article. And it was clear Freddy had won Sykes to his side in all this. From the speculation by "officials requesting anonymity" (which Philip had never heard and didn't believe was real) that Henry Quintana's dealings may have somehow got his daughter hit by the mob. To the Penn professor's comments about Freddy's writing. There wasn't the overall sense Freddy couldn't have committed the murder, but the lack of attention to Mindi, beyond bleeding her father's criminality onto her, seemed to negate the importance of that either way.

Philip read himself described as "a promise unfulfilled, according to colleagues." He had been successful quickly and his potential gleaned by superiors. But he had "tapered," one put it. Freddy, it was noted, hadn't been able to afford a private, more accomplished defense attorney.

Philip picked up a piece of egg and popped it in his mouth.

Michael, on the other hand, was described as a "straight A student." But he had earned his high conviction rate "bringing apples to the courtroom and piling up 'gut' cases for his transcript." Michael had a cramp in his jaw and nodded tersely through this as he had through it all so far.

The portrayal of him amply justified Sharon's nail biting and horrified expression. He was "politically ambitious"; he seemed to an unnamed public official "almost to drool at a press conference." Unnamed colleagues had him climbing over backs for promotions at the DA. It was office speculation that the mayor himself had intervened to have Builder taken from another ADA and reassigned to his son-in-law to be.

"I'm gonna *kill* that sonuvabitch!"

"Which sonuvabitch?"

"If Fitz wants to have anonymous wars in the press, fine, I'll nail his ass to the wall!"

"Are you sure it was him? What about Larry?"

"I can't do anything about Larry."

"Keep reading."

It was thinly implied that his impending marriage to the mayor's daughter was made less in heaven than in some smoky back room. Michael read this without comment. A "close friend" of Michael's: "I like him awfully, but his stats are inflated. The man pleads down whatever he's not sure he can win. Except if the case is in the news. Then he'll never deal, not he. A case like this one? Never. Tough guy when the voters are watching, statistic monger when they're not. But I like him awfully."

Judge Willison read that he was the "bright coin in the muddy change," and that he was regarded in legal circles as one of the most scholarly jurists on any state bench. "He has been twice offered and has twice turned down interim appointments to the appellate Commonwealth courts, explaining he prefers to stay where 'people are people, not paper.'" He still remembered coming up with that and, still liking it, smiled.

19

Pro Bono

February tenth brought the guard to Freddy's cell with two eight-inch packets of mail. Freddy was back in City Hall for a hearing on a motion, and the mail had come by way of Holmesburg, where it had first paid its visit to the censor. The guard tried to stuff the bundles through the bars but they were too thick. Muttering curses, he stretched the rubber bands off and let the envelopes flutter through like several decks of cards. "Fuckin' jerk-offs," he growled lowly of the senders.

"Hey, Mr. Murderer-Writer-Big Shot-Killer, hey, your fuckin' mail's here," he said loudly to rouse the sleeping Freddy. Freddy came around and looked out at the guard, who added, "Next time kill a baby. Maybe they'll make you president."

"Yeah, well, fuck you, too," Freddy said sleepily, rolling out of bed and going to collect his mail. When he had it organized for carrying, he took it with him to the cot and began separating it out into three piles by importance, which he determined by return address. He rubber-banded up the piles, labeled them in pen, "*Writing,*" "*Press,*" and "*Public,*" and placed the packets on the floor at his feet. He leaned back on his fists.

In the beginning—until a few weeks ago—the mail from the public had been hateful, almost without exception. But as time went on, with several more articles by Sykes and the press in general headed in the same direction, attitudes had changed toward the China Manager. The letters now were about evenly divided between those who wished him ill and those who wrote that they understood what the store had done to him, or what the woman had done to him, or that they had read some of his recently published stories and thought them quite good. So that instead of throwing away letters from the public after reading a representative few, he now put them in a pile to read last. Before them he would read the letters from the press seeking interviews, and before them, the letters from agents and regarding submissions of his work—those relating to his career.

In the mail of other days were letters from news producers and correspondents, morning show hosts and radio personalities, all of them handwritten and seeking to convince him in personal terms that they would treat him fairly should he agree to an interview. Such interviews as he agreed to over the objections of his attorney—and only now was he able to be selective—were accomplished usually by taping in his cell or in Visitation, though a few had been live from an administrator's office, where the media outlet had pull or the correspondent or producer was owed a favor. Freddy had even appeared suited at times by scheduling interviews for the mornings of court appearances.

On every local show, he had pressed the writing. Sykes harped on it, too, and Freddy returned the favor by criticizing prison conditions whenever he could. It had paid off. There had been a blurb in the *New York Times* about him solely because of the writing. In the Arts and Entertainment section. Having broken through the national press barrier, *Newsweek*, Court TV, and MSNBC had contacted Philip, and after appearances there, CNN. The magazine had printed an essay written by Freddy, with quiet help from Sykes, on prison life.

His book was coming along, too, though it was less of a novel now than his story, an autobiography of a sort, but beginning with the night he'd met Mindi. Manny visited almost daily to critique and do revisions. He did first-draft stuff, too, based on outlines they worked on together. Sykes was a significant help and in return Freddy toed the party line. He talked about reform issues, the politically inspired prosecution of his case and others, and generally held himself out as suffering from whatever was wrong, according to Manny, with the justice system that day.

Freddy lay back, his head comfortably on his pillow and relived his finest moment to date: *Larry King*.

A *Larry King* staffer whom Freddy would remember in his will had come across some articles about him in planning half an hour of argument about cases in the news, among a panel of lawyers selected from King's coterie. The staffer had first obtained videotapes of interviews Freddy had given the local news, and liked what he saw. Then they prescreened him over the phone and liked what they heard. (Manny had called himself "Cyrano" for a week, though Freddy had waved him off as often as listened to him.) They'd invited him on, sent him a DVD to look at of Erik Menendez's recent call-in appearance—Menendez and his brother had famously murdered their parents with shotguns and were behind bars for life—and Freddy had called in on the appointed night to discuss his case with Larry and his two lawyer guests.

The lawyers had been several cuts above the usual because the first half hour had been devoted to Alan Dershowitz and his views on torture warrants for terrorists. So Dershowitz was joined for the discussion of current cases by another high-end guy, Ferris Cajun, a conservative law professor from Stanford. Freddy read Dershowitz's writing on the issue before the show and discussed it thoroughly with both Sykes and Philip.

Freddy had felt a thrill the first time he offhandedly referred to King as "Larry." He'd just done it and moved on—no big deal. Then, instead of really answering Larry's first question about his own case, he'd articulated his appreciation of Dershowitz's arguments in the first segment, differing with him, though, on important fundamentals. On CNN! Dershowitz had listened intently, and then lent Freddy's arguments credibility with vehement dissent! Cajun had jumped in, defending Freddy's points!

Freddy had mentioned prison reform for Manny, and then his book before they went to commercial. Larry wanted to know about that. It was about, Freddy explained, his captivity in corporate America, the true story of his relationship with the woman he loved but now stood accused of killing, his experiences in prison and as a prisoner of the legal system. His struggle. He mentioned that he didn't have a publisher yet.

After the commercial, Cajun brought up the Son of Sam laws, and Freddy replied that he wasn't writing this book for money—"Though I know what a cover blurb from Larry would mean, and I'm not saying no." That elicited a laugh. No, he was writing to set the record straight and had some other things to say he hoped people would be interested in. And if he was convicted and the money went to Mindi's family, well, he wished it would give them some solace, though he was sure it wouldn't.

"And I'm innocent. I lost Mindi, too. I look forward to my exoneration, not just in court, but in her family's eyes, and the public's."

Freddy sat up quickly and took the *Writing* packet from the floor. Manager of the Year? Unh-unh: Book of the Year.

Reading his mail was sweet like candy was sweet, it was his favorite part of the day and he began doing it now. The first three letters were from literary agents wishing to represent him. He already had one, Marsha Bart, the agent who'd sold Sykes's book on prison reform. The fourth was from a publishing house requesting he or his agent contact the undersigned editor:

"I have worked successfully with several incarcerated authors to overcome the special difficulties presented by confinement. We typically staff such projects with researchers who perform important tasks the author cannot, such as conducting recorded interviews based on author outlines; library, records and site-dependent research; preparation of event chronologies and physical descriptions of people and places . . ."

He put the letter aside for Marsha.

Philip looked up from his work and out through his office window at a gray sky and sheets of rain. It was early morning, he'd been preparing questions for Freddy's coworkers because he was going to Chanet's to conduct interviews today. Freddy's literary agent had interrupted him already with a phone call. And just now he had hung up with another reporter from another magazine who wanted what they all wanted: an interview with the China Manager.

Since Freddy's agent had hired a first-rate publicist, articles about Freddy—his depth, his passion, his eternal optimism that his name would be cleared, his love for his Mindi, his literary promise—abounded. Some of the attention had been national. *Newsweek* and *Larry King* and the frequency with which his fiction was being published had made this a new ballgame and now Freddy enjoyed heavy interest and growing support.

And Leopold had somehow managed to rub the press the wrong way on this one. If Philip knew him, Michael would be thinking of ways to cut his losses. The pressure on him to deal had surely been mounting since the preliminary hearing. But then the case against Freddy was pretty good and Michael might still believe he would ultimately counteract the bad press with a conviction.

Philip went to the window.

Freddy. Who would've thought the bastard would get a literary career out of this? Well, opportunity had knocked, and when it had, Freddy was waiting with its pipe and slippers. Just yesterday in City Hall holding, Freddy had said that it all felt completely natural to him. There was a grotesque unfairness in that. The something wrong was more wrong than anything else Philip had ever let himself be a part of. Freddy was to be tried for murder, and it seemed—was it too much to say he seemed even to enjoy that prospect?

The gray light from the outside had made his office dank; it underscored the municipal heat that was causing his forehead to sweat. His office was quiet, though, there was that. He'd closed the door when the office hubbub began.

He opened the window. Cold air came through the screen that was never changed to glass in the winter and it broke the electric hot. It cooled his forehead and Philip responded gratefully by putting his arms to either side of the window and leaning in to catch the cold full.

The literary agent had asked him to agree not to write any articles on Freddy or the case, nor to give any interviews, that were not first cleared with the publicist. "Conflicting signals," "division of labor," other phrases as reasons had floated past Philip meaninglessly. He did not tell Marsha Bart he had no plans to profit from Freddy's notoriety, nor did he relate that Freddy need only tell him not to discuss the case to preclude him from doing so for a time. He had simply replaced the phone quietly into its receptacle without answering at all.

He wished he'd told the agent to go fuck herself, or that he'd already completed *Helter Skelter II*, and slammed down the phone. The publicist had brought Freddy that book, a host of other "true crime," and the classics: *The Executioner's Song, In Cold Blood, The Trial, Crime and Punishment*. Philip had thumbed through *In the Belly of the Beast* in Freddy's cell and felt sick. Sykes had brought Freddy everything he could find by Wilbert Rideau. Freddy hadn't read any of it. He had told Philip he was afraid it would influence him and he knew what he was doing. He should have slammed down that phone.

He leaned back from the window and closed it. He went to his desk and sat at the edge. Freddy's file was next to him, and his notes from the agent's call, which he hadn't known he'd made. The list of store employees to interview and sway to Freddy's side. Questions to ask them.

The phone rang.

"Hello," said the voice after his, "Sam McDonald here." The man paused for Philip to grasp who it was on the line.

Sam McDonald. Of course Philip knew him; he had watched him

sell his snake oil numerous times, the first with his entire law school trial advocacy class. Sam was a performer like all trial lawyers, just much better, and talked always as if in front of his jury, or what he succeeded in reducing it to. He picked jurors based on the television programs they watched. He quoted the Bible, wore flag cufflinks and lapel pins, even kept an apple pie on the defense table whenever a judge would let him. He forever tossed in horrifyingly cliché sayings as though coined on the spot.

"Hello, Mr. McDonald."

"Got most of us defense guys pretty jealous, you know," Sam said. "The case of the year, at least, and you've got it. Congratulations."

"Thank you, Mr. McDonald," said Philip.

"Sam, Sam."

"Sam."

"Sam, Sam I am," the man quipped. Got his quotes from the books of quotations lining his famed office bookshelves: used Thoreau to get off toxic-waste dumpers, Orwell to get off illegal wiretappers; Frank Purdue and Orville Redenbacher to get off everyone.

"Saw your client on *Larry King* the other night, read about him in the paper again today. Sam, I said to myself, Sam, I said, the boy— meaning you, boy—'s got a good head on his shoulders. Got his client network exposure, turned the press around on him, prepped him so he don't seem like no idiot." He laughed some more to make sure Philip knew his grammatical joke was just that. "And ain't that a feat for an assistant public defender? Ain't that like something us high-priced fellas are supposed to be so good at?"

"Thank you, Sam."

Sam came to the point. "But whatcha gonna do when the trial rolls around?" Philip could just see him biting his lip in concern. As if Philip would never have considered the actual *trial*, and must now be in a spiral over what that would entail.

"I don't follow you," Philip told him coolly.

"Well, I just don't know if you realize what a case of this magnitude requires."

"What does it require?"

"It requires someone who knows the ropes and has the resources. I mean, sure, you've done an enviable job. So far. But whatcha gonna do when the trial rolls around and everything's done just exactly by the book? You're gonna need to go all day and prepare your motions overnight, with every big-time lawyer in the city looking over your shoulder in the papers. That courtroom's gonna run like a Timex. 'Cause no judge is gonna let a thing by him with the national press in the gallery. And, boy, you've drawn Willison. He's the most thorough thoroughbred they've got in the stable, excuse the pun. The smartest, the toughest."

Philip did not respond. Sam went on, a little annoyed.

"And that ain't all. Your client, to paraphrase a wise man, ain't the onliest motherfucker in the world. You got your own self to worry about, too. You're working the press, but you're not working it for you. You're just letting that opportunity slip on by. Get *your* name in the paper, get them talking about *your* strategies, not just your client's hidden talents. Get your own self something out of all this."

"Thanks, Sam," Philip said to indicate he'd like to get off the phone now.

"Let me tell you something," Sam ignored him to say. "Now this might sound harsh. But win, lose, or hang, it doesn't have to matter. You can get him off or get him life and win big either way if you start dealing yourself in. Or let someone who knows how do it for you." Sam let it hang a moment.

"Now I see it thisaways: I come in, take over the defense, you assist me. There's enough here for both of us. And your client, now don't forget him. He gets the best defense money can buy—for free, 'cause this one's on the house. And you get a shot in the arm, which, I assure you, you need."

"Thanks, Sam, but I don't think so. Anyway, the case was assigned to me through the office, even if I wanted to bring you in, which to be honest, I don't."

"You'd resign, I'd bring you into my firm, and I never recruit from the defender. Look, I understand not wanting to share the glory, but you ain't getting much now, outside legal circles, and that ain't where your clients are. Not yet."

"I'm not looking for clients."

"I can get you good press."

"I'm not looking for press."

"I can get him off."

"I can, too."

"I know your record."

"I have a good record."

"You have an all-right record with penny-ante shit. I have an unsurpassed record in the big time. You owe it to your client to turn the case over to me."

"I owe it to my client to provide the best defense I am possibly able. And I owe it to him to promote his interests everywhere, including the press, not mine, and not yours."

"You owe it to him to let him know that the best in the business is willing to take on his case."

Philip paused. "You're right about that. I'll let him know."

Philip could feel Sam believe him, size him up as one of those good-as-his-word guys.

"The China Manager's a smart fellow," Sam said. "I wager he drops you like he dropped his girlfriend."

Philip realized in a flash that drop him was exactly what Freddy would not do. Freddy *was* a smart fellow; he'd know a big personality like Sam McDonald would compete with him. More than anything, Freddy wanted the story to remain the China Manager's.

"Well, son," said Sam, as though the fat lady had shown and he was fixin' to hand her the extension, "you had your chance to be my assistant, but you done fucked it up." And significantly, "You can lead a horse to water, but sometimes you are simply unable to persuade him to partake."

"Possession," Philip returned, he did not know why, "is nine tenths of the law."

"That's fine, 'cause I only need one-tenth to dust your tenth-rate ass on home." Sam hung up.

20

The Man in Bobby Jamison's Office

Philip entered Chanet's through the revolving doors of the main entrance. The store was huge and teemed with shoppers, the crowds stretching before him and expansively to both sides. He'd been here seldom, and not recently; the elevators he'd been told to look for were not apparent. As he scanned for them, streams of customers flowed around him in and out, and he noticed a uniformed guard on his stool just a couple of yards away.

Philip approached him, eyes drawn to his badge which was greasy-dull-disparate from the spanking rest of the place. The guard matched his badge, his face big and tired, dents in his nose. But his eyes were alive, if rheumy, with suspicion. Philip stopped at his side. The man looked like Walter Matthau on a bad day, he decided, and waited to be looked at. But the guard kept his attention on the exiting customers, his watery eyes shifting from faces to bags, from briefcases to garments, for bulks where there should be no bulks, for unpaid-for bulks, for stolen bulks.

"Excuse me," said Philip.

"Restrooms're over there, pay phone's that way," the guard said pointing to the side, pointing in front of him, his eyes never leaving his work.

"No, I—"

"I don't know what department sells those, ask at the information stand."

"I was told to take a special elevator to the management floors," said Philip gripping his arm. "I just want to know where it is."

The guard glanced at him briefly, and then at his briefcase. "Next the escalator," he said.

Philip turned and made his way into the store.

He walked past Cosmetics, where a purple-haired old woman smiled to show him her bridgework. He picked out his wife's perfume, though it mingled in the air with many others, and then his wife by a counter, which flip-flopped his stomach, left him aching, his purpose eroded. Started over to her, stopped, started again, stopped. Stopped. Decided to leave it alone. Backtracked toward the escalators before she saw him, and continued around them to the elevator bank.

There was a sign between the doors:

AUTHORIZED PERSONNEL ONLY
FLOOR 12: UPPER MANAGEMENT
FLOOR 11: UPPER-MIDDLE MANAGEMENT
FLOOR 10: MIDDLE-MIDDLE MANAGEMENT
FLOOR 9: LOWER-MIDDLE MANAGEMENT

He pushed the up button and an elevator opened immediately. Entering, he pushed eleven and, arriving, was directed by a receptionist down a corridor to the last office at the very end of the hall. ROBERT JAMISON it said on removable plastic next to the door. "Bobby," the man had said to call him on the phone two weeks ago. He knocked.

"Come," came a voice from inside.

Philip entered the very narrow office and introduced himself to the rodent-faced man in gray pinstripe behind the desk. He had a few small scars on his pate and seemed the kind who wet his comb in a glass of water to manage his lonely strands. Philip found him strangely familiar, but could not put his finger on why. The man did not seem to recognize Philip by name, which was odd, too, since they had an appointment.

"We spoke by phone," Philip prompted. "I'm Freddy Builder's attorney, Mr. Jamison—I mean Bobby."

"Mr. Jamison is fine," the man corrected.

"I'm sorry: Mr. Jamison," said Philip. He needed this man's cooperation. "We spoke on the phone, if you recall."

"Well, I'm not Mr. Jamison," the man said. "His name plate is still out there, I know, but things move quickly around here."

"Well, sir, I had an appointment with Mr. Jamison—"

"Please," said the man generously, "call him Bobby. That was just when you thought he was me."

"Okay—Bobby. I had—"

"You don't recognize me?" the man asked.

"Should I? I mean, I think I do—" Then it came to him. "You're last year's Manager of the Year."

"That's right." He seemed appeased. "Not to worry, I've taken on B.J.'s responsibilities, and it seems to me I was informed of your visit and prepared—oh, sit down, won't you?" The man gestured to the chair fronting his wood-grain metal desk. Philip did as asked and the man-who-was-not-Bobby-Jamison's phone rang. He picked it up and was silent for a time except for "yes, sirs."

Philip took a moment to look over the office. It was extremely small, there being a foot at most between the desk and the walls on either side, and, he judged, no more than a yard behind it to the windows. "Yes sir, I agree, sir." The wall to the right was of normal plaster, but the left wall seemed comprised of synthetic segments that tried for plaster but failed as miserably as the desk did for wood. "Of course, sir, I think he deserves it, too." The two windows behind the desk, one directly above the other, were each covered with the same poster of a tall office building, which sealed them completely. The light in the room was only harsh fluorescent.

"No sir, neither do I."

On the walls were animal prints. A tiger stared ferociously out from a sea of green grass. The zebra in the print next to it stared out

195

with the same menacing expression, stood the same antagonistic pose. Together the prints told anyone interested they were the work of the same artist, who saw tigers and zebras as essentially identical in character. And across from them was a killer cow, poised, it seemed, to pounce swiftly at either's slightest provocation.

"I sort of felt that at first, too, sir, then, just when you did, I changed my mind."

There were certificates of achievement on both walls, surrounding the prints. They looked like diplomas, the solemn calligraphy recognizing the recipient for *Best Washer-Dryer Quarter*, *Lowest Return Ratio*, *Manager of the Month*, *Manager of the Year*. There was a framed segment of streamer with this man in a Santa Claus beard.

"Oh, yes, sir, Oh, no, sir. I'm very happy for him, sir. Certainly, sir, I'll do it now. Uh, sir, do you know when there will be a decision on me, then? Half an hour? That quickly, sir? Of course, sir, of course. Good-bye, sir." The man hung up and stood. He was shaking a bit. "Would you mind helping me a minute with the desk?"

"Sure," said Philip, standing but uncertain what was wanted of him. The man went to one end of the desk and blocked the enraged cow's view of the tiger. He motioned Philip around to the other end.

"We have to turn it sideways," the man said and left for Catatonia.

"Sideways?" It was ridiculous. There was only one livable place for the desk in this tiny office and it was already there. But the man just stood there staring, and Philip had to lean over the desk and tap his shoulder. Together they turned the desk so that it faced the right wall beyond which there was no more building. Then, at the man's behest, they pushed the desk flush against that wall. The man gestured for Philip to retake his seat and turned his own chair so that they faced each other again, though with no desk between them now. In their chairs, their knees almost touched.

The man made no move to say anything, but when a creaking sound came from the office next door, he sprang up and said, "Better move your chair farther from that wall." Philip, having already helped the man move his desk to its now absurd position, and doubting the man's stability, did not question him. He merely got up, moved his chair to the right two steps, and sat down in it again.

There was the creaking sound, but added now was a squeaking that quickly overrode it. The wall was moving in on them slowly from the left.

"What's going on?" Philip asked, but received no response from the man facing him. Philip looked at him for cues as to how to regard this event: though the man looked worn to his wiring, he did not seem terrified. Philip decided to sit tight, but if the wall started past the door he'd get out quick.

The wall stopped, and the noise, right at the door, the cow, tiger, and zebra on hair triggers. What had been a less than square office to begin with was now a mere sliver a few feet wider than the door.

"That's number three," the man said quietly and used his fingers like tweezers to put back a few wet strands of hair. "The third promotion," he said significantly.

"The third promotion," Philip repeated hoping to nudge him into explanation.

"Yes," said the man, "this is it. Someone was promoted today. They'll either move me up now to upper management or," gesturing to the windows, "out. I'll know in half an hour. Either way, they'll be here soon to clear out the furniture, and then that wall," he pointed right, "meets this one," left. He grinned and poked Philip's knee. "You see, one of the rewards around here is a bigger office. They just move out your wall, and everyone else's gets moved to compensate. Except the guy in the last office." He thumbed at himself and mouthed "me." "They can't make the last guy's bigger 'cause there's nothing to encroach on." He thumbed the right wall. "So, three times, then they promote you or, sshhhoooo—" he pointed down with his thumb "—and the guy before you is in the last office."

"That's too bad," said Philip.

"Too bad? You think that's too bad?"

"Yes," Philip told him, "I really do."

The man nodded. "Is it too bad enough to kill someone over?"

"What?"

The man smiled tolerantly.

"I asked you if it is too bad enough to kill someone over."

"That's not something I can discuss with you."

"Think of this: This is life. Unfortunately, except for a few lucky, lucky people, this is life. Is your job any different, any different really?"

Philip said nothing.

"How is it different? Nothing pointless, no one wicked—everything you hoped?"

Philip gave no response.

"And have you ever been devastated in love, like your client?"

"Yes."

The man pursed his lips. "I've read everything about your client and by him. I've read his short stories, I watched him on *Larry King*. He thinks he deserved better than this store."

"That's safe to say."

"He thinks—he thinks it was part of his destiny for Mindi Quintana to die. That she lived only so he could kill her and become what he was meant to become."

"What makes you think that?"

"It's there to be gotten. And I would have felt sorry for him. I mean all the little stupidities here that point to the big ones. He exploded. I might have forgiven him the explosion."

"What can't you forgive him?"

"The book." The words fell like pebbles on Formica.

Philip said nothing.

"The book and the rape."

"What rape?"

"Oh, well, see, he's not sorry. How dare he not be sorry! He's raping that woman in her grave. He's changing what she was. He's actually turning her into what he killed her for not being: a cog in the

198

wheel of his destiny. The rape is of her life, of her death, of her memory, and of her meaning. How's that for rape?"

The man was silent for a moment.

"I'm right, aren't I?" he asked, laughing and pointing at Philip.

Philip wanted to answer but didn't.

"Aren't I?" the man repeated.

"I'm not going to discuss it with you," said Philip.

"All right, then." With another crazy shift, this time down to business, the man took a typewritten sheet from his desk and handed it to Philip. "This is a list of the people you asked to speak to and where they are located in the store. We've made a conference room available for you on nine. Except for the Chocolate Manager. You'll have to interview him at the stand."

While Philip looked over the list, the man leaned to paperwork on his desk and made little wrist-flick check marks on it.

Philip finished reading. "Thank you," he said, folding the list lengthwise and putting it inside his jacket. "If you don't mind, though, I'd prefer to interview everyone at their workstations. I don't want to make them nervous."

"As you wish."

Again, a change in the man. He slumped and seemed to slip into himself. Wistfully he said, "Did I tell you I was a wonderful floor merchant?"

"I bet you were. But maybe you need a rest." Philip stood. "Well, good day," he said.

"Oh, good day," said the man, standing and shaking hands absently. "Aren't I?" he said.

Near the door, the man clapped Philip on the back. "Say hello to the wife-kids."

The man's phone rang again and he lunged for it as Philip closed the door behind him. As he moved down the hall, the most unguarded wail followed him from behind that door.

21

Aren't I?

Out of the elevator, a puffy-faced youngster stood crying in the clutches of his mother. She was pinching jeans against him to see if they would fit, the veins in her arms disappearing and reappearing like blue swirlies in some flesh-colored Jell-O. The boy was struggling and she was smacking him to stand still, pinching the pants to him with three more pairs folded at her side.

"You little shit. Hold still," the woman said to her son, Philip going around them and stopping a store employee, who directed him to the chocolate stand.

As he came close to the stand, the man who ruled the island kingdom of sweets killed the childhood associations triggered by the smell of chocolate and candies. The fitted suit, small-knotted tie, razor-perfect hair, the way he had folded his apron wherever possible to minimize it. The way he drew on his cigarette *en filtero* and blew out the smoke in hair-thin lines like final breaths. And moved slowly to fill the candy bins from Tupperware barrels, wearing an expression of unspeakable humiliation.

Philip made a pretense of perusing the candies, and watched him. In the center of the stand there was a peach-colored Formica island with an inset stainless-steel sink. Atop the table was an empty metal bin. The manager sprayed the bin with spray from a sprayer and wiped it sparkling, spotlessly clean, but only methodically. Then he slowly spun a roll of ribbon, taking up the excess on its spool, and closed a pair of scissors, placing it near the ribbon.

Philip approached the register and stood there, the man dragging himself over. Philip extended his hand. "I'm Freddy Builder's attorney," he said. The chocolate manager's head shot up, fear on his face. Almost immediately, though, it was gone, replaced by a bitter smirk.

"Of course you are," said Jamison.

"What do you mean, of course I am? I am."

"I admit, when you called, I was taken in," Jamison said. "I mean, it seemed natural that Builder's attorney would want to meet with me. I don't think I was being gullible. But when I was demoted two days later, and then was allowed to hear snatches of conversation—cut off as I got near, but not before I heard comments about 'the attorney's' visit—well, I knew immediately who you were."

"Who?"

"An actor," said Jamison. "Hired by the store. I'm to be part of next Christmas's festivities." Jamison peered over Philip's shoulder. "Where's the camera?"

"There is no camera." He opened his jacket, bewildered.

"So this is it." Jamison screwed his cigarette out of the filter and dropped it. The floor inside was covered with butts.

"Really," said Philip, "I don't have any idea what you're talking about. So this is what?"

"It. The end of my career. I'm to be chocolate terminated, in some amusing way." He screwed in another.

Now Philip understood. "No, really, this has nothing to do with that. I'm not here to fire you. I'm here as Freddy Builder's attor—"

"Oh, no? Do you have identification?" Jamison blew smoke in his eyes.

"Yes, I do." He removed his wallet and took out his public defender card and driver's license.

"Of course you do," Jamison said, his eyes darting about to be sure he made contact with the camera. "Don't you guys realize," he said to his audience, "that I know how far you'll go to make these things work? Mine was the best ever, remember?" He looked back to Philip as though bored and held out his hand. "May I examine your credentials, *counselor*?" Philip handed them over. Jamison went immediately to the Formica table, held the IDs in front of him, and cut the cards in half with the scissors. "Heavens, I'm sorry. They slipped." He cut the halves into fourths. "My! Again!"

"What the fuck are you doing?" Philip yelled.

"That was very good," Jamison said coming back. "Very convincing." He flipped the pieces on the counter in front of Philip.

Philip brought up his briefcase and slapped it down on the counter. He sprang the catch and yanked it open. "Here, look," he said, pulling out papers and a legal pad. "These are official papers." Jamison held out his hand for them but Philip kept hold. "This is the criminal complaint against my client," he said showing it to him. "This is a police report, this is an autopsy report, these are my notes. I'm Freddy Builder's attorney."

Jamison studied the complaint charging Freddy with murder, while Philip kept a grip on it. He flipped through the pages of Philip's notes, reading excerpts at random, Philip careful nothing volatile. Jamison waved the papers away.

"You're not here to fire me."

"No. As I explained on the phone, I'm here to talk with you about Freddy."

"Freddy," Jamison repeated. He had collected himself. "He liked to be called Frederick."

Philip knew it. "I believe—or at least I believed from what Freddy told me—that you were fond of him. Please stop making it difficult for me. He's in very deep trouble and I came here to find out if you would help him."

"He said I was fond of him?"

"Yes," said Philip, "was he wrong?"

"No, I was fond of him. I recognized his talent two years ago, and I kept the uppers informed. I, you might say, discovered him and the uppers rewarded me for it down the line. Most recently, they added my lower teeth to the dental plan." He pulled his gum down to show a set of corroded lowers so at odds with his perfect upper palate. "I was about to take advantage of that. Oh, I was a middle-middle back when I was given the sales figures for his first few months as china manager. I saved his ass."

"What do you mean?"

Jamison pulled his shirtsleeves out a little from his jacket. "There was talk then of making him chocolate manager. Vendors—wholesalers and manufacturers—were all complaining that he refused to put their merchandise in prominent display positions, positions these vendors warranted based on the business they did for us. I was supposed to study the situation and make a recommendation. I recommended keeping him and he became the best we had. I was doing well on my own, mind you, and the upstairs attention he started receiving didn't hurt. They decided to make Freddy Manager of the Year, and I was the only sub-upper told. By then I was just three offices away from senior upper-middle. I took Freddy to lunch, told him we weren't going to name him, just to heighten his reaction in case he was expecting it. I told that to the uppers and they let me fire the two people ahead of me for the end office." He smoked again but the dream in his voice was gone when he continued. "Thirty-four, I was thirty-fucking-four years old, and I was senior upper-middle. I could've been the youngest upper in store history. That bastard."

"What bastard?"

Jamison took another Benson & Hedges from his apron pocket and twisted out the old one. "Your client."

"I take it that you are no longer fond of him."

"Very good," quipped Jamison, puffing. "You should be a lawyer."

"What happened?"

"They came to me on the day of the arrest and asked me what we should do about him. I said, strip him, of course, strip him now or he'll bring us down. So we do. We choose a replacement Manager of the Year, spend hundreds of thousands of dollars putting his picture on bags, ribbons, gift certificates, make up new ads, what happens?

"Your fucking client gets popular. It's the old joke: we cut off the wrong leg but the bad one's getting better. The store fills up every day, customers want to see where the 'China Manager' worked. They strip his display clean, they strip his *department* clean, and it's too late to remake him Manager of the Year. Someone on eleven suggests we hire ex-convicts as floor managers, figuring some of them will do it again, and my office gets smaller. I come in one day, and my second window's got a building on it. The next day, my cow's gone. The day after, you phone, the day after that Freddy's on *Larry King*, and the day after that there's this apron on my desk chair." Jamison blinked back tears. He dragged on his cigarette for full seconds.

"I understand and I'm sorry," Philip said. "And I know Freddy will be, too, when he hears about . . . your troubles."

Jamison waved dismissively.

"I need to ask you just a few questions. Do you think that Freddy is the type to commit murder?"

"I wouldn't have thought so from what I knew of him, no. He was very controlled."

"Can you tell me what his reputation was among his coworkers."

"He had an excellent reputation. He was a gifted floor merchant."

"If I put you on the stand, would you tell that to the jury?"

"If you put me up there, I'd say he'd been talking about killing the bitch for a month."

There were screams near the front entrance and a general flurry of people rushed by them in that direction. Philip asked an employee on his way briskly past, "What's going on?"

"Bobby Jamison on eleven. He jumped." The man pulled away. It struck Philip immediately who he meant. "I just talked to him," he said out loud.

"Bummer," said Jamison.

Another employee ran by. "Bobby Jamison just jumped!"

"Better him than me," Jamison said and laughed. But he coughed like he'd caught the bouquet.

"Excuse me," said Philip somewhat disoriented, "I'm going outside—I just talked to the man."

"Go, go, enjoy," said Jamison. "Tell your client I hope he dies."

After the police removed the stuff from the pavement, Philip went home and sat on his stoop. When it began to rain he stayed outside, feeling it was the least he could do. Finally going in, he climbed the stairs and peeled off his suit in the bedroom. Pulled his shirt open, the buttons popping onto the floor, also for the man he'd probably been last to see alive. And climbed null and void into a hot shower.

22

Autobiography

The next day, a guard took Philip to Freddy's cell. Through the bars, Freddy sat cross-legged on his cot. Manny Sykes was in a chair, hunched over a pad on his knee. Arrayed atop the prison blanket with Freddy were stacks of typewritten pages, newspaper articles and photocopied material, legal pads. On the floor before Sykes were more piles, some topped with white bond labeled "Chptr. 1," "Chptr. 2," and so on. The two were in intense though quiet conversation, the key in the lock and the door sliding back caused them no pause. As Philip stepped in, Freddy lifted a hand for him not to interrupt.

"What you had was fine," Sykes was saying, "but I think it sounds better this way." He read from the pad. "'Mindi reached out to me, and I to her. A bond was established between us, we realized, its roots in our chance meeting on that winter night six years before, and in our relationship then. We were discovering that the bond had lain dormant but had never been severed.' Then we move right into china department dialogue and dates one and two. What do you think?"

"Aaagghhh," Freddy complained. He shivered. "Mushy."

Sykes laughed and threw his pen at him. "I know, I know. But that's what you want, isn't it?"

"It is," Freddy assured him. "It's fine. Dormant bonds, though. Boy."

Sykes stopped laughing. "That's how you used to talk about it, Frederick."

Freddy got serious, too. "That's the way it was."

"You talk about her differently now."

"Drop it."

"Dropped."

Philip broke in. "We have some things to discuss," he said to Freddy.

"That's okay," Sykes said, standing. "I'll go powder my nose half an hour. Will that cover it?"

"Plenty," Freddy told him. "Take chapter two with you. I need to seem stronger. Tormented, yes, fine, but quietly, and with talent others see, even though I don't see it myself. So I'm miserable, right, but I shouldn't be. If I knew myself, I wouldn't be. See what I mean?"

"Mm-hmm." Sykes turned to Philip. "The book's about a failed criminal justice system," he said, hands on the back of the chair. "I hope you won't mind my interviewing you for some of the later chapters."

"What do you mean 'failed'?" He kept his voice low by habit against guards and other prisoners. "He hasn't been convicted yet, or acquitted. How do you know which will happen? Which would be failure?"

"The system failed long before boy met girl, friend," Sykes said.

"Oh. Well, off the record, girl had a name," Philip said. "Mindi Quintana. And some boy killed her."

"Right. And she's not coming back. The only one we can help now is Frederick," said Sykes. He pushed straight from the chair.

"Help him?" Philip thumbed at Freddy, who was searching for something on the cot and did not notice. "He risks his case every time he opens his mouth to you."

"We're careful. I know the ropes," said Sykes.

"Powder your nose," Philip told him.

Sykes fetched chapter two from the floor. He went to the bars and yelled for the guard. Several silent moments later he was keyed out.

Philip approached Freddy, who'd found what he was looking for and was studying it.

"He's right about how you talk about her," said Philip. "You'd better watch it."

Freddy put the page down. "I watch it all the time," he said. "But I'll bite, how do I talk about her?"

"Like her murder was the expression of something profound in you rather than the expression of the profound lack thereof."

"Very good, come up with that in the car?"

"Boy meets girl but with a twist," he said. "Of her neck. I came up with that in the car."

"You're trying to make me mad. I'm not sure why." Freddy laughed. "But, see, as of today I've got three publishers interested in my book, which, you will notice, is moving along pretty nicely. It's just kinda hard to work up a good mad right now. And really, please consider this. Who cares what you think? Nobody even knows your name but for the rest of your life you'll be hearing mine. Builder on *Nightline*—they already want me back on. Builder donates proceeds—which I'm planning to do if Son of Sam doesn't stop me. Builder's new book. Et cetera."

"All of that for just one girl's life," Philip said. "Quite a bargain."

Freddy shook his head sadly.

"Not a word about Mindi, Freddy. Not a word from where you really live."

Freddy shifted on the cot, sat with his back against the wall. He fanned through a chapter pile in response to Philip.

"Well," said Philip, "your literary career aside, there's still the small matter of your trial for you to think about. Though I gather you're not too worried."

"If I'm convicted, what am I up against?" Freddy put down the chapter and leaned forward. "Honestly now. Answer me like you're my lawyer for a goddamn change."

"I don't think they'll convict you in the first degree. I've told you that. There's no guarantee but the evidence hasn't shaped up that way.

The press sure hasn't. It's a third-degree case on the evidence and, in this climate, there's a shot and a half at voluntary manslaughter. They'll parole you first chance."

"It'll suck but I'll live," Freddy said. He moved back against the wall.

"And I could be wrong. You could get more time or they could come back in the first degree. Or you could be offered a deal."

"No deals."

"Right, I know. There are still some points I need to clear up with you if I'm going to prepare you a defense. Do you think you can fit that into your busy schedule?"

"I'll make time."

"Today. Three o'clock for two hours. I've got another client here till then."

"All right."

Philip went and took his interview notes out of his briefcase. "I saw some of your coworkers. Jamison, Beryl Lamber—"

"Who?"

"The former chocolate manager you gave advice to several months ago. And I interviewed some over the phone. Furniture-Dilton and Jewelry-Stevestre, for example. Dilton and Stevestre will testify to your managerial prowess, dedication, if aloof interpersonal style. Jamison is disinclined to testify at all on your behalf."

"I thought the bastard liked me," Freddy said surprised.

"He blames you for his demotion to chocolate manager."

"You're kidding, they made him chocolate manager?" Freddy fell on his side laughing. "It must be killing him!" He sat back up still grinning and straightened the papers on his bed. "And you say there's no justice."

"Lamber, on the other hand, your chocolate pretzel friend, would be happy to testify for you."

"Come on."

"He doesn't know you were part of that 'by committee' thing, or were going to be. Which they apparently went ahead with, some alien abduction scenario. He actually thinks you tried to help him."

Freddy broke into another grin. "Don't look at me like that," he said. "He let the store beat him. He was gone, nothing I could do."

Philip took a step forward, kicking over one of the chapter stacks on the floor.

"Hey—" Freddy started and Philip stepped around.

"I got a call from Sam McDonald. Know who he is?"

"I know he doesn't have a farm or a fast food chain." Freddy smiled. "He's been recommended."

"Sykes?"

"They're acquaintances," Freddy said, getting off the cot and fixing the pile.

"He wants to take over your case."

"If he did, Sykes would have told me."

"No. Professional courtesy, if you can call it that. He called me first. He'll defend you no charge. If he'd known Court TV wants to televise, I'm sure he'd have offered to pay you. It's okay with me, Freddy."

"If I wanted him, I'd have called him," said Freddy and went back to the cot.

"Too big a personality, huh?"

Freddy didn't answer.

Philip put his papers away, went to the bars and called for the guard. "Three o'clock," he said to Freddy and waited to get out.

23

Cherry Tobacco

They are at Murphy's.

"I didn't think you'd want to talk to me," is the first thing he says when they find a table and order drinks.

"I do," she says.

"I just thought—because she was your best friend."

She says nothing.

It is she who suggested Murphy's when he asked her to meet. She explained Mindi liked it. He wonders if she wants him to feel guilty. He wonders if it is smart to be here at all.

"What was she like?"

"I didn't think you would ask me questions like that."

And he isn't sure why he has. "I wasn't," he says. And after a moment, "What did you think I would ask you?"

"Things about them together, I guess. To see what kind of case you have." She's drinking her Tanqueray and tonic and there's a Seagram's in front of him. He hasn't noticed the waitress put them down. There is something alive in his stomach. It is wearing ice skates and cutting him open. "I need to know what she was like." He's trying to smile but should probably give up.

"We used to come here," she says.

He thinks she's going to cry. "Tell me about her! I have decisions to make!" He couldn't have yelled at her, maybe he hasn't. But a few heads have turned. He's stirring his drink and taking one of her cigarettes. He doesn't smoke but there's no time like the present. He's sure he is a lunatic.

But, "Don't yell at me," she says. "I don't know. She understood me." She is shaking her head as if this isn't good enough, and he is stirring a neat whiskey with the last person's swizzle. "She worked hard, she wanted things." He swallows his drink, coughs on his cigarette. She says, "I don't know what to say." Bitter now. "She had long black hair. She understood me. She worked hard. She was . . . nice." Tears fall on the wood. "Nice! She was five foot six! She's dead and you're defending her murderer!"

"Don't cry." Someone has slipped him a voice strangifier. His drink is crying out for more stirring. The cigarette wants him to smoke it. He wants to reach out but whoever was skating in his stomach has put on golf shoes.

She's saying, "It's like looking for photos of someone and not finding any. I can't explain her."

He tells her, "I've talked to some of her friends. They were hostile toward me. I don't blame them. They tried to tell me."

"Did it help?"

"No." The waitress appears. He points at both glasses and she goes away. Mindi's name is carved into the wood next to his glass.

"No?"

"Uh, unh-unh." He shakes his head. "But it's me. I just can't get the feelings. For personal reasons." Why has he alluded to them? Why does his voice sound like it's on a tape recorder? There's the question he's raised in her eyes and then the answer. He doesn't want to talk about that.

"The only time I think I saw a little of Mindi was when you testified at the prelim. In you. And her family. That did affect me. I guess I want you to know that." He'd move on to the interview now. Just the facts ma'am, please, just the facts. *Please* just the facts. The golfer has changed into sneakers and is kicking funny bones inside him. He starts shaking his head.

Someone, probably Lisa, wants to know, "Why are you shaking your head?"

He's laughing now, chuckling it off, wishing for a drink to stir, a cigarette to cough on because he feels like he is coming apart. "No, no nothing." He's chuckling weakly. "Where were we?" He is looking at his empty glass.

"What's the matter?"

"Nothing." He struggles to be light. "Nothing," protesting. But again there is his empty glass. He feels the touch of his upper and lower back teeth. Funny bones go off inside him and he is afraid to move. He wonders about the inappropriate nature of his behavior. But he makes no move.

She is looking at him, concerned but unalarmed. Concern for the lunatic. "What's the matter?" Her "I'll help you" washes over him.

"I don't know," he says. "I really don't. I really, really don't."

"Think," she tells him.

"I don't know you. I'm sorry. This is inappropriate."

"I don't care. It doesn't have to be appropriate." She pauses. "I'll help you," she says.

He is quiet.

"I'll help you."

"Really?"

She nods.

He thinks, "I'm so far away." He laughs and shakes his head again.

"What do you mean, far away?"

So he's said it. "I don't feel anything," he says. "I haven't been able to. I used to. And I can't anymore because I've lost my capacity."

"No, you haven't. People without emotion don't say things like that."

"I've lost my capacity."

"No. Soon. I promise, believe me."

"I want to die, I think. That's the strangest thing I ever said about myself, and I don't even know if it's true. It doesn't hit me to say it."

"You don't want to die, that's not it. You're just sticking yourself with pins. You're just trying to shock yourself. You're sticking yourself with needles to see if you are alive."

He must stop this nonsense, straighten and be forceful. He has maybe just told her he wants to die. But he has a tie on. He has a suit on. So maybe he hasn't. His briefcase is leaning against his leg so that he'll know if anyone tries stealing it. So maybe he hasn't. "I shouldn't be saying this to you. I came about a case." Two more drinks have appeared.

"It's okay," she says. "Let it come."

Let what come?

"Come on," she whispers.

"There's nothing to come!" Fine, the heads are turned again. "I've tried that—I can't." Great, now he's shaking inside. Great, now he's going to start shaking outside and she's going to have to call the nets in. He'll worry about his briefcase and they'll smile and tell him, "Now that's all right, we have Crayolas at the farm." They'll take his tie and belt away. Stamp will get a new trial out of it, Michael will get a kick out of it, Freddy will get a chapter out of it, McDonald will get a new case out of it, Sykes an article, Cindy—Cindy won't care.

"My wife left me."

She has her hands on one of his. "I know."

"I thought we were in love," he says.

"Did you find her with someone?"

"I found her suitcases."

"What did you do?"

"I confronted her."

"What did she say?"

"I don't want to tell you."

"You can tell me if you want to."

He knows if he tightens his grip any more the glass will break. He tightens it. The glass breaks. He looks at her face to see if his hand is okay. She is wiping up the mess. No blood on the napkin. "She was sitting on the couch. She said, 'I want to be in love.'"

She stands. "Let's go outside."

"I used to be able to use my outrage to make decisions." He stands up. His briefcase hits the floor. He looks at that weird thing; it's for papers, official important papers that don't mean anything. He should leave it here. People's lives are in it, though. He picks it up, but it is unfamiliar. During the day he uses it to negotiate sidewalk traffic, for everything from catching closing elevator doors to intimidating dangerous drunks. He would probably take it to an auction and use it to bid. He should shed it. Everyone would get new trials. He is dazed, some pre-faint stage it feels like, but he will let himself have it. Maybe he is sick, maybe he *will* faint. But it is an excuse to follow her like being drunk can be an excuse.

Lisa is holding the check up to the waitress and mouthing, "Tomorrow." She says to him, "Come outside."

Through Murphy's outside to a deserted Market Street. The stores are closed, the winter is mellowing.

"I don't remember her from the Lincoln Ball," he says.

"I wish you did. I wish you knew her."

There are boxes and candy wrappers, cigar butts on the pavement. Can tabs and broken bottle glass and they are so interesting.

He says, "This is weird, I know. Don't go away yet, though. I'm not gonna freak out or anything. I'm not usually like this."

"I know you're not going to freak out."

They start walking. "A man jumped at the store. I don't feel anything for him. Your friend was murdered. I don't feel anything for her or her family. I don't feel anything for you."

She lets him talk.

"My outrage used to tell me what to do. I could count on it. I should be outraged: the man who jumped, Mindi. Do you understand?"

"Yes."

"I can't hate Freddy, but I know I hate him so much." She isn't asking why he hates Freddy. How can he thank her for that? "Lisa?"

"Yes."

"Thank you for not asking. Lisa?"

"Yes."

"You painters are so lucky. I always wanted to be like you. I thought I was going to be." He's rambling but she's next to him listening. "You walk in the city. I get through it. As quickly as possible. I have to get things done despite it. You get things done because of it—"

"What do you smell?"

"—and I never have time."

"What do you smell?"

He takes a deep breath through his nose. "I smell Chinese food, I smell cherry tobacco, I smell the winter, I smell exhaust, the city."

"What do you see?"

"That beat-up car going by."

They have turned onto Tenth and are near Vine. "That billboard kills me," he says. It's black with green letters that seem to glow in the lights from up top. "BEAUTIFUL FURNITURE IN 24 HOURS."

"I haven't painted a thing since Mindi died," she says.

"Will you ever?"

"Oh, yes."

"When?"

She shrugs. "Soon. Come here. Follow me," she says. "You're almost there."

"Where? Where are we going?" He follows across Vine. They take their time in the wide, empty avenue. She walks a few circles around him just to show him it's possible and sits a few seconds in the road. Watching her feels like going through a red light when there's nobody around. He's stopped doing that. On the other side, she climbs a chest-high fence, and he follows, going with her into a grassy lot, the sound of their footsteps changing.

She touches his arm. "Stop." They are in the center of the plot that divides two lit parking lots. Some light from each side spills over onto the grass, but where they are there is only a hazy glow. Vine Street and Race border north and south, Ninth and Tenth, west and east. They are in the center of a rectangle, in the center of a square. Everything is far away.

"Lie down on your stomach," she says.

He does. He does not question her.

"Look at the grass. It's different at eye level, isn't it?"

And it is. "Yes. The ground is thawing. I can smell the mud."

"Take the time. You've got nowhere you've gotta be tonight. Please. Relax. It's really different being here, isn't it? There's nothing you have to do. Shhh. Pick out a blade you like."

In a moment he says, "I've got one."

"What's it like?"

"I picked a green one, I think. It's moving now, it's really distinct."

"Is the ground cold?"

"Uh-huh."

"Okay."

A car is starting easily somewhere in the east parking lot. An easy giggle and lower male voice float over from somewhere west. A horn, so far away, maybe that car's horn, but some people who are alive whom he would never know. He remembers taking trains to Baltimore and seeing the laundry on lines from his window, and beat-up little wading pools, rusted cars in yards and being amazed that people who didn't know him bought things that got washed and old.

"Can you tell me more about the blade? Please, I want to know. Remember? Like you wanted to know about Mindi."

"It's the first time I've ever looked at it like this. Maybe when I was a kid. I feel like I remember. It's quiet . . . It moves when I breathe."

"That's her."

For a moment nothing. Then, "Whoosh," Lisa whispers, her hand on his neck, his body heaving under it.

Later, they walked to Lisa's apartment in a converted Walnut Street warehouse. His briefcase weighed a ton by the time they got there, and she seemed as tired as he. His suit was ruined, his briefcase was muddy, mud and grass were caked in the opening mechanism. He leaned against the building while she found her keys. They came in from the street and he saw an instant of overhead light fixture with dead bulb and the next locked door before she shut out the street light behind them. She led him back through a lit hallway past some elevators into her apartment. And into her bedroom where, without turning on any lights, or talking, really, they undressed and climbed into bed, wrapping themselves around each other under the quilt.

He awoke with his arms around her.

His watch said seven-thirty. He got up quietly and looked around the place for his clothing. It was lying in the far corner of the room, but before he got to it, he stopped at a group of easels with paintings on them. One of them he recognized from Mindi's apartment. It had been hanging on her wall above the couch near where they'd found her.

"I painted it for her," said Lisa from the bed. Her voice startled him. "The police said it wasn't evidence. I can't even look at it."

Philip looked at the painting closely. The flush peach primary coatings, roughly laid on. Purple strokes, kind of wild. A glittering black that reminded him of last night. Red dots with tails from the left, that as they hit must have moved across until the canvas finally held them. They had dried with a high gloss. There was a darker reddish-brown smudge that had the same leftward movement but had dried thick and crusty. He put his face nearer the canvas and found the fingerprint in it. He straightened slowly. "Oh, Christ." The police had arrived several hours after the murder. It could not be a policeman's print.

"What?" She came over and put her arms around him. "I didn't hear you."

"Nothing," he said.

"At some point, I'm going to hang it in the living room."

"Let's have breakfast," he said.

She kissed him. "Let's have it in bed."

24

The Plan

March fifteenth had Philip and Lisa making love in Philip's bathtub. Next to them on the sink was the new can of shaving cream she'd bought for him after twice observing him shave with watery dregs from the old can. On the hamper was a small zippered bag with her makeup in it. She'd left a pair of earrings on his night table last week, and they were still there. He had found a bra in his laundry and a pair of her jeans was folded on the floor of his closet.

She had brought bubble bath with her last night and he explained that he could envision no circumstances under which he would take one. She'd hidden a capful near the tub, and poured it in fifteen minutes ago. She'd claimed it was an accident: She'd meant merely to show him the capful of bubble bath. He didn't believe her. Then she pretended that *she* was angry because *he* had poured the bubble bath in without consulting *her*. He didn't get defensive; they both knew who poured the bubble bath. She said, well these were the circumstances he'd had trouble envisioning the night before, and he should thank her for opening his eyes. He excused himself for a moment, shivered and dripped downstairs, came back up and poured barbecue sauce on her head. He said it was an accident.

Afterward, as they dressed in the bedroom, she asked, "Are you going to be sad to leave?" Two days after their meeting at Murphy's his real estate agent had found a buyer for his house. The closing had been quick, last week, and he still had the rest of the month to find a new place.

Tying his tie in the mirror, he said, "No, not if the new place has a bathtub." In the glass he saw her notice the earrings on the night table and pick them up casually. She would put them in her pocketbook, she was wearing a pair already. Then she dropped them back down and met his eyes in the mirror with a complaining look.

"My hair still smells like barbecue sauce."

She was going to New York for the gallery today so he kissed her good-bye and ate breakfast by himself. An hour later, he was waiting at the bottom of his office building for the elevator.

There were things he couldn't do, like bring back Mindi for Lisa or save the dogs yelping now in the elevator corridor, but over the past few weeks he had thought very carefully about the things he could do. He could go into his office and make that call to Michael. He could make that call to Michael, and maybe stop the rape of a dead girl, stop the coming-to-be of her killer.

He hadn't told anyone about the painting. He'd alerted no one to the conflict he now had because of Lisa, and had not yet resigned from the case. Because he had a plan. He was going in to think it into final form. And then he would call.

By early afternoon, Philip was prepared. He dialed the DA's office from memory, was transferred to Leopold's secretary, and held while she checked if he was available. He held quite some time.

"Phil!" Michael cried suddenly as if elated to hear from him.

"Hello, Michael, how are you?"

"Fine, fine." And he sounded it. "Sorry to keep you waiting exactly five minutes." He said in a lower conspiratorial tone, "That was Condi Rice again. Whadya think about Kazakhstan, Mike, what about Sierra Leone? My apologies, pal."

"How is the secretary?" Philip played along.

"She doesn't like you, either." Michael got serious. "I've got a lot to do today, Phil. Spit it out. You want to plead down the Manager. Right? Come on, I want to hear the words."

"I want to set up a meeting."

"You want to capitulate."

"You're awfully arrogant for a guy with a shaky case and a shakier political future."

"Fine, let's get together. And let me make an admission that should scare the shit out of you. If you hadn't called me for a meet, I would have called you." Why would Michael concede that now unless he believed he was dealing from strength?

"Do you want to let me in on what you think you've got?"

"Mmmm," considered Michael. "No, I don't think so. I'll let you think on it a bit. Really, though, you might want to have someone pull a motion for pretrial conference. You're gonna want to change your plea once we talk."

"I don't care what you have, Mike," Philip said, because the truth of it was big. "Nothing would be good enough to get me to switch pleas."

"That's a pretty stupid thing to say in ignorance," Michael said. But Michael didn't know Freddy Builder. And Builder was the boss. Michael said, "When you hear what I've got, you're gonna jump at a guilty plea like it's your heart medication. My office, four o'clock, be there, aloha."

"I can't make it at four."

"Okay, then, four it is." The line died.

Far from playing final cards, Michael should have been about ready to turn his up. The plan that Philip spent his morning honing would have saved Michael's butt, if only as a necessary feature, but Michael had him thinking it was his own butt that might need saving. Maybe Michael had the painting. If he did, he would somehow have had to find out about it this morning after Lisa went home and before she left for New York. He checked his messages. She hadn't called. He tried her cell and left a voice mail.

Philip pulled out Freddy's file, which now occupied almost three full file cabinet drawers. He placed the various red jackets by his desk and started through them one by one. He needed to be sure Michael's bombshell was not something he should already know or be able to deduce. He placed a call to Freddy at the prison and questioned him minutely about things he was still unclear on. They had an in-depth plea bargain discussion in which he laid out all the possibilities and got Freddy's final decisions. No surprises.

At one point he looked at his watch, saw it was two-fifteen, and made the automatic calculation that told him he'd have to leave now for the gym if he wanted to release some tension with a workout before the meeting. He'd slipped some documents into his briefcase, pulled on his jacket and overcoat, was about to pull open the door when he remembered he had not been to the gym in over five months. He was no longer a member of the gym. He opened the door. In the elevator, he checked his wallet for his credit card.

At the Rittenhouse Square Fitness Center, he lay flat on his back on the bench and pushed up the barbell, glaring at the ceiling and gritting his teeth. He wore silly swim trunks and a T-shirt he'd purchased hurriedly on the way over, and his black socks with no shoes.

He could handle forty pounds less than his workout bench of five months ago. The weight was not important to him, he loved the exertion again. He told himself, three sets of eight and he'd kick Michael's ass, three sets of eight for that spark that made the difference. On the last rep of set three, he grunted loudly and strained, lifted his ass off the bench, waddled the bar up by the inch with his eyes fluttering slits until his elbows locked.

Some Big Pecs in tank tops turned to see the owner of this great grunt (a pale man in loose flowered trunks and black socks) put up one forty-five, leap off the bench holding up his shorts with one hand and whoop like he'd cinched the gold for his weirdo country. Three sets of eight, an act of will. He had a will. He retied his trunks. He leg curled, pulled up, sat up, pushed down, pushed up another fifteen minutes, then went to the locker room. His arms trembled as he sweated and figured out the knot in his drawstring.

Philip showered leisurely, dried up and dressed. A few minutes later he stepped outside through the glass doors into the sparkling cold day. He went to Eighteenth and walked north, his hair slicked back, his shirt tucked in without a wrinkle and his collar open, his tie loosely knotted. He felt starkly alive, in bold relief against the street.

He was already ten minutes late, but he took his time. Bought fruit salad from the Koreans at Eighteenth and Chestnut and ate it next to a newsstand at the corner. Gave a bum five dollars and said no to making it an even ten. Said no to the guy on roller skates who wanted to sell him a Chagall. Took a free packet of condoms when it was offered, and filled out a questionnaire for a sleepy-looking girl from People Against Caffeine:

> Name: Juan Valdez
> Occupation: Coffee harvester
> Work phone: No, work coffee field.

And so on.

After that he started onto Chestnut toward the district attorney's office about a block down. By his watch he would be forty minutes late, which was about good. A secretary retrieved him from the waiting area and took him back to Michael's office. Michael's name was on a blue name plate on the wall outside. The secretary knocked and opened his door.

Philip entered and stood just inside the office, the secretary closing the door softly behind him. Michael looked up briefly from behind his desk of paperwork and said, "You're late," and looked expectantly for an explanation.

Philip offered none.

Michael nodded and said, "Well, now I have to finish this, I'll be a few minutes." He went back to his paperwork and Philip pulled out the slat of coarse wood from the back of the desk designed for visitors. He opened his briefcase and took out the documents he'd brought, placing them on the slat. He sat and perused them, determined to make use of the time, or seem to.

Michael finally finished, looked up and clicked his ballpoint. "Philip." He said the name reflectively, as if he'd awakened from meditation, his karma cleansed, to find Philip, his dear friend, had joined him. Or, more aptly, as a victorious gladiator would, sword at the bested man's neck, the death part not to be rushed. Michael pointed at him with the pen.

"You first. Why'd you want to meet?"

Philip lied. "We plead to manslaughter and you tell the judge no recommendation at sentencing."

Michael shook his head sadly as though Philip had wanted to trade Electric Company for Park Place and Boardwalk.

"Very gracious of you," he said and stood to bow. "But, as I told you this morning, I'm afraid I'm going to have to insist that you plead your client guilty to the charge as it stands. Murder."

"And as I told you this morning, there are no circumstances under which I could be persuaded to do so."

"Yes, you did, indeed, you did tell me that," said Michael.

"Mike," Philip said, "let's cut it out. Get to what you've got already."

Michael quickly stood. He walked from his desk to an Oriental dressing partition about two feet from the sidewall. He made a show of removing his handkerchief, bending and breathing to fog a spot on a lacquered panel, and polished the small area. Then he "leaned" on the partition as if it were a wall, of course not placing any real weight on it for that would have knocked it right over.

"Like art, Phil?" Michael asked cheerfully.

Philip smiled widely. "Some," he said lightly. "Do you?"

"Hate it. Stuff's ugly," Michael responded heartily. "But I like the painting behind this partition very much. You might recognize it, Phil—I'll let you see it in a moment—but I'm sure you won't understand its significance. Really," he said, beaming uncontainable pleasure, "it's the most beautiful painting I've ever seen. Do you want to know why I love this painting so much? Can I tell you what it's going to do for me?"

"Go ahead," Philip told him drily.

Michael put his hands together at chest level. "Well, this is the painting that is going to send your client to jail for a substantially lengthy period. And this is the painting that is going to get a quite mediocre PD"—he pointed at Philip—"out of my hair and back into obscurity where he belongs; no, where he aspires to be. It's going to end, friend, without further ado, a situation that might have otherwise caused me some real trouble."

"Gee," Philip said, "how's a painting gonna do all that?"

Michael turned and gathered the sectioned panels together, yelling "Voilà!" as he did so. He closed it in as nearly a graceful and singular movement as possible, which wasn't very of either, and his "Voilà!" lasted several seconds. He was unflapped, however, and stood beside the painting proud as if he'd painted it.

"This is a painting Lisa Bianchi did."

"I recognize it."

"It's supposed to be Mindi Quintana," Michael said, squinting at it. "But I don't see it."

Michael moved very close to Philip now. He put a hand on the back of Philip's chair so as not to miss a shard of shattered PD. Carefully, he asked Philip, "Now, do you have any idea what is wrong—or from my point of view, right—with this picture?"

"I dunno," said Philip looking back into Michael's eyes. "Could it be there's a bloody fingerprint in it?"

Michael's smiling face froze but not before shock leapt to his eyes to freeze with it.

Philip jumped to his feet. "You're kidding," he shouted, as if he'd gleaned from Michael's expression the incredible accuracy of his joking guess. He rushed to the easel. "There *is* a fingerprint! Jesus Christ! Jesus fucking Christ."

He turned to the fast-defrosting Michael.

"Is it Freddy's? It can't be Freddy's! Have you checked?—maybe it's a cop's!"

Michael was watching with half-closed eyes and wide nostrils as if this were his favorite meal wafting from the kitchen.

"I took the imprint myself and had the comparison done informally. Did the blood type, too. We'll do the official tests and DNA tonight." He came over to Philip for a closer view. "It's his. No doubt about it, it's the China Manager's print in the Quintana girl's blood."

Philip asked quickly, "Who else knows about this?"

"Nobody. I've got a press conference in half an hour."

"No one else knows?"

"I'm interviewing Lisa Bianchi at her apartment this morning and I ask about the painting in the crime scene photos—I mean, I almost didn't. So, she shows it to me and there it is," he said amazed all over again, motioning in wonder to the area on the painting, "all blood-brown and . . . beautifully crumbly." He gave himself a shake. "Shit— I bet forensics missed it because, wet, it looked just like more of that glossy red paint." He laughed, remembering. "I said, 'Madam, if you won't let me have your painting I'll just have to subpoena it and have you arrested for obstructing justice,' even though I couldn't really have her arrested, but in my best DA's voice."

He looked at Philip evenly now. "Sit down."

Philip obeyed, moving over to his chair and lowering himself slowly. Michael followed and leaned next to the slat with Philip's papers on it. He looked at Philip, trying to get him to maintain eye contact but Philip wouldn't.

"Here's what you're going to do," Michael told him. "You will draw up a motion for pretrial conference. At that conference you will move to change the China Manager's plea to guilty as charged. I will not oppose your motion. Your client's sentence—if Willison doesn't fix degree at murder one—will be less severe, of course, than if he'd cost the state the time, expense, and trouble of a jury trial."

"Nothing in return, Mike? No agreement not to go for murder one?"

"No way. I'll go for whatever the market will bear."

Philip looked up. "Michael, be fair," he said, "I can't agree to that. The print only means Freddy killed her. This is still a third-degree case, judge or jury. If you're gonna go for one, I'd rather have a jury fix degree after a trial than Willison at a sentencing hearing. And with a jury, at least I've got a shot at manslaughter. I'd still have to go to trial."

"That's not true and you know it. To get him on one, all I need is the intent to kill her—could have formed in an instant at any time. I could show it easy. Against you, I could prove he shot Lincoln. And the manslaughter bullshit's bullshit. Nobody's gonna believe she provoked him once they hear the evidence, fuck the newspapers.

"But, okay, Philip, to spare the Commonwealth one more trial in an already overburdened system, to save the taxpayers another million bucks on this, I'll let him cop to third. I'll recommend max, but Willison'll give him less than if you make me put on the show." He straightened slightly and pulled his elbows behind him until his back cracked. "File that motion tomorrow." The meeting was over.

Philip crossed his legs. "I won't be filing any motion."

"Excuse me?"

"No deal."

"I do believe he's trying to bluff me," Michael said to an imaginary fellow on his shoulder. And then to Philip, "Oh, God, please, you're breaking my heart. I've hit you with the big stick. You're dead, have the class to fall over. You've got nothing to bargain with."

"That's right. All I've got is a bottom line: no deal."

"You've got no choice. I've got him cold on three. At least."

"Maybe. So why don't you tell me—your concern for the court's docket and the taxpayers aside—why it is you're willing to bargain at all."

Michael pushed to his feet and stood over him. "Because I feel sorry for your client, because I'm busy with my other cases, because shirts are on sale at Boyds, because God in the form of a hairy grape told me to, what the fuck do you care why? You have a client to represent! The first assistant district attorney has just offered him a deal better than anything he could hope for in court and it's your duty to jump on it. Which you'd better do forthwith or I'll withdraw it, take your incompetent ass to trial, and win hands down!"

"Which means you lose hands down. Go ahead, withdraw the offer. I bet you won't."

"I will withdraw it if you're not careful."

Philip stood. "I'm waiting!"

Michael spoke through his teeth. "That wouldn't be fair to your client."

"Come on. Let's go to trial. I'll plead not guilty, you argue murder one. Or lower it to three. Trial should be in about three months. Three more months for Freddy and the press to have their pretrial fun. Three more months for your booming political career. You think the painting will make a difference? Most people already figure he might have done it. That's why he's interesting to begin with.

"And when you win, Michael, and it's time to make a sentencing recommendation, I'd like to know, are you going to go long—public opinion, bad press be damned, your treatment in Freddy's book be damned—or will you go short and show yourself for what you are at bottom: shine for your campaign shoes? Christ, Michael, that painting is the worst thing that ever could have happened to you. Without it you might have had the good luck to lose." Philip sat back down.

"If you don't take the bargain, you're open to the same criticism. That you want a Court TV trial and are giving your client bad advice to get it." Michael jabbed his finger at him. "I'll get that across, you can be sure."

"You forget—I ain't running for nothin'. I belong in, no, I aspire to obscurity, remember?"

"You are duty bound to present my offer to your client. If you won't, I'll petition the court to replace you and the next guy will take it to him."

"I'll present it to him. The point is, he won't take it."

"Of course he will. He'd be crazy not to."

"Like he was crazy not to let Sam McDonald represent him pro bono?

Michael said nothing.

"He'd do anything to assure a trial for the same reason you'd do anything to avoid one," Philip told him.

"He'd trade away years of his life? To get published?"

"To be someone. Yes. That's just what he's decided to do."

"I'd consider voluntary manslaughter."

Philip just shook his head. "He needs a *trial*, the sustained interest, the press coverage, the controversy. A plea is a blanket on the fire. He cannot plead."

"Christ." Michael went around his desk and sat. "I don't believe it," he said, though clearly now, he saw the truth of it.

Philip let him imagine the coming few months. Then he said, "My hands are tied. Freddy's tied them. There's only one person who can save you, Michael."

"Who?" His interest was minor.

"You."

"Me? How?"

Philip said softly what he'd come here to say. "Drop the charges."

"Drop the charges? Drop the fucking charges?" Michael gave a self-pitying laugh. "How can I drop the fucking charges?"

"Just do it. You say the evidence is insufficient. You've been uncomfortable with its quality all along, it's interpretable either way. If Freddy did have a relationship with Mindi, and you've come to believe he did, then the hair, the prints are all explainable. The broken hand? You think he fell down the steps just like he says he did. Throw in the bar if you think it helps. The press and the public will hail you as a man of conscience. If they don't think he's innocent now, they will with the charges dropped and after your statement. Freddy's insisted on his innocence, I have, the press pays lip service at least to the possibility, and now the closest person to the evidence, someone with a prosecutorial mandate, says the evidence as developed doesn't justify trying him.

"You add a statement to the effect that you *apologize* to Mr. Builder for the disruption of his life, and that you are unwilling to let it continue. You'll have some trouble with your boss, and there might be some minor speculation by the astute as to true motives, maybe, but if law school taught you anything it taught you how to balance. So balance the criticism from within against what will happen to your life if we go to trial. Do you think your people will stick with you through that anyway?"

"What about the painting? You've forgotten about the painting."

He hadn't forgotten it but had come up with his plan before knowing Michael had it. Now he had a decision to make. Michael was saying, quite correctly, that to drop the charges, there had to be some doubt as to Freddy's guilt, and that the existence of the painting removed that doubt. He was asking Philip how he could drop the charges *now*?

Philip had come today knowing Freddy would profit from either his trial and conviction or his trial and acquittal, and having decided to stop him by showing Leopold a way out. But now, with the painting discovered, Philip's role as attorney, and the law itself, came directly into conflict with what he believed necessary. Michael could not drop the charges with that painting as evidence.

Small picture versus big picture; instant, substantial, individual justice versus justice in the numbers, the most justice, most often, for the most people; the resurrection of the meaning and validity of Mindi Quintana versus the actualization of a murderer, a rapist, a Freddy Builder, as Frederick, as writer, as lover of the girl he'd murdered.

That's what judges were for. He knew. That's what juries were for. He knew. Society had already decided the question in constructing its machinery for justice as it had. He knew this, too. And he was Freddy's *advocate*, he had a role to play, had pledged to play it, would be subverting it. He would be breaking his oath. He would be committing a crime. He could not stay a lawyer afterward. He knew all of this.

But if ever a punishment fit a crime, and if ever a crime needed to be punished, and *prevented*. If society, the judge, the jury knew what Philip knew, if they knew Mindi, knew Freddy, knew what Freddy had done and was doing, wanted and was getting, believed about Mindi and was making the truth, they would find a way to this outcome for Freddy.

"Give the painting back to Lisa. Tell her you were mistaken, it's not evidence. We'll scrape off the blood."

"I'd want it destroyed."

"That's not necessary. You won't have to worry about her. I've gotten to know her very well."

"Fucking prosecution witnesses now, are you? I'd rather take my chances with a trial than have that painting hanging over my head for the rest of my career. It would have to be burned."

Philip stood and put the documents in his briefcase. "I'll let you know."

"By the end of tomorrow," Michael said. He got up and came around to face Philip. "As far as I'm concerned I told you about the new evidence and offered you a cop to third. You refused and I told you we'd proceed with our case. Try convincing anyone of anything else and I'll have you disbarred." In a lower voice he added, "I'll have you killed, too, I swear to God."

Philip walked to the door. Before he opened it Michael said, "You hate your client that much?"

"Yes, I do."

"You're no lawyer."

"I know it." Philip put his hand on the knob, and took it off. He turned back. "But it's not just that I hate him, Michael."

Michael gave him a questioning look.

"It's that I know what happens next if I don't do this. I know *you*."

"What do you think happens next?"

"You can't win winning and you can't win losing." Philip shrugged.

"So I go for a draw. Sure. But do you know what the draw is?"

"There is no draw, there'd still be a trial. Freddy pleading would have been a draw."

"But now I know he won't. Do you know what I'd do now?" Michael studied him.

Philip nodded. "You'd lower the charge to voluntary manslaughter. You'd hope it'd take some of the heat off, giving everyone half a loaf."

Michael leaned past him and opened the door. "You were never dumb, Philip. Just not ambitious."

25

Justice for One

"Burn it?" she whispered. He had told her about the fingerprint and his meeting with Michael. She stood up and he made her sit back on his bed and took her hands. She pulled them away. "How could you ask me to do that?"

"I'm not asking you."

She hugged herself suddenly.

"But you want me to."

"Yes."

She stood again looking at him and moved away toward his desk. Then whirled back, her ponytail coming over her shoulder. "It's crazy. You're crazy!" she yelled at him. "He killed Mindi! He should go to jail! What are you doing?"

Philip got up and went to her. "He wouldn't go for long, Lisa, I've explained that to you. A few years at most."

She turned, arms crossed, to stare at him dumbly.

"Think about it," he said. "He gets everything he wants if he goes to trial. If that happens, the murder is a success. I'm trying to stop him."

She shook her head. "No, you're trying to get your client off. That's all." She dabbed her eyes with the sleeve of her sweatshirt.

"No, Lisa, listen." She swung away again refusing to face him. "Lisa, I'm through with this case either way. We're together, I can't represent him." He reached out and took her arm to bring her back but she yanked it away.

"I saw the print weeks ago," he told her, "and I didn't say anything.

I wanted to try and force Leopold to drop the charges. To *hurt* my client. Don't you see?"

She didn't answer right away. "No," she said finally, striding toward the bedroom door, "I don't see."

He started after her. "Lisa—"

But she stopped at the door and sat down in the chair there. Realizing he'd thought she was leaving she looked at him. "No," she said, shaking her head. Then she took a sweatshirt of his from under her on the chair and used it to dry her eyes. She looked ahead of her at the floor. "Continue."

He went and sat on the bed again.

"He's so proud, Lisa. Look how interesting he is now. Look how fascinated people are. Look how everyone wants his interview and is waiting for his book. He has an agent, a publicist, a reporter helping him write. He loves what he's becoming—a prisoner-celebrity, poet-murderer, a writer, someone with opinions people listen to."

"I know that's all true," she said nodding.

"He's a coward but now people think he's brave. He's missing something but they think he has something extra. And they think he killed Mindi because he *loved* her."

"Yes," she said leaning back, her hands fists on the arms of the chair.

"And he believes them: that he killed where others don't because he's special."

She hit the arms of the chair so hard it startled him. "And he should go to jail for it!"

"Maybe," he said regretfully. "But I don't see how that would be punishing him." He stood and went halfway to her. "I think if there's a trial, he gets everything he wants. It's *accusing* him and *trying* him that makes him controversial, fascinating. But if the charges are dropped now, in the way they would be, I think he fails. No trial, and Leopold will go to great lengths to say he should never have been accused at all, that he was only ever a hapless department store manager. I think his book goes away—I've spoken with his agent, his publicist. They're counting on this trial, they're counting on Court TV, they're counting on more *Nightline* and *Larry King*, they're counting on controversy, speculation, disagreement, strong feeling, *interest*."

She was nodding.

"Do you remember the BTK Killer?"

"Yeah," she said looking at the floor. She gave a couple quick nods. "Yeah, I've thought of him, too. Standing so smug there in court. Bragging over the details. Like they made him somebody. Like, yeah, you thought I was a little man—but now you know. Yeah." She continued to nod, and blinked a few times as what was the same became even clearer.

He said, "Or Gary Gilmore? They made the guy a poet—a nobody, a nothing, a killer. Or Jack Henry Abbott?"

This time she shook her head.

"These guys, Lisa, they can't make it through the front door so they go in the back. And we let them."

"She said that. That he wouldn't work. She said he wanted it to happen to him, like winning the lottery."

"Let's rip up his ticket."

With this she put her face in her hands and sobbed in frustration.

He said, "I'm suggesting we destroy evidence. It's a big deal, I—"

She took her hands from her face. "I don't give a damn about destroying evidence. That painting is the only way Mindi lives anymore!"

"For you, honey. For herself she's dead all the time."

She pushed up angrily from the chair. "And what if he kills someone else?"

"Lisa, he's seen five different shrinks since he's been inside. One at the prison, one of mine—and three prosecution shrinks, because Leopold can't find one who'll say what he wants. This is a *type* of murder. Builder is a *type* of perpetrator. He snapped. It's impossible—in anyone—to predict future violence and be right every time.

But this type of murder—highly situational, relationship with the victim—and this type of perpetrator—a person with no history of violence or even minor lawbreaking, no testing indicating a propensity to violence—isn't likely to repeat. And after a few years of prison, believe me, he'll be *more* likely to be violent again, if anything."

Lisa went and stood right in front of him. "I couldn't even look at the painting after she was killed," she said. "But I knew I'd be able to as the years went on. When I had a different life and she was starting to fade."

"The man who killed her is still erasing her *now*, changing who she was. You've told me that her friends talk about her differently now. That sometimes you get mad because they refer to Freddy and Mindi as 'them,' as if there was a them."

"Then they never knew her!" she said with more conviction then she felt.

"Okay, Lisa, listen." He waited until he was sure that she was. "It's not only that he lies. It's that he's making his lies the truth. Because in five years what he does with her today and tomorrow will be history, too, just like her life and her murder. She *will* have been his stepping stone."

She went to his desk and sat on it, feet on the chair. She started shaking her head.

"What?"

"I hate that I can understand him not being able to accept himself. Wanting more than china displays."

"Would you have killed someone?"

"If I couldn't paint? I don't think so. Maybe myself."

"How about the rest of it? The book—"

"Never!" She stood quickly. "The mother*fucker!*" she shrieked and burst into tears. "I want to kill him! Kill him!"

He went over to her and held her. "It's not enough to put him in prison a few years."

"No, it's not enough," she said.

26

The Defense Rests

"Judge Willison will see you now," Willison's secretary said to Philip and Freddy.

A lawyer emerged from Willison's chambers mopping his face. The judge's laughter and that of, presumably, a clerk could be heard behind him. The man said to Philip as he passed, "He's having fun with us today."

Philip checked his watch. Michael was not late yet but he had better hurry. If judges were anything, they were not punctual, but they expected their attorneys to be. Philip went in first, followed by Freddy and a guard.

Willison's close chambers smelled of books and old wood. Texts and a century of commonwealth case law covered two walls, an escritoire at the back with pipes, tampers, ink jars, and tobacco tins in its cubbyholes, a manual typewriter on its surface. The judge was behind his desk spooning soup from a bowl, a clerk seated next to him. In front of the desk on a dark faded rug were four leather armchairs in various positions with small antique lamps on a stand for additional light. A court reporter sat in the corner, his machine resting on the uneven floor beyond the rug.

Willison used his free hand to motion Philip and Freddy to seats, but the movement still caused him to spill soup from his spoon. As the two went to chairs and pulled them close, the guard took standing position behind, and the clerk tore a paper towel from a roll and applied it to the spilled soup. The process seemed of inordinate interest to the judge who watched, absorbed. After, he looked up at

Philip with heavy significance. He extended his finger to its full wondrous length, spilling more soup in the process, and pointed at the roll of paper towels.

"Bounty," he said as if lives depended on it, "the quicker picker-upper." Philip waited for the judge to go on or look away, but Judge Willison did neither.

"Yes, your honor."

There was a knock and Michael stepped into the room.

"Mr. Prosecutor," the judge said, gesturing with exaggerated politeness. "Why don't you take a seat by the PD." Michael moved a chair next to Philip, glancing at the guard who still held his eyes to the back of Freddy's head.

"Now why don't you tell us what it's all about, Mr. Prosecutor," Willison said. "What is so urgent that it can't be disposed of at trial?"

Michael stood. "Your honor, the People have requested this conference—"

"My honor, the People have requested nothing," Willison interrupted. "You have. Save the gobbledygook and just get to the point."

"Your honor, we're dropping all charges against Mr. Builder."

There was the slightest of delays before Freddy was on his feet yelling, "What? What? What?" and then, "*What?*" and the guard was restraining him, pushing him back down into his chair. "What do you mean?"

"Quash that outburst now!" the judge ordered. "Or I shall have you removed to holding and conduct this conference without your presence."

Freddy stopped resisting and dropped the few inches left to his chair. He leaned to Philip and whispered vehemently in his ear, "Find out what the fuck's up and fix it."

Philip looked at him evenly. "It ain't broke."

Willison paid his attention to Freddy. "I'm confused," he admitted, "by your less than joyful response to the news." Now he looked at Michael. "But I'm even more perplexed as to the ADA's reasons for wanting to drop the charges. Please enlighten me," he commanded Michael.

"Your honor, let me explain simply and briefly," began Michael nervously. "Let me encapsulate things for you so that the situation is broken into its component—"

"Enlighten me!" the judge roared.

"The evidence no longer supports the charge of murder one," Michael blurted.

"So why aren't you charging a lesser degree?"

"I—" began Freddy.

"Be quiet!" Willison ordered.

"The evidence, Judge, does not support the conclusion that he killed her in any degree, that he killed her at all."

"That makes no sense," said the judge leaning forward on his desk. "The evidence has supported the charge for months. I ruled that it does support the charge. Why the sudden change?"

"Your honor, this is no sudden change. The evidence has always been circumstantial—not that circumstantial evidence can't be compelling, but its strength depends on the probability that the inferences we draw from it are true."

The judge closed his eyes and shook his head slowly.

"So far," said the judge to Michael with eyes still closed, "you've told me nothing." He opened them. "I suggest you start telling me something."

"At first I believed from the evidence that Mr. Builder killed Quintana, your honor," said Michael, spreading his arms. "The prints, the hair, the statements of Lisa Bianchi, especially his hand and the calendar. Rejection of his advances as the motive. We had a case. The smart-money inference seemed to me that he'd done it." He shook his head. "Looking back, part of it might have been my fault. This was a case with great public office—I mean interest—and there was much pressure from within the *office* and the mayor's *office* to prosecute. I may have responded to that pressure. And I may have been so incensed by a brutal crime that I rationalized my doubts away to pursue a conviction. But, your honor, I am a man of conscience. I can no longer justify *or* rationalize prosecuting this man."

Michael paused here and Willison whispered something to his clerk, who bent over his pad and began writing. Philip stared ahead at the judge, ignoring Freddy's desperate looks at him.

"Two things specifically have happened," Michael continued. "First, in discussions with Lisa Bianchi yesterday and today, I find she can no longer say with assurance that Mindi did not tell her that Mr. Builder had called to cancel their date. I find, too, that she's now unsure about certain other points on which she was formerly firm. Second, and really most important, I have been listening to Mr. Builder speak of his love for Quintana for months, I have been reading his very ably written accounts of their relationship, I've studied those circus photos, and, well, I've simply come to believe him. I have watched his face and read between his lines, and he's convinced me." Michael had wound up at Willison's desk, resting his fingers on it.

The judge did some more consulting with his clerk. "These are jury questions," he said.

"The evidence must reach a threshold of reliability and validity before it can be put to a jury," Michael said. "You may think it reaches that threshold, Larry Fullbody might, I no longer do. Your honor, trying a man at all leaves his guilt or innocence, even if he's acquitted, forever controversial. He would be linked in the public mind to a heinous crime for the rest of his life. For that reason, and for the added reason that I simply will not prosecute a man I personally believe to be innocent—it's abhorrent to every instinct in my body— I am formally moving you to nol-pros the case." He paused a moment. "We plucked a man from life, called him a murderer, and made him a household name. He was only ever a harmless department store manager who, but for us, would have had his day as Manager of the Year."

"No!" shouted Freddy. But no one was paying him any attention now.

Michael backed away from the desk. "Your honor, I issued a statement to the press before coming here today. In it I stated my intention to drop the charges. I explained in the strongest terms that the office and I personally were convinced that Frederick Builder was wrongly accused."

"You did that without waiting for my decision whether to dismiss?"

Michael sucked in his breath. "Judge, if you refuse to dismiss the case, I still will not prosecute. If you are so inclined and are able to convince the district attorney to continue with the case, I will resign from the office and make my views known publicly. I think you should consider that I am the person most familiar with the evidence from the prosecution standpoint and that my opinion might carry great weight. And I don't think the case will be number one on Fullbody's list to personally intervene in."

There was no whispering to the clerk. "You've sought to tie my hands," said Judge Willison.

"No, sir. I've sought to act on my conscience."

"Have you spoken to DA Fullbody about this?"

"Yes."

"Before or after the press release?"

"After."

"What did he think of your act of conscience?"

"He didn't like it."

"What if I confess?" Freddy interrupted miserably. The judge just looked at him. The clerk just kept scribbling.

"You'd look like an attention-seeking nut, for one thing," said Michael.

"And that's a very different book," said Philip. "Doubt Sykes would help out with it."

"Okay," said Willison. "Why would you confess now that he wants to drop the charges, when you have maintained your innocence to date?"

Freddy stared blankly at the judge.

"Prison has been a strain on my client," Philip said. "Being unjustly accused has been a strain on him, sir."

"Judge," said Michael, "I do feel partially responsible. If he persists, I would feel compelled to move for new psychological evaluation."

"I'd have to also so move," Philip said. Softly, to Freddy, he added, "What would being crazy do for your literary prospects?"

Michael looked at the court reporter. "To prevent the compounding of state liability in the event of a civil suit, I suggest his honor dismiss the case, if he is going to, and release this defendant as quickly as practicable. Psychological injury and civil rights violations attributable to after today would be injury the state might reasonably have avoided." Michael returned to his chair and sat down.

The judge and his clerk stood and stepped back from the desk.

Freddy turned to Philip. "You did this."

Philip leaned over to him and whispered in his ear. "Yes."

"Well," said Judge Willison, sitting down, "I'm going to dismiss the case with prejudice. I will sign an order to that effect as soon as you present me with one."

"I've got the order and the memo now, Judge Willison." Michael handed everything to the clerk.

"Fine." Willison went on. "We should be able to release Mr. Builder in a few hours. Until then he is to remain in the custody of the sheriff." To the guard Willison said, "You can put him in holding downstairs when we're done."

The judge looked at all of them now.

"The prosecutor is to be commended for his act of conscience; that will be my position." He pointed a thoughtful face at the ceiling and then down at his lap.

"You know," he said, "the law is a funny thing. It never really works by itself. Justice does not flow merely from the written word, our statutes, our case law, nor does it from the rigid black letter of court rules of procedure, rules of evidence, this infrastructure we've built so painstakingly to bring the law to bear. No, justice must always depend on the people in the process. I should like to point out in this regard that the Constitution with its first ten amendments, a beautiful and inspiring document though it is, reserves no greater individual liberty on its face, boasts no greater concern for freedom and justice with its words, than the beautiful documents of brutal societies. The difference, as I say, lies in the intentions of the people in the process in carrying out the mandate.

"Today we have an act of conscience on the part of one attorney not in keeping with the conduct expected of him by his colleagues. Where would we be if he had read only the law's letter?" The judge looked at Freddy. "An undeserving man would have met an unjust fate."

Now he looked at Michael. "Get out of here," he told him.

"In a few hours you'll be free," said Philip as the guard cuffed Freddy.

"Free for what?" asked Freddy, the guard pulling him up.

"I don't know. Maybe they'll take you back at Chanet's."

27

——

Ashes

Late in the afternoon, Philip and Lisa arrived first and drove along the Northeast Philly street that bordered Pennypack forest. Lisa knew the thick woods well from a childhood spent nearby. The street was small and of a texture that crunched under their wheels as they went slowly down for a parking spot; it had dried already from the earlier downpour. Cars were parked tightly on both sides, but finally someone came out of a house and drove one away. Inching forward and backward several times, Philip made the space. He turned off the ignition and they stepped out of his aging Buick as it coughed and finally quieted. They sat on the hood to wait for Michael.

They stared over the line of cars, their feet sharing the front bumper of Philip's car and the back bumper of the next car. Philip got up and began kicking small chunks of the street toward a fire hydrant. The rough jags on the street surface had broken over time under feet and car tires, skateboard wheels, so that there was a gritty miniature rubble mixed with windshield and beer-bottle glass. The sharp stuff that sits on such streets and lays in the bottoms of potholes, that flies when cars pass to sting faces and hands, that sends children into houses holding elbows and knees, that causes old people to slip and break hips, and gives the street an uncertain feel, as if one's leg might suddenly crunch through to the thigh. The cars and feet and skateboards grinding the stuff into the street again to cut more of itself, leaving the surface with new jags to be broken again, to cut again, to sting faces, break hips, abrade knees again.

He watched Lisa on the hood. She had her knees up, her arms

around them, and was staring ahead. The black portfolio she'd brought for the painting lay beside her. He looked over to the house side of the street. Leafless trees were spaced intermittently in the uneven concrete sidewalk. The duplexes were box shaped and identical to one another down to the nailed-on shutters and strips of weeds separating them.

The parked cars stretching forward without break formed a line it seemed the neighborhood was not allowed to cross. Their dents and bald tires, their models and sun-shorn interiors, their bent chrome car dealers, missing hood ornaments, dust and caked dirt told the story of the neighborhood that ended with them and like them. He went back to Lisa now.

"There's Leopold," she said.

Philip turned and Michael nodded slightly from where he stood across the street. He wore a suit, had the painting in brown paper, and was carrying a knapsack and a flashlight. He looked like he wasn't sure what he wanted out of life, though he knew probably better than anyone.

Philip gave Lisa a hand off the car. She continued past him and went to Michael, taking the painting from him without a word. Put it in the portfolio. She went back to Philip who removed a flashlight from the car and cut with her into the woods. Michael followed but kept the street's width between them. They trudged into the perimeter, dusk descending, through pockets of tree trunks with butts and Buds and rain-pinked Marlboro packs, last night's teenage sex, until they came to a rusty railroad track thick with weeds and grass, strung everywhere with vines, and followed farther in.

Though the world outside the woods had dried hours ago—even the thick muck the street stuff and water made in Northeast Philly potholes—the woods were still wet, water still hung in the trees. The rain had busted spring's humidity, and when they brushed bushes and overhanging branches, the drops that rolled onto them or dropped on them flatly were cold.

"It takes longer for the forest to dry," said Philip shaking a slug from his sneaker.

"It's just that a city can't get very wet," Lisa said. "The rain can't get in so it lies on top."

The stirrings of insects and small animals, alive again after the winter, out again after the rain, came to them with the steady sounds of their hiking. The air was sweet with mud, moldering railroad ties, and the dense foliage.

After a while, Lisa turned away from the tracks, Philip with her and Michael a moment later. They proceeded through a grouping of trees into a clearing that had been visible from the tracks at an earlier bend.

"Rocks," Philip said and looked for some nearby. Lisa followed holding the portfolio by its handle. Soon Philip had arranged a circular pyre. Michael opened his knapsack and started to pour wood shavings into the circle. Lisa grabbed the bag from him.

"Get away," she said without looking at him, and he went to the edge of the clearing. Philip stood next to her and she handed him the portfolio.

Lisa turned from him and let the contents of the knapsack fall into the circle. Her aim strayed since her eyes were full and so Philip lifted a corner of the bag to correct it. When it was empty, he let go and Lisa dropped the knapsack on top. Michael protested from the edge but did not come over. Lisa knelt and took the painting from the black case. She took off the paper, and Philip balled it up and put it under the knapsack, on top of the shavings. She laid the painting face up on the rocks, backing away a step and looking down at it.

Truly Extraordinary stared up from the right corner.

Philip brought out matches and she took them. The sun was straight ahead now and it cast a deep red through the forest behind the rocks and painting.

"Mindi, this is all I have of you," she whispered too softly for anyone else. "I'm taking the chance of losing you over the years. Don't let me. I hope I'm doing the right thing."

She struck a match. Bright blue inside yellow inside the red in the blackening sky. She held the match to the shavings until they caught.

The painting burned quickly. After a minute, all that was left was a bright orange rectangular cinder, which finally collapsed into the circle, sending up embers.

Now it was done. Philip snuffed out the fire with damp leaves and ground. When he was finished, he aimed the flashlight and saw that Michael was gone. Lisa picked out small charred pieces of the frame, some with black pieces of canvas still clinging to them. She put what she gathered into the portfolio.

"Ashes," she said.

Lisa took his arm as they made their way back along the tracks.